REVIVE

NINA LEVINE

REVIVE

Copyright © 2014 Nina Levine
Published by Nina Levine

Cover designed by Louisa @ LM Creations
http://lmbookcreations.wordpress.com/portfolio/

Cover Photography by Christopher John @ CJC Photography
http://www.cjc-photography.com

Cover Model: Joseph Troisi

Stock Image from Dollar Photo Club
www.dollarphotoclub.com

NINA LEVINE

**_USA Today_ & International
Bestselling Author**

ALSO BY NINA LEVINE

STORM MC SERIES
Storm (Storm MC #1)
Fierce (Storm MC #2)
Blaze (Storm MC #2.5)
Revive (Storm MC #3)
Slay (Storm MC #4)
Illusive (Storm MC #5) – COMING 2015
Command (Storm MC #6) – COMING 2015

HAVOC SERIES
Destined Havoc (Havoc #1)
Inevitable Havoc (Havoc #2) – COMING 2015

CRAVE SERIES
All Your Reasons (Crave #1) – COMING 2015

Keep up to date with my books at my website
http://ninalevinebooks.blogspot.com.au

DEDICATION

To all the women who have had their self worth
crushed by someone they loved.

To all the men who have been too strong and proud
to admit when they were struggling.

And to those who picked up the pieces
and helped put us back together.

To love.

A NOTE ABOUT THE STORM MC SERIES

Each book in this series continues on from the previous. While there won't be major cliffhangers in each book, there will be parts of the story that won't be resolved so please be aware of this.

It is recommended that each book be read in order.

REVIVE

(Storm MC #3)
Nash & Velvet's Story

WARNING

PROLOGUE

NASH

Three years ago

MEMORIES WERE A DOUBLE-EDGED SWORD. FOR ME, they were mostly a sword that never failed to leave another scar on my heart. And today was no different. Mothers Day; the beginning of my yearly cycle of remembrance. It always began on Mothers Day and lasted for nearly two months. Had been this way for seven years now and I figured it would continue until Gabriella took her last breath.

I re-read the text she'd sent me.

Happy Mother's Day asshole.

There was no need to reply so I slipped my phone back in my pocket. The pain she'd stirred up hurt like a motherfucker, but I was skilled at dealing with it now. I shoved it away and focused my attention on finding a distraction for the night.

"You okay?" Velvet asked as she slid into the seat next to me, a concerned look on her face.

My gaze dropped to her legs as she crossed them. And then it shifted up to admire the curves of her hips and tits that were encased in the hottest black dress I'd seen in awhile. Her long, brunette hair hung half way down her back. She was a stunning woman, but the thing I loved about her the most was her heart and soul. Caring and kind on the inside, fearless on the outside.

"Yeah, sweet thing, don't worry about me."

"I do worry about you, Nash. A lot. And tonight, you're giving off a vibe. What's going on?"

I'd known her for a year now, and she had a way of reading me, of knowing when I was struggling with something. But I didn't want friends like that; friends who pushed you to play with your demons. I pasted a smile on my face. "Just had a busy day, babe. I need to relax, maybe have some fun." I winked at her. "You wanna help me with that?"

"You never give up, do you?"

I'd lost count of the number of times I'd hit on Velvet. To her credit, she put up with me and let me do it, all with a smile on her face. She'd almost given in a couple of times but even I knew we'd reached the point where it was unlikely to happen. Velvet had chosen our friendship over sex, and for some reason I couldn't fathom, I was more than okay with that. Still, a man had to try. You never knew when a woman would give in.

I shrugged. "One day you'll succumb to my cock, sweet thing. I can be a patient man."

"I've got plenty of other cock to keep me occupied, Nash. It's your heart and your mind I'm interested in. Maybe one day you'll give me those."

"Baby, you say the sweetest things but truly, once you've had my cock, my heart and mind will be distant memories."

She leant closer to me and whispered, "One day you're going to be knocked off your ass by a woman who will own all three. It'll be a sight to see, Nash Walker."

"Sorry, babe, but the only item on the menu is my cock. My heart and mind were trashed by a woman a long fuckin' time ago."

More like fucking annihilated.

Her eyes widened and she sat back, processing what I'd said. Before she could say anything else, I stood. "I'll see you tomorrow night, yeah?"

She nodded, disappointment clear on her face. "Yeah, Nash. I'll be here and I'll come and find you for a chat."

I forced a smile. "Good," I said, and walked away from her without a backwards glance. It was all well and fucking good to have friends, but what I needed was pussy. That's what would make me feel better. Losing myself in it helped me forget. And Mothers Day was a day when I really needed to forget.

CHAPTER 1

Lookin' For A Good Time ~ Lady Antebellum

NASH

STORM.

My boys.

As I watched them give J shit about something he'd done, I thought about some of the stuff we'd been through lately. A lot of people didn't understand our club, didn't understand what we stood for. When it was all said and done, we stood for family. For loyalty and trust. Things that were hard to come by these days, and things that when broken, could never be repaired. At the moment, our loyalties and trust were being put to the test.

Griff lifted his chin at me before walking my way. "You and J good at the moment?" he asked.

"We're working on it, brother. It's been two months since his wedding, and Madison's done her best to push us together."

"I can imagine."

I chuckled. "Yeah, she's running herself ragged holding get togethers all the fuckin' time. I think J's had enough; I know I have."

"Never thought I'd see the day you and J talked like civilised men. Madison's a miracle worker."

"Fuck you." I grinned at him. "We all know J was a dickhead when it came to his caveman attitude towards Madison, so that was all on him."

"Takes two to fuck it up," Griff muttered, his gaze drifting to Marcus who'd just hit the clubhouse.

It was Friday afternoon and all the boys were gathering for Friday night drinks. Tension within the club had hit an all-time high over the last few weeks. After the fallout between Marcus and J a couple of months ago, Marcus was strengthening his ties with some of the boys. It looked like he was using those ties to create a divide between them and those of us behind J.

"He's a sly bastard," I said.

Griff turned back to me. "Marcus?"

I nodded. "Yeah. Some of the boys told me the shit he's been spinning them. Making them promises of huge payouts if Storm runs drugs again. What I can't fuckin' work out is why the hell he got us out of drugs years ago if he's just going to dump us back in that shit."

Griff was quiet for a minute. "Been trying to figure that out myself."

J and Scott joined us, and J glared at Marcus. "What the fuck's he promising them now?" he snarled.

"Christ knows," Scott said as he downed some of his beer.

I eyed him. "How you holding up, VP? That's some shit Marcus threw your way this week."

Scott scowled. "He can throw as much shit as he wants at me, at all of us; if he wants any of us out, we're not going quietly."

It was clear Marcus wanted J out, but it looked like he was trying to turn the boys against Scott too. We'd heard rumblings that he wanted a new VP. And it appeared his plan to achieve that goal involved spreading lies about Scott, which was what he'd started doing this week.

"Wilder tell you anything more?" Griff asked Scott.

"Thank fuck for that prospect," I muttered. Wilder had been with Storm for almost a year, and as far as I was concerned, should be patched in right now. He was quietly behind J and Scott, and passing on information about Marcus.

Before Scott could answer, Harlow and Velvet walked in. I straightened at the sight of Velvet, on high alert for what she might have to say to me. We hadn't spoken in months after a disagreement. However, watching her now, she didn't appear to be mad at me. In fact, she seemed happy enough to see me. I ran my eyes down her body, and my dick jerked as I took in the skin tight black pants, and fuck me heels she was wearing. I had no idea how women managed to walk in shoes that high, but I wasn't fucking complaining. My gaze settled on her tits that were pushing their way out of her tight black top. She had to be a double D cup at least. Christ, one day I had to get my hands on them.

They came over to where we were, and Harlow began telling Scott some shit about her day. It was white noise to me as I zeroed in on Velvet's tattoos. In amongst the ones she had on her arm, there was a new one. It was some sort of flower and swirl design. I wondered what it meant, because Velvet was deep where her tattoos were concerned. She had a lot of them on her arms, stomach and back, and they all symbolised something in her life.

She was watching me. I jabbed my finger in the direction of her tattoo. "What's it mean?" I asked her, quietly.

"It's a lotus flower. New beginnings, growth."

"The colour in it looks good."

Shit, this whole conversation felt stilted. I yearned for the easiness we used to have. And what new beginnings was she talking about?

"I used your girl again to do it. She's good."

I'd put Velvet onto my tattoo artist awhile back after she had a bad experience with the guy she was using. He'd hit on her and hadn't been happy when Velvet said no. I was livid when I found out, and had paid him a visit. "Yeah, she might be an angry dyke but she's damn good at what she does."

Velvet's gaze shifted to my arms. "You get any new ones lately?"

I chuckled. "It's kinda getting hard to find any bare skin to ink."

She smiled; the kind of smile that makes a man forget where he was and what he was doing. "Yeah, I guess." And then her eyes twinkled with the Velvet mischievousness I'd really missed. "What about your ass, Nash? Is it inked?"

My face broke out in a grin. "You wanna see it? Happy to show you any part of my body that you're interested in, sweet thing."

Her eyes continued dancing. Hell, she was flirting with me now, and it felt fucking good. "Can we keep that invitation open? I'm fairly busy at the moment but I think your ass might be worth seeing."

"You've no idea, baby. But I've got other body parts that are far more worthy of seeing, and anytime you're up for that viewing, you just call. Don't care what time of the day either."

She tilted her head to the side. "Those body parts inked?"

I leant in so I could whisper in her ear, "That's for me to know and for you to find out, darlin'."

As I moved my face away from hers, I didn't miss the glazed look in her eyes. I'd affected her as much as she had me. This sexy tango we'd been locked in for years always aroused me. Flirting with Velvet was one of my preferred activities, but fuck, I'd much rather she take me up on my offers.

Harlow cut in on our conversation. "You ready to go, Velvet?"

Velvet battled to drag her eyes from mine. "Yes," she murmured. It was evident she would have happily stayed. And that thought right there made me a happy asshole. Perhaps we could move past what had been said two months ago; forget it and move on.

She gave me one last smile before leaving. It confused the hell out of me. It was the kind of smile that says 'well, it was fun while it lasted'. I'd obviously misread the flirting for something it wasn't. Shit, women and their fucking mixed signals.

They left, and Griff brought up the one thing I didn't want to think about. "What are you fuckers doing on Sunday?"

Mother's Day.

It was ten years this year, and my mind was already overwhelmed by thoughts of it. And that was without whatever Gabriella would fire at me. The anger and hurt that was never far away, surfaced. And along with it, came the suffocating pressure on my chest. My heart thumped and my skin burnt with the rage that I desperately needed to get out of me; the rage, that as much as I tried, I could never escape from.

"I'm doing lunch with Harlow's mum," Scott said.

He was oblivious to the shit swirling in my head at the moment. So was Griff. I'd never told anyone; only my family knew. And Kick, but I didn't see him very often.

"You're not seeing your mum?" Griff directed at Scott.

"Haven't worked that out with her yet. I think Madison's trying to organise dinner with her so we'll go to that I guess."

"And you?" he asked me.

I pushed through the rage to answer him. "Lunch with the family."

"What are you doing, Griff?" Scott asked.

Shit, it came back to me in a rush. Griff's parents were both dead. Maybe he needed somewhere to go; a distraction for the day.

He shrugged. "I'll find someone to spend the day with. There's always plenty of offers." He aimed for nonchalance, but I wasn't so sure it was what he was feeling. I left it alone though; Griff wasn't big on talking about shit like this. And besides, most days, he

8

preferred his own company anyway.

My attention was diverted by a pair of sexy legs that walked by. I followed the legs up until I hit big tits and knew I'd found my fun for the night. I slapped Griff on the back, and grinned at him and Scott. "Have a good night, boys. I'll be over there if you need me. That is, until she agrees to ride me, and then you won't see me for at least a day." If I could, I'd lock myself away with pussy for the whole fucking weekend. It was always a welcome distraction from my thoughts.

CHAPTER 2

One Last Breath - Creed

NASH

MOTHER'S DAY HIT LIKE A BITCH.

First I had to deal with the chick I'd screwed last night. Then, I received instructions off my sister, Erika, to pick up groceries on my way to lunch. I'd had a run in with a dickhead at the store and arrived at Mum's house in the worst mood.

I juggled the groceries in my arms and kicked the half open door all the way open so I could enter. "Carla, a little help please, babe," I hollered down the hallway.

Carla didn't appear. Of course she fucking didn't. My sister's life revolved around herself and we only got the time of day when it suited her.

"Fuck," I muttered as the bags of groceries threatened to fall out of my arms. I continued to make my way to the kitchen, doing my best not to drop any of the bags. As I passed the lounge room I caught a glimpse of Carla out of the corner of my eye. And I didn't like what I saw. The groceries all fell to the floor as I saw red.

"What the fuck?" I yelled, as I stepped over the bags and stalked into the room. Carla was on the lounge underneath a guy, and he had his mouth all over her and his hands on her ass. It wasn't so much his hands on her that pissed me off; more so, whose hands they were. At the sound of my voice, he turned his head to look at me. He smirked and I lost my shit completely.

"Get the fuck off her," I thundered. Blood pumped through my body and rage filled my vision.

Red, fucking rage.

I wanted to knock the shit out of this motherfucker.

And I tried. I ripped him off her, spun him around and shoved him to the ground. A moment later my fist connected with his face and I punched him so hard that blood flew onto the carpet. I continued my assault, oblivious to the world around me. All that mattered in that moment was my uncontrollable urge to make him hurt. I pummelled him with punch after punch. What Carla was doing with a dickhead like him was beyond me. And for him to fucking smirk at me like that just proved to me that he wasn't worthy of her. I knew his type. And hell would fucking freeze over before I allowed my sister to give herself to someone like him.

"Nash!"

My arm stopped mid-punch and I looked up to see my mother standing in the doorway with her hands on her hips. She was pissed off.

Fuck.

Pissing my mother off was not a good move, and doing it on Mother's Day was a really fucking bad move.

Begrudgingly, I straightened. I divided my attention between my mother and the asshole on the floor. My pleasure at seeing him almost unconscious was short-lived when both my mother and Carla started ranting at me.

"You can be a real asshole, Nash," Carla fumed, her face clouding with anger. She tried to shove past me to get to her boyfriend.

Jesse.

Who the fuck names their son, Jesse?

I blocked her attempt, holding my arm out to keep her away. At the same time, Jesse groaned and caught my attention. His face was covered in blood; I'd probably broken his nose.

He deserved it.

Motherfucker.

I twisted my head to look at Carla. "What the fuck are you doing with him again?"

"That is none of your bloody business." Quick tempers ran in our family and hers flared up instantly.

"Like hell it isn't." I slashed my hand in front of me in a circular motion, pointing to my mother and other sister, Erika, who were glaring at me. "It's all of our business after what he did to you the last time."

Carla sucked in a breath, but her anger didn't dissipate. "I've forgiven him and you need to let it go."

I shook my head. "No fuckin' way, babe. And you need to have more self respect."

Hurt flashed across her face, but she covered it quickly. My sister was good at hiding her pain from the world. Christ, my whole family was good at that shit. She took a step back; it looked like she was getting ready to flee. Another thing we were good at; running. "Nash, I'm a twenty-two year old woman, for God's sake. I'm old enough to make my own decisions. I don't need you stepping in with your fists to sort out my life. You should spend your time and energy sorting out your own shit rather than screwing your way into oblivion and getting in my face."

"Enough!" my Mother finally stepped in. "Nash," she pointed towards the hallway, "Kitchen. Now."

I scowled at the room. How the hell had this become my fault?

At that moment, Jesse pushed up off the ground and turned on me. "You're a dickhead, Nash, and you'd better watch your fucking back."

His face was a wash of blood and that made me fucking ecstatic but he had to be hallucinating if he thought I needed to watch my back. I shook my head at him and his naivety. My rage hadn't calmed though, and I decided it was best to walk away from him now. For my Mother. It was Mother's Day after all. But I stepped into his space one last time. "You fuck with my sister again and a broken nose will be the least of your problems." We glared at each other for a moment, hostility churning between us, and then I stalked out of the room.

★★★

"What's up your ass today?" Erika asked as she entered the kitchen. Just over five feet of fierce female energy packaged in the softest and most feminine looking woman I'd ever seen. Erika was one woman I didn't mess with. She'd retrieved the groceries I dropped and thrust the bags at me while hitting me with a dirty look.

"You can't tell me you're happy that Carla's back with that dickhead," I muttered.

"No, but it's her life, Nash. At some point you've got to stop being the overprotective older brother and give her the space to make her own choices." She raised her hand at me as I opened my mouth to reply. "And you've got to let her fail."

"Fuck that. I don't want her to fail." My eyes narrowed on her. "Why would you want her to fail?"

She sighed. "I don't *want* her to, but it's how we learn in life. You know that. Shit, with all the screw ups you've made in life and all the shit you've been through, you know that failing teaches us how to be better; how to do better."

"Yeah, and with all the shit I've been through, I want to use what I've learnt and help her not make the same mistakes." I blew out a long, frustrated breath.

She started unpacking the groceries and putting them away. Erika never could stay still for very long; she was always on the go. "Tell me something; if someone had advised you not to do the things you did that ended up being mistakes, would you have listened to them?"

"Maybe."

She stopped what she was doing and trained her eyes on me. "Bullshit."

Why did she always have to be right? Begrudgingly, I admitted, "Okay, so maybe not."

"How about, definitely not? You were a handful; so determined to get into all kinds of shit. And don't even get me started on the stuff you did after Gabriella -"

I cut her off right there. Fury circled the room. It reached into my soul and forced its way into my mind. As hard as I tried to control it, to stop it gaining any power over me, there was no way I could. I was no match for it. I towered over Erika and let the fury explode out of me and shatter around us. "She does not exist to me so don't fucking say her name. Ever. Again."

I remained standing over her, panting heavy breaths and trying desperately to get my shit together. My mind was a mess of thoughts; thoughts I didn't fucking want in there. Thoughts I'd spent years jamming into the dark recesses to avoid them. My chest tightened into a painful knot of heaviness and the demons beckoned from hell, calling my name with a lustful resonance .

I needed to get out of here.

Now.

But I couldn't.

Fuck.

I shoved my hand through my hair and attempted to calm my breathing. This day started off bad and had quickly escalated to completely fucked.

"I'm sorry." Erika snapped me out of my inner turmoil and forced my attention back to reality.

My eyes darted to hers and I processed the distressed look on her face.

She laid her hand on my arm.

Gentle.

Soothing.

Calming.

I focused on breathing.

In. Out. In. Out.

"Nash." She tried to reach me but I was still clawing my way out of the abyss.

Give me a minute. I'm nearly there.

I sensed movement behind me; sensed another presence in the room. Noise and talking. But I couldn't drag myself out yet.

And then arms wrapped around me from behind.

Love.

Tenderness.

Carla.

I forced out a long, harsh breath and gulped for air.

"Fuck," I muttered.

Carla squeezed me, not wanting to let me go. I placed my hands on her arms. "It's okay. I'm okay. You can let me go now."

"You sure?" She hesitated.

"Yeah."

Her arms released me and I turned to face her. She looked as distressed as Erika had. Worry coloured her face and I hated that I'd put it there. Me and my shit. I pulled her into a rough embrace. My hand cupped the back of her neck, and my lips brushed across

15

her forehead.

We held each other for a moment and then she looked up into my eyes. "You need to deal with that once and for all."

"I have."

She shook her head. "No, you haven't, Nash. And it's time you started being honest with yourself about it." Her voice held no judgement; there was only love there. And for that, I couldn't be mad at her.

★★★

An hour later, I wandered back into the kitchen. I'd just spent the last forty minutes working on Mum's car.

Erika was cooking dinner and gave me her attention for a moment. "All fixed?"

"Yeah, but there will be something else next week. That car is a piece of junk and she needs to get a new one."

"She won't spend the money, you know that." She told me something I already knew.

"One day it'll disappear out of her garage and there will be a new one in it's place. I'm not a mechanic anymore and the only engine I want to work on is my own."

"You can't just replace her car, Nash. She loves that -"

"Piece of shit," I finished her sentence, and then continued, "You watch me."

She fell silent for a moment before asking, "What time is Jamison arriving?"

I watched her juggle stirring the casserole and scrolling on her phone. "What the fuck are you doing?" I eventually asked.

She hit me with a dirty look. "I'm trying to see what the next thing is to add to this casserole. And you didn't answer my question."

Our brother was always late. "He'll be here soon," I answered as I walked towards her. "What are you cooking?"

"That beef casserole that Mum likes."

I peered into the pot and then eyed her. "Seriously? You need to read the recipe to make that?"

Another dirty look from her. "You want to make it?"

Leaning my back against the bench, I muttered, "Well I sure as shit wouldn't need the recipe. By the looks of it, you need to add the mushrooms now."

She continued to scowl at me, but did as I suggested before saying, "Mum doesn't like Carla's boyfriend either. You know that, right?"

"I figured. Not sure why she lets him in the house though."

"Because Carla still lives here and she respects her enough to let her live her own life."

It was hurting my ears to listen to this shit. "Babe, you've got ten years on Carla and I've got twelve, and we both fuckin' know that she can do a lot better than that prick. He shared his dick around the last time they were together; I'm not sure what makes her think this time will be different."

"She's young, Nash. She grew up with no father figure except for you and Jamison, and while you both did an amazing job, she's suffered because of Dad leaving us. Her self worth is shot to shit and so she lets guys treat her like Jesse does."

"Fuck, Erika, why do you always have to be so fuckin' understanding of stuff? For once, why can't you join the rest of us and admit what a prick he is? And that Carla needs to open her eyes and see what's right in front of her."

"I'm not understanding," she huffed, "I'm just giving you my opinion on why she is the way she is."

Before I could say anything more, Jamison made his entrance, his arms full with flowers, wine and chocolate. He lifted his chin at me before filling the kitchen table with his gifts, and asked, "You in trouble again, shithead?"

"Always," I grinned at Erika who rolled her eyes at me. I nodded at the stuff he'd put on the table, "What are you sucking up to Mum for?"

"It's Mother's Day, you're supposed to bring presents. You were probably too busy screwing some chick to go shopping, weren't you?"

I smirked at him, "Well, if you've got it, use it. Next time you feel the urge to hit the shops, just send your woman over to me; I'll take care of her for you."

"Now see that's where you're wrong, little brother. The way I treat a woman when I take her shopping? Guarantees me the best fucking orgasm when I get her home."

Erika butted in, "God, will you two ever grow up?" She'd finished with the casserole and was now cleaning up. Pointing at the cupboards, she said, "Nash, you need to set the table; Jamison, you can help me with the food."

Anyone would have thought that Erika was the oldest from the way she bossed us around. I saluted her. "Yes, boss."

She paused for a moment, and asked, "Why can't you always just do what I say?"

"My middle name's not easy, babe."

Jamison chuckled. "You sure about that? I reckon we could find a football stadium of women who would disagree with that."

Grinning, I nodded, "Probably right there, asshole."

Erika just shook her head at me and Jamison continued laughing. The earlier tension between my sister and I had eased but the heaviness in my chest lingered. Mother's Day never failed to fuck with me and today she'd dug her claws in deep.

★★★

"Will I see you again this week?" my mother asked as she hugged me goodbye.

"Probably not, I've got a lot going on at the club."

She let me go and I reached for Carla. Wrapping my arms around her, I whispered in her ear, "You need to ditch that asshole."

She tried to pull away from me but I tightened my hold on her.

"Nash, let me go," she complained, fighting me.

Doing as she asked, I stepped back and caught her gaze, "You deserve so much better. I wish you could see that."

"Yeah, like you do too," she countered.

"I don't fuckin' deserve anything," I muttered, and turned to Erika. "You still having problems with your neighbour?"

"Yeah, he's getting worse, playing his music loud till all hours and yelling abuse at me whenever I try and talk to him about it. I actually think he's got a mental health problem, because he's so up and down."

I scowled. "Doesn't excuse his behaviour. Call me the next time it happens, okay?"

She sighed. "Nash, you'll only make things worse. I think I'll just call the police next time."

"Fuck that, Erika. They'll do jack shit. You let me talk to him once and he won't give you grief again."

She raised a brow. "So you'll talk to him? Or will you resort to your favourite way of dealing with stuff?"

"Babe, my favourite way of doing stuff *is* with my mouth." I winked at her. She was far too uptight.

She rolled her eyes. "You know what I mean."

"I'll only punch the motherfucker if he needs it. He listens to what I have to say, and promises not to annoy you anymore, then we'll all be happy and no-one will end up with broken bones."

She slung her bag over her shoulder and murmured, "Something tells me he won't listen to you so I still think it's best if I just call the police. I don't want you to end up back in prison."

Fuck, why did my sister have to be so headstrong? "I'm not going to end up in prison again. Just promise me you'll call me."

She'd already started walking towards the front door and yelled out over her shoulder, "Promise."

I followed her out, with Mum, Jamison and Carla on my heels. Even though I didn't believe her promise, I kept my mouth shut. There was no way she was going to agree to what I wanted so I simply decided to follow it up at some point during the week and sort the asshole out myself.

As she said her goodbyes to everyone, I received a text message.

Gabriella: Happy Mother's Day, asshole.

Fuck.

The red rage blinded me again. It reached into my chest and threatened to squeeze the life out of me. At the same time, the pain engulfed me. Ten fucking years and the pain never left. It tore through me, lacerating my heart; the cold, patched together heart I still had even though I'd done my best to rip it out and throw it the fuck away.

"Nash!" My attention was drawn back to my family around me.

"What?" I snapped, looking wildly at them; my mind unable to focus clearly on what they were saying as it tried to process jumbled thoughts and the relentless anguish that wouldn't let me out of its grip. The anguish that on most days I dealt with, but on this fucking day, I struggled with. No fucking thanks to Gabriella.

My mother looked at my phone and then back at my face. "Gabriella?" she whispered.

My voice was caught somewhere in my chest so I simply nodded.

20

"You need to change your phone number," she suggested, her kind eyes watchful over me. Hesitation was clear in her eyes too; she knew from experience that I wasn't good at taking advice.

I fought the urge to ignore them all, jump on the back of my bike and get the hell out of here. That would be a lot easier than dealing with this shit. Again. I blew out a long breath. "No." I was emphatic. I'd never do that. As hard as it was to negotiate this pain, I needed to remember what we'd done; what I'd done.

Annoyance flared on my mother's face. "It's been ten years since Aaron -"

"No!" I roared, anger pumping furiously through my body. That was it; I was done. I pushed past them all and stalked to my bike. Voices floated through the air but I had no idea what was being said; the only thing that mattered to me in that instant was getting the fuck out of here. Getting the fuck away from the memories and the pain, and finding a reprieve from the living hell I was in.

CHAPTER 3

Hard To Love - Lee Brice

VELVET

"SEE HOW THAT COLOUR BRINGS YOUR EYES OUT?" I asked.

Harlow leaned forward and assessed herself in the mirror as I packed up the eyeshadows and makeup I'd used on her. She smiled and I knew I'd achieved my goal. "You're right!" she exclaimed, and eyed me with excitement. "I'm not sure why I've never experimented with that colour before."

"It's easy to get stuck in a rut with your makeup; we all do it."

"Thank you so much for forcing me to let you play with my makeup."

"You make me sound like a bossy bitch."

A voice boomed from behind us. "If the shoe fits."

I turned and glared at Scott.

He shrugged. "What? You are a bossy bitch, Velvet."

"I have to be where you and the guys are concerned, but I'm not usually bossy with Harlow."

Harlow backed me up. "Yeah, she doesn't boss me around but

I'm glad she did on this because I love what she's done with my makeup."

Scott walked to where Harlow was and grabbed her around the waist. He kissed her and then murmured, "I'm heading out but I'll be back at the end of your shift to pick you up. You all good?"

I tuned them out; watching lovestruck couples together was not something I enjoyed doing. Instead, I packed away my makeup and finished getting ready for work. It was a longer shift than usual tonight because one of the other strippers was sick, and Cody had asked me to cover for her. Fortunately for Cody, I liked him, so I'd said yes. Hell, in the four years I'd worked at Indigo, Cody was the best manager they'd ever employed so I was doing everything I could to make sure he stayed.

Scott's voice pulled me back into their conversation. "Nash is out front, Velvet. Something's pissed him off. You got five minutes to check on him?"

"Christ, Scott, Nash is always pissed off about something lately. I doubt there's anything I could say that would help him."

Scott's eyes narrowed on me. "What happened between you two? You've been good mates for years and now you're hardly talking."

"Nothing, unless you count the fact I told him a little while ago to clean his shit up, and stop fucking every chick he sets eyes on."

Harlow sucked in a breath. "Really? You said that to him?"

I scowled at the memory. "Yes. Someone had to, because seriously, I'm concerned his dick will need resuscitation soon. Surely that thing has had enough pussy to last it two lifetimes."

Scott snorted. "Make that three lifetimes and you're getting close."

"My point exactly. So yeah, he didn't take that conversation very well and he's been avoiding me ever since."

Scott pulled Harlow close for another kiss and then gave me

his attention. "Talk to him; he might surprise the fuck outta you."

He left me and Harlow alone and I stood staring after him, shaking my head. I didn't want to talk to Nash for a couple of reasons. Number one was that our friendship really did seem to be dead after I'd said that to him. And the second reason was that he'd actually hurt me by cutting me off. We'd been friends for as long as I'd been working at Indigo; not close, close friends, but when we hung out together at the club we got on really well. There was an easiness to it that I liked, and he was one of the only guys who hadn't hit on me. Well, he flirted a lot but he'd never put the hard word on me and I loved that about him. I'd felt like our friendship had gotten to the point where we could be open and honest so that's why I'd said that to him. Nash screwed any woman that would have him and I felt like he deserved better. I knew there was something inside him that made him treat himself the way he did; looking at him some days was like looking in a mirror. I'd been where he was. The only difference was that I now respected myself enough not to do that shit anymore and that's what I wanted for Nash.

"You gonna talk to him?" Harlow asked.

I sighed. Of course I was; I couldn't let a friend down. "Yeah."

She smiled. "Nash is lucky to have you as a friend."

"He fucking is, but we'll soon see if he realises that."

★★★

I found him ten minutes later, sitting alone in the club watching the stripper who was currently working the stage. It was still early in the night; only a handful of men were here so far. However, the ones that were here recognised me as I walked towards Nash, and whistles and suggestive comments followed me.

One guy yelled out, "I'd like to lick your pussy and then come all over your face before sticking - "

This shit wasn't new to me but this guy was a complete dick. I'd seen the way he treated the other strippers and I didn't like it. I turned and challenged him, "Really? Is that how you sweet talk all your women? Cause I've gotta say, it doesn't turn me on and there's no way I'd let your tiny dick anywhere near my face."

His friends laughed and cheered me on, and I watched in satisfaction as his face turned a lovely shade of red. I shook my head in disgust at him and continued on my way to Nash. As I approached him, I realised he was watching me with an intense stare; it kind of unnerved me.

"Remind me never to piss you and your acid tongue off," he said as I sat next to him.

"Well, you already have."

His brow arched. "How? I just arrived."

I leaned in close to him. "You pissed me off awhile ago, Nash, but I decided to let you off from my acid tongue."

"How the fuck did I piss you off?" His body tensed with anger and frustration which only served to irritate me; I hadn't said or done anything to warrant the amount of hostility he was projecting.

Sitting back away from him, I replied, "When I was trying to be a friend to you by suggesting you stop screwing around, you cut me off."

He glowered at me. "Friends don't tell you how to live your life, Velvet."

"Then they're not your real friends," I threw back at him with no hesitation.

He stood up abruptly. "Fuck, I don't need this shit from you, too," he muttered, raking his hand through his hair.

I sat calmly; I wouldn't allow him to rile me up on the outside, even though my insides were seething with annoyance. "Maybe you do, Nash. If you don't have any other friends who will be honest with you, then I'd say you do need this shit from me."

He turned so he was staring directly down at me. Leaning forward, he rested his hands on either side of my chair and shoved his face into mine. His green eyes were blazing with wrath, and he spat his words out. "Today is not the fuckin' day to mess with me. I've had all I can take from my family and I sure as shit don't need to come here and cop more from you. So keep your fuckin' mouth shut and leave me the hell alone." With that, he pushed himself away from me and strode out of the club.

Well, shit. I had no idea what that was all about, but something told me Nash probably needed a friend more than ever right about now. Unfortunately, I started work in ten minutes so it wouldn't be me helping him tonight. Sadly, I knew he would find solace in the arms of a stranger but it would be temporary solace at best.

CHAPTER 4

Stupid Boy - Keith Urban

VELVET

I UNLOCKED THE BOOT OF MY CAR AND STARTED unloading my groceries from the trolley. It was only ten am and already the idiots were out in force, which meant my day so far hadn't been the best. People never failed to irk me. Perhaps I should seriously think about doing all my shopping online.

As I struggled to lift the box of coke cans I'd bought, into my car, a pair of strong hands took over and lifted it for me. I looked up at Nash's face in surprise. It had been just over a week since I'd seen him; since he'd abused me. He hadn't been into Indigo in that time and I wondered if he'd been avoiding me because he normally lived at that place.

He laid a huge smile on me and that just pissed me off. I slammed the boot shut and pushed the trolley into the trolley bay before returning to my car. He was standing there with his arms folded across his chest, smile still in place.

I glared at him. "So this is how you're going to play this out?"

"Play what out?"

"I haven't seen you for a week and the last time I saw you, you told me to back the fuck off. Now you show up and act like nothing happened."

His smile disappeared, and he rubbed his hand over his face. "Can we pretend that didn't happen?"

"No, Nash, we cannot pretend that didn't happen. I'm not a fake friend who is happy to let shit slide. If you want that, you won't find it with me, so I suggest you go back to your skanks, who I'm sure would be happy to provide you with a shallow friendship and a place to stick your dick." God, he riled me up lately and I couldn't even begin to understand why.

"Fuck, Velvet, you make it hard on a man."

"Oh good Lord, get over yourself," I muttered, and tried to shove my way past him to the front door of my car.

He placed his hand on my shoulder and stopped me before I could get past. "I'm sorry for being a prick the other day," he forced out. His eyes flamed with displeasure, and his shoulders tensed; this was hard for him to do, but I wasn't going to make it easy for him.

"And what about the fact you've been a prick to me for months now?" I challenged him.

He opened his mouth to say something, but snapped it shut straight away and stared at me. I waited to see what he would say but nothing came out; he simply continued to stare. As much as I tried to figure out what he was thinking, he was unreadable. To me, anyway.

"Fine!" I huffed, and turned away towards the front door of the car, ready to leave. But before I left, I had one more thing to say, so I spun back around. "We've been friends for four years, Nash. I've always felt like you were there for me and vice versa. It upsets me that you've shut that down, but I'm not the kind of person who will allow someone to keep treating me like shit which is what you've been doing to me for awhile now. So, if you want to still be friends, you know where to find me and what you need to do. Until then, I'm done with this."

I didn't even wait to see his reaction; I got in my car as fast as I could and sped off. It had hurt to say that to him, but there came a time in a friendship where you had to put yourself first and refuse to be walked all over.

★★★

As I pulled into my driveway, I realised with a sinking feeling that my day was about to get worse. My ex-husband was leaning against his car, waiting for me.

"Shit," I muttered, and psyched myself up to deal with him.

"Velvet," he greeted me in his smooth, honeyed voice. That voice could charm the habit off a nun. I should know; he'd dazzled me years ago and smooth talked his way into my heart.

"What do you want, James?" I snapped.

"Someone's having a bad day?"

I didn't have time for small talk with him. "I haven't heard from you since the day you trashed my heart five years ago. I'm guessing that the only reason you're here today is because you want something from me."

His cool composure was momentarily challenged, and I saw the darkness cross his face fleetingly, but he quickly pulled himself back together and walked towards me. He'd kept that darkness hidden from me for most of our relationship but when I'd not performed in the manner he'd wanted and had failed to provide him with what he desired, his dark side had shone through and slapped me in the face. I'd been naive in my love for him and he'd taught me that love is a fickle master; one to be avoided at all costs.

He moved into my personal space; he knew I hated that. "I

29

have a proposal for you."

"I'm not interested in any proposal of yours."

"This one will interest you," he stated with the arrogance I knew so well.

I pushed past him and began walking towards my front door. "The answer's no."

He reached out, grabbed my arm and pulled me back to him. His grip was hard and I was sure it would leave me bruised. And shit, he scared me. I'd spent years building my walls up against any further hurt this man could inflict on me and here he was, smashing those walls down with ease. "You should know by now that the answer is never no, Velvet," he threatened on an angry breath.

My heart raced with fear. "What do you want from me?" I tried to hide my anxiety, but my voice cracked slightly; just enough for him to notice, and just enough for him to be able to play his manipulative games knowing that he held all the power.

He kept me in his tight grip. "That's my girl," he said, his voice washing over me like poison, "It's very simple really. I'm going to offer you a lot of money and in return you're going to keep your mouth shut if anyone should ever come and ask you questions about me or us."

I broke free of his hold and stared at him. "Why?"

"I'm going into the family business."

Politics. No wonder he was sniffing around me now. I had the power to shatter his dream.

My anxiety eased a little and I faked the confidence I desperately craved. "Make your offer and then get the fuck out of here."

He visibly struggled with my attitude. This was a side of me that James was not acquainted with. "My lawyer will be in touch with the details," he finally said. "And, Velvet, that language is very unbecoming."

My blood boiled. "I don't give a shit what you think of my

language. I'm not your doormat anymore, so I can say and think whatever the hell I want."

Disdain dripped from him. "I was right to get rid of you years ago."

His words pierced my heart. As much as I knew he was an asshole, and as much as I knew I was better than what he thought of me, it still hurt to have the man I'd loved and given everything to, say those words. He'd ruined my self belief years ago, and I'd slowly healed myself; I now feared he had the ability to bury me under a layer of self doubt and loathing all over again.

CHAPTER 5

This Is Who I Am - Vanessa Amorosi

NASH

Erika was wrong. Her neighbour didn't have a mental health problem; he was just a dickhead. I'd confronted him ten minutes ago about her issues with him. He wasn't happy about it and had proceeded to have a go at me. I let him hurl obscenities at me which he did like a pro. He was obviously experienced at abusing people; he didn't even stop to take a breath.

Once I was sure he was finished, I took a step closer to him and snarled, "You finished?"

I was slightly taller and bigger than he was, but he held his ground; he didn't even blink at my intrusion into his space. "No, one last thing. You tell your sister that this is my fucking home and I'll do whatever the fuck I want whenever the fuck I want to do it. And if she wants to get her big brother involved, tell her to bring it on."

I was already in a foul mood after my earlier conversation with Velvet, but this guy's smugness tipped me over the edge. Even if I'd wanted to contain my fury, I wouldn't have been able to.

"You're the big fuckin' man, aren't you? Treating women like that must make you feel real fuckin' good about yourself, motherfucker," I growled. "You know what makes me feel good?" I continued in a menacing tone. He had the good fucking grace to register concern, but my lust for violence had been fueled, and there was no turning back now. I raised my fist and smashed it into his face, taking great joy in the blood this produced.

I'd caught him unaware and he tried to get in the game, but I was two steps ahead of him and punched the other side of his face before jabbing him hard in the gut. He doubled over, but I wasn't done. I grabbed him by the shoulders and shoved him back into the brick wall behind him. The thud he hit the wall with was satisfying, as was the look of alarm on his face.

"Stop!" he managed to get out while clutching his stomach, and trying to shield his face from me.

My arm was raised and ready to rain more blows down on him, but I paused and eyed him. His face was a bloody mess and he appeared to be in some pain. I'd probably done enough damage to make him think twice about bugging Erika again. Lowering my arm, I demanded, "We got an understanding here, asshole?"

He didn't hesitate. "Yes, now fuck off and leave me alone."

"Just one more thing: you fuck with my sister again and I'll be back." I paused, and then threatened him further, "And I won't be alone."

He nodded and once I was convinced he meant it, I shoved him one last time and then left him to it. I was fairly certain that Erika wouldn't hear about this from him which was the way I wanted it. She had a tendency to stress too much about shit and the last thing I wanted was her worrying about me. God knew, she already did that enough.

★★★

Five hours later, I met with Scott, Griff and J to discuss where we were at with our investigation of Marcus. Griff was full of bad news.

"You're kidding, right?" I asked in disbelief.

Griff looked at me and shook his head. "No, the lead was a dead end. Marcus has covered his tracks well."

"Fuck," J swore and slammed his hand down on the table. "We're never gonna get this motherfucker, are we?"

I felt his frustration. We'd spent the last two months trying to get a handle on what Marcus was up to and none of the leads went anywhere. Either Marcus wasn't up to anything or he was skilled at hiding shit. We all believed the latter scenario.

"Patience, brother," Scott directed at J.

Unfortunately, patience wasn't J's strong suit and he was pretty agitated with this latest development. "Maybe I need to go back to Adelaide and talk to some of the boys down there. Someone's gotta know something for fuck's sake."

Scott considered this and then gave Griff a questioning look. Griff nodded, and Scott turned to J and agreed, "Okay, you go down there and see what you can find. But you're going to have to keep it quiet, brother; the last thing we want is news travelling back to Dad. You know if we can trust any of the boys down there with this?"

J contemplated that, and then replied, "There's two of them who I'm pretty sure can be trusted."

Griff stood. "Contact them and set it up, J." He checked his watch. "I've gotta go, got a hot date with a brunette."

"Since when do you date?" I asked. I'd never known Griff to date.

"Date is probably the wrong word for it, brother," he smirked, "But I have dated before."

"Must have been before I came to town."

Scott stood as well. "Long time before you came to town, Nash. Griff's a moody bastard; kind of makes it hard to find a woman to stick around."

"That and it's hard to find a woman who won't fuck you over," Griff muttered as he left us.

"That's the fuckin' truth," I agreed as J and I stood too.

"You heading out," Scott asked me.

"No, I'm going to stick around and find a bit of fun for the night."

"Yeah, I bet you are. Heard you haven't been in here for over a week; you having withdrawals?"

I chuckled. "Smartass."

J cut in, "Nash, Madison wants you over for dinner soon. Can you sort that out with her when you speak to her next?"

"Will do," I agreed. J and I still had an uneasy relationship but we were working on it for Madison's sake. Hell, I'd do anything for that chick.

He nodded and then they left together. As I watched them leave, a blonde chick caught my attention. She had her back to me and what a fine sight that was. I watched as she chatted with two men; it looked like she was doing all the talking, because their attention was on her body and it didn't look like any words were coming out of their mouths. I couldn't blame them because she was fucking spectacular in her tight, black dress that hugged her curves and barely covered her ass. Her back was exposed, and most of her skin was covered in tattoos. It looked kind of familiar to me, but I couldn't place it, and as I was wondering if I knew this chick, she turned around and started walking towards me.

Fuck.

It was Velvet in a blonde wig. My fucking dick was hard, and as I took in her killer tits and hips, it only got harder. Shit, who was

I kidding; I'd had a hard on for her for years. She inspired it in a man just by existing. I'd flirted hard with her when we first met, doing my best to get her into bed. We'd come close a few times but she'd managed to resist me and block every attempt I made to get her panties off. She'd used the excuse of not wanting to sleep with people she worked with so I'd calmed my flirting down thinking that she'd eventually come to the party. However, we'd become friends and for some fucked up reason, I didn't want to screw that friendship up by screwing her. So here I was, with a four year old hard on, and no chance in hell of getting it taken care of by the woman who caused it.

She didn't stop when she got to me, and she didn't acknowledge me; she kept walking without a backwards glance. I'd really managed to piss her off this time. She was a feisty woman and over the years we'd had our arguments because she was the kind of woman who gave it to me straight. If she didn't agree with something I said or did, she didn't hesitate to tell me. But we'd always moved past every argument; we always knew we could count on each other. When she'd told me to stop getting my dick out for every chick I met, she'd caught me in a bad moment and I hadn't taken it well. And I'd reacted by cutting the friendship. It'd been a lonely few months without her, but being the asshole I was, I'd refused to own up to my shit. But fuck, I'd missed her. I'd realised how much just having her to sit and talk with meant to me. I might have wanted to rip her clothes off over the years but if you gave me the choice between fucking her and talking to her now, I'd give up the sex in a heartbeat. And that realisation right there had done my head in so I'd kept my distance ever since it'd hit me.

Watching her walk away from me without a word exchanged, hit me in the chest. It was painful; not as painful as some things in my life but it fucking hurt. *Shit.* I raked my hand through my hair. I had to fix this. But first I had to fix the raging hard on I was stuck with. I scanned the room looking for someone to help me with that. Tonight I'd take care of pressing matters and tomorrow I'd take care of my friendship with Velvet.

CHAPTER 6

Golden - Lady Antebellum

VELVET

As I opened the cupboard to start putting the groceries away, my mother complained, "You've got to stop spending your money on me, Velvet. I can buy my own groceries."

Why did she always have to whinge about the shit I did for her? Sometimes it felt like I couldn't get anything right where she was concerned. "Mum, we've been over this a million times. I know you've struggled ever since that asshole boss of yours fired you and I like to help you when I can."

"You did enough for me when you moved in and looked after me while I was sick. Now that I'm better and you've got your own place again, it's time for you to live your life and stop worrying about me."

I looked at her like she had two heads. "Like that's ever going to happen."

She huffed. "I just want to see you happy. You deserve that after all the shit you've been through. And fussing over me is a waste of your time."

I stopped what I was doing and gave her my full attention. "I am happy, Mum. Yeah I've had some hard times but I feel like I'm getting my life together. My beauty course is nearly finished so I'll be doing that full time soon and I've made some good friends the last few months. I've got savings in the bank for the first time ever and I've paid off my car. And, I have you and Anna back in my life which makes me very happy." I smiled as I thought of all the good things in my life. The good had been missing for a long time, but it finally felt like I was moving past that phase of my life.

A slow smile spread across her face. "The day you came back to us was one of the best days of my life. Promise me you won't ever leave again."

Regret sliced through me. I'd been so selfish and self absorbed when I walked away from my family all those years ago. I'd cut them out of my life like they were a disease that needed to be eradicated. And for what? To make me feel better about myself by forgetting where I came from. To please a man who could never be pleased. I'd walked away without a second glance thinking my life would be so much better without my white trash family in it. Little did I know that my life would be so much darker and desperate without my family to provide the love and support that my new family didn't have in them.

I pulled her close and hugged her. "I promise, Mama."

She broke the embrace and gave me a concerned look. "James was here this morning."

"Shit. He came and saw me yesterday, said he has a proposal for me. Turns out he's going into politics after all."

"I thought he said he never wanted a bar of that."

"He said a lot of things that weren't true." The memories of all the lies he'd ever told me punched me in the gut. I'd been so dumb to believe anything he'd ever said.

Mum smoothed her hand over my hair. "I know you feel stupid

for believing him but that's not on you, Velvet. That's on him and he's the fool for treating you that way. He's the idiot who is missing out on everything you would have given him."

My mother had a way of saying the exact right thing just when I needed to hear it. She might be a difficult woman a lot of the time but when her mothering instincts kicked in, she rocked the mother gig.

"Thank you," I whispered.

"What kind of proposal does he have?"

"He wants to buy my silence. Obviously he realises what a shit he is and knows that it would end his political career if people ever knew what he'd done."

"Are you going to take it?"

"God, no!"

"Maybe you should think about it. You could do with the money."

"I don't want to touch his dirty money. He can shove it where the sun don't shine." I barely contained my anger and she felt it.

"It was just a thought; there's no need to bite my head off. I figure you may as well get what you can out of him seems as though he screwed you over in the divorce."

"I've been free of him for five years and that's the way I want to keep it. If I take this money, we're tied together forever; he'll find a way to hold it over me. Plus, I won't sink that low. I've got no intention of telling our story to the world but I don't need to be paid off to do that; I've got more integrity than that."

She listened quietly while I spoke, and then said, "It's one of the things I love the most about you."

"What's that?"

"You hold your head high and live with honesty; you always do the right thing."

Her words meant a lot to me; I was glad I'd come over today

because I'd really needed the boost they'd given me.

★★★

I arrived early for work that night. James had played on my mind all afternoon after talking about him this morning, and I needed the calm that being at Indigo gave me. I loved working at the club. Scott and the other Storm guys had welcomed me into their family from the beginning; I'd never be a part of their club, but they looked out for me like a family did.

The only thing against being at Indigo at the moment was Nash. His silence was a clear indicator that he wanted nothing more to do with me, and that hurt. But I'd vowed years ago not to take shit from a man ever again and I was sticking to my guns on that. Not even Nash could make me change my mind.

I sighed as I thought about him. He was sex incarnate and I'd be lying if I said it hadn't crossed my mind that sex with him would be out of this world. And it wasn't like he hadn't tried his best to get me into bed. The thing about Nash was that while he was a well built sex God that every woman wanted a chance at turning into a one woman man, I actually really liked spending time with him. He was intelligent and funny, and I always looked forward to that time right after I finished my shift when I got to sit and unwind with him. We had that easy relationship where nothing was forced and it was just as comfortable to sit in silence as it was to sit and talk about anything and everything. So I'd made the decision a long time ago not to go there with him; I valued our friendship more than I wanted the bliss of a few hours with him and his body.

Harlow interrupted my thoughts. "What are you doing tomorrow at lunch time?"

"Sleeping." Tomorrow was Saturday and I had the day off. I had the entire weekend off for once and I planned to shut myself away from the world and have some Velvet time.

She grinned and I eyed her suspiciously; Harlow was always plotting and planning stuff and I wondered what she had dreamt up this time. "Nope, you're coming to Scott's for lunch. I've convinced him to let me take over his kitchen so you can't say no."

I groaned. "Really? You're going to make me get out of bed on my weekend off?"

"Yes, and no complaints. I'll make you lemon meringue pie."

"Damn you and your food bribery," I muttered. Harlow's food was out of this world and she used it often to get what she wanted. I felt bad for Scott; he was so screwed when she pulled out the big guns.

She grinned again. "Twelve o'clock and don't be late." And with that she waltzed out of the room.

I dropped my head into my hands and rued the fact that I couldn't resist her charms. She was so unlike any of the friends I'd ever had and although it had taken us a little while to warm to each other, I counted her as a close friend now.

"She's got mad skills at persuasion, hasn't she?"

I looked up to find Nash standing in the doorway, his intense gaze burning into me. My skin tingled at the way he was looking at me; a feeling I desperately tried to switch off. "Yes, she has," I agreed. I remained guarded, not knowing what his intention was with this conversation.

He leant against the door frame and crossed his arms over his chest. The intensity in his eyes remained, and a new tension settled in the space between us. Something was going on here; I didn't know what it was but my body buzzed with anticipation.

"I owe you an apology," he finally said.

"Yes you do," I agreed as I fought with the butterflies in my stomach. Where the hell had they come from?

He didn't say anything, just stood watching me. The look in

his eyes was beginning to fluster me; a feeling that was foreign to me. I waited in silence for what he would say next.

Pushing off from the doorframe, he came towards me, the muscles rippling under his fitted black t-shirt. I tried like hell not to look at those muscles, but I doubted there was a woman on earth who could pull that off. His voice dragged my eyes back to his. "I'm sorry for being a bastard to you. Please forgive me because I miss the hell out of you."

His apology was simple, but the emotion tangled in his words was real. He meant every word he'd just said. I blinked. He'd stunned me; I'd never expected him to come to me with an apology. And certainly not a straight up one like he'd just delivered. The honesty and vulnerability in his words meant more to me than he would ever know.

I needed to lighten the mood so I went with sass. "I've missed you too, asshole. Don't ever pull that shit again, okay?"

He grinned, and visibly relaxed. "Thank fuck."

I stood and moved closer to him. His musky scent filled the room and did things to me I wished it didn't. I did my best to ignore it; I had something else that he needed to hear and I didn't want to be distracted. "I meant it when I said I'm the friend who will always be honest. I look out for my friends, Nash. And I only want the best for them."

His grin sobered but he didn't shut down on me. "I know."

I pushed him. "Can you handle that?"

He took a moment but he nodded and murmured, "Yeah."

I smiled. "Good."

It was a charged moment; there was a shift in our relationship and I felt it strongly. By the look on Nash's face, he'd felt it too. But it was clear that neither of us knew exactly what it was or what to do with it.

Eventually he blew out a breath and took a step backwards.

"I've got to go. We're good, right?"

"Yeah, we're good."

He nodded and then he left. And I slumped down into my chair, overtaken by confusion. What the hell just happened?

CHAPTER 7

Dayum, Baby - Florida Georgia Line

NASH

FUCK.

I had to get out of here.

Now.

I'd salvaged my friendship with Velvet but what the fuck had I just gotten myself into? There was a reason I didn't do relationships with women; they demanded more than I was willing to give. And, fuck, I'd just thrown all my rules out the window for Velvet. I hadn't been able to stop myself when she'd pushed me for more. Christ, I'd just gone in there to say sorry, but somehow she'd found a way to break my resolve. Up until now we'd just been casual friends; now it felt like we'd gone past that boundary.

I'd hightailed it out of there pretty damn fast and was now at a loss as to what to do. I'd planned on kicking back at the club tonight, but I needed to put some distance between me and Velvet. I was heading towards the front door to leave when a blonde approached. Her hand snaked out and landed on my chest. "Nash, where are you going?" she purred.

My dick stirred but I wasn't interested. *What the hell?* She was hot and just what I needed tonight, but I wasn't feeling it. "Heading home, babe," I replied as I removed her hand.

She wiggled her hand out of my grasp, and went in for the grope. I still didn't want her, and pushed her hand away. "Sorry darlin', I'm not interested tonight."

Her eyes widened in surprise. "You're always interested. I've never heard of you saying no."

She said it like an accusation and my dick certainly took it as one. *You're fucking letting the team down here, he screamed at me.*

"Yeah well, not tonight. I've got other things to take care of tonight," I muttered. Like a stern talking to myself about rejecting women who clearly wanted to be fucked.

"I could come over after you're finished with that," she offered.

Christ, couldn't a man say no in peace? I wouldn't know because I'd never done it but surely there were men who did that shit all the time. I changed tactics. Smiling lazily at her, I suggested, "Not tonight, darlin' but maybe another time."

She moved closer to me and rested her palm on my chest again. "Well that would be fun too, but I'd really like you to fuck me tonight. I've heard ah-may-zing things about your talents."

Fuck me! This chick had it all happening and was all over me, and I still felt no desire to go there with her. My mind went into overdrive; what the hell caused this shit to happen to a man? In my thirty-five years, I'd never once had lack of interest issues.

I started to move away from her when a hand curled around my bicep and a warm body pushed itself into my front. "Nash is with me tonight. Sorry, hon."

And at that sultry voice, my desire jumped to attention.

Velvet.

She had her arm around me, and was engaging in some kind of girl warfare with the other chick. I waited to see where this all

46

ended up.

Finally, the chick huffed out a breath and muttered something under her breath about sluts and strippers that I didn't quite catch before she turned and stalked away from us. Velvet loosened her hold on me a little and turned to look up at me. I raised my eyebrows at her but didn't utter a word. I was still mentally dealing with my malfunctioning desire.

"What?" she asked, her eyebrows raised back at me. "You needed rescuing so I rescued you." She let go of me completely, and the pussy in me wanted to reach out and pull her back.

I nodded. "Thanks, sweetheart. Means a lot to me." The words dribbling out of my mouth were not in my control. Nothing I was saying or doing was in my fucking control tonight.

She gave me a strange look that I couldn't comprehend and then said, "Sure thing. But you should go now before she tries to latch on again."

"Yeah, I'll see you later," I muttered, and then exited the club before I fucked anything else up tonight.

★★★

An hour later, I found myself at Scott's house.

"Hey brother," he answered the door, surprised. "What's up?"

I pushed past him, and started walking down his hallway. "Nothing's up, just felt like some company."

He chuckled. "I'm not really your standard type of company, am I?"

I scowled at him. "You'll fuckin' do for tonight."

"Trouble in Nash paradise?"

"Yeah, fuck you, asshole. Just make me a coffee," I grumbled and sat at his kitchen table.

Laughing, he did as I'd demanded, and then sat with me.

"What's wrong, man? You've been off lately."

Scott was a perceptive guy, often sensing when shit wasn't right with people. I'd always managed to stay off his radar; probably because my shit was packed so deep in my soul that even I didn't feel it. But the last decade was catching up with me, and I could feel myself slowly falling apart. And for the first time in those ten years, I didn't know what to do.

I exhaled in frustration and anxiety, my heart hammering in my chest as I contemplated letting the monsters out. I'd locked them away for so long that just thinking about them distressed me. Talking about them scared the fuck out of me. "Do you have things in your past that no-one really knows about? Things that you don't even want to know about?"

"Brother, I've got things in my life now that I don't want to know about, let alone shit that happened years ago."

"Yeah," I murmured, lost in my thoughts.

"You need to talk about it?"

The concern in his voice was clear; I knew I could trust Scott but I didn't trust myself with this stuff yet. I shook my head. "No, I'm good. Just been thinking about shit lately."

We sat in silence for awhile. It was exactly what I needed and the anxiety I'd been feeling started to ease out of me. Once I had myself under control, I eyed him and asked, "You ever had a problem with your dick not working?"

Surprise flickered on his face and he smirked. "Never thought I'd hear that shit come out of your mouth."

"Yeah, yeah. But fuck man, have you?"

"Can't say I have, Nash."

"Shit."

"Yours giving you grief?" The bastard was laughing at me.

"Not my dick so much but my desire to use it. First time it's ever happened so you could say I'm a little concerned."

"Maybe Velvet was on to something when she said she was worried your dick would need resuscitating soon."

"What the fuck?"

"She told me that she'd said something to you about screwing every chick in sight."

"Fuck, why can't women keep stuff to themselves?"

He shrugged. "Beats the shit outta me too, brother."

I stood up to leave. I'd gotten what I'd come here for.

Scott followed me out. "Shit, I forgot to tell you that Harlow's cooking lunch for everyone tomorrow. She wants you here."

"What time?" Nobody passed up a meal cooked by Harlow.

"Around twelve."

I slapped him on the back. "Thanks, man. I'll be there."

I avoided the thought that Velvet would also be at lunch. And how fucking happy that made me.

★★★

VELVET

I STOOD BACK and watched quietly as everyone greeted Nash. He'd arrived nearly an hour late for lunch and Harlow was giving him grief. I was dealing with the thought that I'd been disappointed he was late. It shouldn't have affected me that much, but it did.

He finished hugging Harlow and caught my eye as he pulled out of the embrace. A slight smile touched his lips before he shifted his attention to Madison. He reached out and dragged her into a tight hug, whispering something in her ear that made her laugh. A pang of jealousy hit me, and I quickly turned away and headed into the kitchen to escape the unwelcome feelings I was having.

Scott was in there and his watchful gaze made me uncomfortable. "Why are you looking at me like that?" I finally asked.

He settled back against the counter before answering me. "Had a visit from your ex husband yesterday."

My concern about James spiked as dread filled me. "What did he want?"

"He wants me to fire you, and in return he offered me a lot of money."

"You're fucking kidding?" I exploded. Dread gave way to anger; how dare he fuck with my life like that?

Scott shook his head. "Nope, not kidding. You sure picked an asshole there."

"You have no idea."

"What's his story? He didn't tell me why he wanted me to fire you, just made me the offer."

I sighed. James was supposed to be out of my life for good but here he was, right back in it. "His family has a long history in politics and although he swore he'd never go into it, he seems to have changed his mind. He showed up out of the blue the other day and offered me money too. He doesn't want me to talk to the media about him."

"Got some nasty shit in his closet, has he?"

"You could say that."

"You accepting his offer?"

"No."

He nodded and pushed off from the bench. "Good. Me either."

I'd known he wouldn't accept the offer. I didn't even have to ask him. Scott Cole was a good man, even if most people took him for an asshole. He looked out for those he loved, and I knew that he loved me like family. He'd shown me that too many times for me not to know by now.

Harlow breezed into the kitchen, and Scott grinned at her.

"Can we eat now?" He asked as he reached out and smacked her on the ass. She shooed him away with a slap to his arm. This only encouraged him more, and he wound his arm around her waist so he could pull her into him and plant a kiss on her neck.

"I'll leave you two to it," I said, more to myself than them because they were too engrossed in each other to hear me. I headed out to the back deck, and closed my eyes for a moment, taking a deep breath of the cool air. We were having a cooler autumn than usual and I was enjoying it. I despised the muggy heat of a Queensland summer, and we'd had a hot one this year, so this was a welcome change.

I pulled up a seat and relaxed into it. Exhaustion was claiming me after a busy couple of months finishing off my beauty course and working full time throughout it. I hadn't wanted to get out of bed this morning, but I knew that Harlow would be disappointed if I didn't make it, so I'd forced myself to come. I closed my eyes and let sleep claim me.

That was, until a husky voice startled me awake. "Lunch is ready."

Nash.

My eyes flew open and desire pulsed through me at the sound of his voice. I jumped up and landed on unsteady feet. His strong hands caught me and his eyes searched mine; looking for what, I wasn't sure.

"Hi," I breathed out.

He blinked and for the first time ever, I saw Nash unsure of himself. His face was a blank mask and his breathing was uneven. "Hi," he stuttered, and released me from his grip once it was clear I was okay.

I took a deep breath. This was so awkward, and I had the sudden urge to get out of here and run far, far away. Instead, I rallied my bravado and said, "I'm starving. What's Harlow cooked?"

"Umm, not sure. She just told me to get my ass out here and bring you in," he replied, his usual composure returning.

I faked a smile. "Okay, well let's not keep her waiting."

I didn't wait for his reply; rather I started walking inside. His footsteps behind me indicated he was following me, but he didn't utter another word either.

Harlow smiled at us as we entered the house; it was a strange smile though, the one I usually associated with her when she was dreaming up one of her schemes. "Glad you could join us," J drawled, as he settled into the seat next to Madison and draped his arm over the back of her chair.

"Fuck off," I muttered, and he grinned. I shook my head and returned his grin.

There were two seats left at the table; two seats next to each other. I sat but Nash mumbled something about getting a drink. I tracked his movement to the fridge and he caught me staring at him when he turned and asked me if I wanted a drink. My face flamed red; I knew it did because it always happened whenever I was embarrassed to be caught out at something. His eyes narrowed as he took it in, but he didn't acknowledge it; he simply held up a can of coke and a can of lemonade with a questioning look. I pointed at the coke and mouthed a thank you before turning to Madison and asking her an inane question. "Have you gotten any new tattoos lately?"

She looked surprised, but answered me, "No, not since J and I had our tattoos done after the wedding."

I mentally slapped myself. What a stupid conversation to start. And so out of character for me to be babbling on about shit.

Nash slid into the chair beside me, and handed me my drink. I ignored the fluttery sensation his fingers grazing against mine gave me.

"Velvet, how much longer have you got left on your beauty

course?" Madison asked as she passed me the salad.

I started loading salad onto my plate. "Just over a month left to go."

"And then what will you do? Will you leave Indigo or do both?"

Scott cut in. "I'm trying to get her to keep working one night a week." He laid a huge smile on me before continuing, "Going to have to make you an offer you can't refuse, I reckon."

I smiled. We'd had numerous conversations about this and he knew I didn't want to do stripping once I found a new job, but he kept pushing me anyway. "I told you, Scott, I'm getting too old for stripping. Your clients don't want to see an old woman getting her bits out."

Nash almost choked on his drink and gave me a bewildered look. "You're what? Thirty-two? That's hardly old," he muttered, "And fuck, Velvet, have you taken a look in the mirror lately?"

Warmth spread through me at his words even if I didn't agree with them. "Ah yes, I have, and let's just say that I haven't got the goods that I once did."

Nash's eyes dropped to my chest and, holy hell, that did things to me. It was no secret that I liked the attention of men, hell you wouldn't strip if you didn't, but having Nash's eyes on me, turned me on more than I had been in a long time.

He raised them back to my face and murmured, "Sweet thing, I've seen a lot of goods in my time, and let's just say that what you've got are spectacular."

Desire pooled between my legs. Nash flirting with me was not new, but this conversation had a different tone to it; things had definitely shifted between us and I sensed new meaning behind his words. And I realised that I couldn't deny it any longer; I wanted to have sex with him, wanted his hands on my body and his lips whispering dirty talk in my ears.

He'd rendered me speechless, but Harlow kept the conversation going for me. "I agree with Nash, you're hot. I've got a girl crush on you and your goods." She winked at me and I could have kissed her for her kind words. I truly believed that women needed to stick together rather than trying to tear each other down, and a compliment like that from a woman sometimes meant more to me than if it had come from a man.

"Thank you." I blew her a kiss.

J waded into the conversation, "If anyone's fit to be the judge of goods, it's gotta be Nash, babe. I'd be listening to him if I were you."

I looked around the table at Scott, Harlow, J, Madison and Nash; they really were the family I'd chosen and this lunch just proved it to me more. Smiling, I said, "I'll take that as a compliment, J."

Madison laughed. "You should. It's definitely a J compliment; trust me, I should know. I can be having a down day and the way he tries to make it all better for me is by telling me how hot my tits are or how much he wants my legs around him."

J grumbled, "Well it's true, you do have great tits and legs, and I figure you need to hear that shit when you're down."

Madison leant her face close to his and said, "Thanks, baby, but what will you tell me when I get old and grey and my boobs are sagging?"

He grinned. "You'll still have lips, right?"

Madison smacked him on the arm. "You're a dirty man, Jason Reilly."

"Fuck yeah, babe. It's what you love about me the most."

Nash shifted in his chair and muttered under his breath so that only I heard him, "Fuck, do we really have to listen to this shit?"

I turned to look at him and for the first time, noticed the tiredness that marred his face. "You okay?" I asked, softly, "You look tired."

His response was unhurried. "Yeah, just got some stuff on my mind at the moment."

"You want to talk about it?"

He smiled tightly. "Thanks, but I don't really even want to think about it let alone talk about it."

"Sure, I get it. If you change your mind, you know where to find me."

"Yeah. I do."

I contemplated what I wanted to say, not sure how he would take it, but then decided to hell with it; we'd come this far now that it was just too bad if he didn't like me saying it. "I worry about you, Nash. I wish you would talk to me about stuff when it's upsetting or worrying you." I rested my hand lightly on his arm as I said it. His reaction was swift; his arm jerked and surprise flickered across his face.

He pulled his arm away and stood abruptly. Looking down at me, he asserted, "You don't have to worry about me. This stuff will go away soon and I'll be fine." Shifting his gaze to Harlow, he apologised, "Sorry, Harlow, but I've gotta go."

She gave him a disappointed look. "Really?"

"Yeah, got shit to do." He didn't elaborate. And then he was gone. And I was left stunned yet again by his behaviour. Nash wasn't being his usual fun self lately, and now I was really concerned for him.

CHAPTER 8

Scream - Usher

VELVET

THE SOUND OF MY RINGING PHONE PULLED ME OUT OF the deep sleep I was in. Squinting my eyes, I checked the caller ID. Shit, it was James. How the hell had he gotten my phone number? I dropped it back down on the bed; I wasn't answering his call. Instead, I rolled off the bed and traipsed into the kitchen to get a drink. The time on the clock caught my eye; five o'clock in the afternoon. It was Sunday and I'd spent most of the day in bed, drifting in and out of sleep. The rain was falling on the roof and I couldn't believe my luck that I'd been blessed with rain on my day off. Rainy Sundays in bed were a favourite of mine.

I downed the glass of water I'd just poured and cursed when my phone started ringing again. Ignoring it, I gave my attention to Bella, my kitty. She was rubbing herself up against my legs, demanding I feed her. Hell, this cat was always asking for food; she really should have been fatter than she was with all the food I gave her. I couldn't help but give in to her demands every time.

The phone stopped ringing as I poured some food into her

bowl. She looked at me with her 'you've gotta be kidding me' look.

"That's all you get," I said to her and with one last cranky look at me, she began eating.

Deciding I must smell bad, I headed into the bathroom for a shower. Just as I leant in to turn the taps on, my phone rang again. What the hell? Now he'd pissed me off. I stalked into the bedroom and retrieved my phone. "What the fuck do you want?" I snapped at him.

"Lovely to speak to you too, Velvet. Do we really need the language every time we talk?" he chided.

"Yes, we fucking do," I swore for his benefit.

He sighed. "Your lawyer has my proposal. Has he contacted you?"

He had, but James didn't need to know that. I figured it was my turn to muck him around after all the shit he'd ever put me through. "No."

"Can I suggest you get in touch with him?"

"It's Sunday, James. Surely you don't mean for me to call him today."

"Velvet, I think you are underestimating the seriousness of this situation."

"No, James, I think you're underestimating the lack of fucks I give about this situation." This man seriously made my blood boil. I had no clue how I ever thought I'd loved him.

Silence was followed by the nasty snarl I knew so well from years ago. "You're still the gutter trash you were when I met you and saved you. Getting rid of you was the best move I ever made and it's no wonder that you don't have a man in your life, because I can't imagine anyone choosing you over the other women out there."

The rational part of me knew his words were worthless and not to be given any attention to, but there was a part of me that was powerless when it came to James. He used his words like weapons and they annihilated me every time. They shredded their way through the self belief I'd spent years building and circled their way through my body in a painful spiral of doubt, loathing and fear.

I froze, unable to form words to shoot back at him, and he took my silence and fired more poison at me. "Your life is shit, Velvet. It's been shit ever since I kicked you out. The offer I've made you is the best option you have to make it better. I suggest you get back to me soon to tell me you'll take it, because it won't always be on the table."

He hung up and I slowly removed the phone from my ear. His words hung heavy in my mind as I tried desperately to sort through them. I needed to shove them out of the way so I could think straight; so that I could acknowledge them for the lie they were.

"Shit!" I yelled at the empty room. Why the hell did I let him get to me? Every fucking time!

My heart started beating faster and I broke out in a light sweat. Bella's wary eyes were focused on me and she looked like she was ready to run. I scooped her up and patted her. "Sorry, baby. I didn't mean to yell but that asshole just fucks me off," I whispered. Her eyes blinked and she began to purr. Once I was convinced she was settled, I placed her back on the ground and headed back into the shower. I was going out and I was going to have a lot to drink. James was going to be banished from my mind tonight if it was the last thing I did.

★★★

NASH

I ENTERED THE club, scanning to find what I was looking for. Tonight I was making my cock my bitch.

I found what I was looking for in the corner of the club; blonde, stacked and sending me the signal that she was up for it. She also looked like she might have a friend who would play with us; the more the fucking merrier I thought. It'd been a long week of no sex mixed with confusion about Velvet, and I needed to fuck like I needed air. My dick grew hard just thinking about it, and I picked up the pace as I made my way across the club. I was a starved man and I was going to fucking bang these chicks into tomorrow.

My destination was almost realised when I caught sight of Velvet out of the corner of my eye. I came to a dead stop and sucked in a breath. She was wearing the shortest, tightest dress that barely covered her ass, and she was bent at the waist, whispering something in some guy's ear. The displeasure I felt stunned me, and I had to hold myself back from stalking over there and tearing her away from him. I tried to drag my eyes away but I couldn't; I couldn't fucking move my legs either. She had me transfixed. I let my gaze roam over her body and soak in the beauty that was Velvet. She was the most beautiful woman I'd ever laid eyes on; I'd known this for four long years and I was done trying to deny it.

As I stood staring, she flicked her hair and caught my gaze. The smile she gave me reached out and stroked my dick. It was pure fucking heaven that smile, and it propelled me forward; towards her. She turned her body to face me, a move that signalled she was done with the guy she'd been whispering sweet nothings to. Her feet moved her in my direction and we met in the middle.

"Nash," she said, her voice breathy.

Sex.

Velvet oozed it and I wanted it.

With her.

I didn't care about the consequences; I couldn't even begin to wade through that minefield tonight when all I could see, smell and touch was her.

Her hand landed on my chest and my dick jerked again. Hell, this woman commanded my attention like no-one ever had. Not even my ex-wife. I curled my hand around her ass and pulled her to my body. When she brushed against my dick, she moaned, and her eyes fluttered shut for a moment. When she opened them again, I leant my mouth to her ear and murmured, "Sweet thing, I want to take you home and fuck you. And I'm not taking no for an answer tonight. We've been dancing around each other for too long now and my dick is so fuckin' hard for you that if you don't do something about it, I won't be held responsible for my actions."

She moaned again before saying, "You had me at sweet thing."

"Fuck," I growled. Grabbing her hand, I led her out of the club and to my bike.

This was going to be the fastest ride I'd ever fucking taken.

★★★

I unlocked the door and pushed it open, dragging Velvet behind me. She stumbled and giggled which was strange. I'd never heard her giggle before. Stopping my mad rush to the bedroom, I looked at her. "You're drunk, aren't you?"

Her sexy smile turned me on even more if that was possible. "Not really; just a little bit tipsy."

Yeah, like fuck she was only a little bit tipsy. Shit. I couldn't take advantage of her when she was drunk. I raked my hand through my hair and told my dick to shut the hell up when he screamed at me to keep going. "Velvet, I can't fuck you like this."

Confusion crossed her face. "Like what?" Her hands landed on my ass as she said this and shit, it felt fucking amazing. My two heads were engaged in a screaming match right about now.

"Don't get me wrong, I want to fuck you like I haven't wanted to fuck a woman ever, but I don't want to do it when you're drunk and not thinking straight."

One of her hands moved around to rub my crotch and I groaned in pleasure. "Nash, don't be a pussy. Just fuck me. It's what you do, so do me."

"Velvet, you're different. We're friends and I don't think you'd want this if you were sober." I couldn't believe the fucking words coming out of my mouth. Since when did I give a fuck about shit like that?

She scowled. "You'd be surprised what I want from you when I'm sober."

Christ, what did that mean?

I hesitated, and she used that moment to thrust her body closer to mine, grinding herself against me. I fought to contain my hard on. My resolve was seriously struggling; if she kept this shit up, I doubted I could restrain myself from throwing her over my shoulder and taking her to bed.

"Nash, for fuck's sake, we're adults and both know what we want. If you don't take care of me tonight, I'm just going to go and find some random guy to do it."

Hell, no fucking way was she doing that. I'd take care of her before I'd let another guy get his hands on her. "You just remember you fuckin' said that, okay?" I growled, and resumed dragging her towards my bedroom.

When we hit the bedroom, I spun around and pulled her roughly to me. My mouth came down on hers and I devoured her with my lips and tongue. She tasted of bourbon and smelt like some kind of lolly I couldn't quite work out in my lust filled haze. I ran my hands down her back and over her ass, letting one hand slide down between her ass cheeks. I slightly parted her legs while at the same time, lifting her closer to me. She moaned into my mouth and her tongue frantically sought mine.

We kissed each other for another heat filled few minutes before

I pulled my mouth from hers. I moved one of my hands around to her front and slid it under her dress, in search of her panties. Quickly finding what I was looking for, I slipped a finger into the wetness that was her pussy. With the hand I had behind her, I tilted her ass so that her pussy lifted up and forward, and she whimpered at the pleasure that caused.

"You like that, baby?"

Nodding, she begged, "Please, don't stop."

I brushed my lips against hers again before promising, "There's no chance of that, sweet thing."

My finger continued to trace the inside of her pussy and I added another while using my thumb to massage her clit. Her head lolled back, and her mouth spread out in a sexy smile before she bit her lip. Fuck, I craved those teeth on me. I dipped my head to her neck and licked a trail up to her lips. She opened her mouth and let me in, and I took it; I took everything she offered and more. My fingers worked harder and faster; the need to make her come consumed me. I was so fucking turned on by the sight of her writhing in pleasure, the smell of sex in the air and the sounds she was making that my mind was exploding like fucking fireworks on New Years.

Her pussy tightened and convulsed around my fingers as she found her release. When she orgasmed, she cried out my name and it was the sweetest fucking thing I'd ever heard. My dick banged against my pants, demanding to be let out, but my mouth won out in it's intense desire to taste her.

I held her tighter as she sagged against me. "My mouth wants your cunt, Velvet," I rasped.

Her eyes found mine and she smiled again. She brought her face closer and flicked her tongue out to lick my lips before pleading with me, "It's all yours, Nash. You have no idea how much I want your lips on me and your tongue in me."

A growl escaped from my chest, and then I gave her what we both wanted.

I dropped to my knees and pushed her dress up. The sight that greeted me nearly made me blow my load on the spot. A strip of black lace barely covered her pussy and a bow sat at the top of it. Like a fucking present for me to unwrap. Gripping her ass with both hands, I pulled her to my mouth. Her scent was intoxicating and I couldn't hold myself back; I inhaled her pussy and memorised the smell so I could remember it in times of need.

Her hand clutched my head and desperate fingers pulled my hair; pulled my face closer to her. I wasn't arguing; my need was as frantic as hers. The strip of black lace hit the ground less than a minute later and Velvet's glory was revealed to me. I feasted on the sight for a moment before I moved in to enjoy the feast with my mouth.

Heaven.

Velvet's cunt was like the Garden of fucking Eden.

She pulled harder on my hair and moaned as my tongue entered her. Her moans caressed my cock and fueled my greed for her, and I licked and sucked her in a frenzied rhythm.

"Nash....yes..." her throaty voice begged me to keep going.

I could have eaten her for fucking days, she tasted that good. Pussys were my forte; I'd fucked enough of them to know what I was doing, and I couldn't get enough of them. But a newfound hunger was filling me; a hunger that, even in my scrambled, Velvet-filled mind, I was sure only this pussy would sate.

Her hand moved from my head to the side of my face, and her gentle touch jolted me. It had been soft, but it affected me in a way I hadn't been affected in years. I growled and yanked my face away from her and stood up. My cock had finally won the battle; I was going to fuck her now like she'd never been fucked.

The room was silent around us, but we were screaming at each other with our eyes, with our bodies. This night had been coming for too long, and we both needed a release from the built up sexual tension. I stepped closer to her and pulled her dress over her head. My eyes dropped to her chest and I sucked in a breath. Velvet was more beautiful than I'd remembered.

"You like the goods?" she asked, cutting through the haze I was in.

Without taking my eyes off her tits, I murmured, "Oh baby, you've got no fuckin' idea."

She reached out and undid my belt and then lowered my zip. Her hand slid into my pants and a moment later, bliss gripped me when she held my cock for the first time.

"Fuck," I hissed.

She cupped my chin and lifted my face so that our eyes met again while her other hand stroked me. "I need you to show me what you can do with your cock."

I grinned, and ripped my shirt off. "Babe, how 'bout you take the rest of my clothes off and then I'll give you the ride of your life. This cock was made for your fuckin' pleasure."

She continued to lazily massage my dick, and I raised my brow at her.

"What?" she asked with a teasing glint in her eye.

I crossed my arms over my chest and played along with her. "Don't mind me, darlin'. I'm enjoying what you're doing, but I thought you wanted me to fuck you."

"Nash, I've wanted you to fuck me for years. I'm good at waiting for things."

"Christ, Velvet. If you wanted me all that time, why the hell did you make me wait so long?"

Smiling lustily at me, she replied, "Because I knew you'd make it worth my wait. I know your cock is going to make me scream louder than I've ever screamed for a man in my life."

That was it. I was done with waiting. Pushing my jeans down, I kicked them to the side at the same time as I ripped her bra off. I grabbed her and pulled her close. "You've got a dirty fuckin' mouth woman, and it's turning me the hell on. Between it and your cunt, I'm a dead man because I think you're gonna kill me tonight."

I lifted her and she wrapped her legs around me as I carried her to the bed. Depositing her where I wanted her, I took one last look at her body before I knelt on the bed and positioned myself over her.

"You ready?" I growled.

Her wild eyes gave me the green light, and her hands pushed my ass closer to her. Nodding, I reached over to the bedside table, grabbed a condom and sat back so I could roll it on. Even though I was way past ready to get inside her, I did this slowly to tease her. It worked a fucking treat too. She moaned and muttered, "Hurry the hell up, Nash. I want that cock in me."

I grinned, and leant forward to kiss her. "Good, because that's exactly what you're about to have, sweet thing."

Holding myself over her, I thrust hard and fast, filling her sweet pussy completely. She screamed out my name, and I withdrew and thrust again. Holy, fucking sweet heaven; Velvet felt so good around me. I thrust one more time and savoured being inside her for a moment before pulling out and sitting back on my knees.

Craving deeper penetration, I kneeled and pulled her legs up and spread them so they rested on my arms just below my shoulders. Leaning forward between her legs, I thrust back in and out, setting a new rhythm. Our eyes locked and I fucked her deep and dirty, just the way I liked it.

"Nash!" she screamed again, and it was so loud that I bet I'd made good on her belief I could make her scream the loudest she ever had. Her pussy clenched around my dick and I struggled not to come; I wanted to get her off at the same time.

"You close?" I grunted.

"Yeah," she managed to get out in between moans, and then she came. Her orgasm shattered around me and, fuck, it felt amazing. My dick was rock hard and began to throb as my heart started pounding in my chest. Her wet pussy kept contracting around me and I was sure I glimpsed nirvana, as a lightning bolt lit up my brain with the kind of pleasure a man only dreams of.

Euphoria hit me and I came hard. Long and fucking hard. The space around me blurred as I lost focus, lost sound, lost taste. I was drunk on her and grappled to get back to her. I needed to see her; I craved a taste of her. But I was lost in the orgasm and the sensations spreading throughout my body.

Finally, I came to and opened my eyes. Her head was turned to the side and her eyes were closed, a look of happiness on her face. She must have sensed me watching her, she turned to look at me and smiled.

We didn't say anything for a moment, just enjoyed the moment in silence. Then, she purred, "You sent me to heaven, Nash. Everything I've heard about you was true."

My mind was in overdrive; the new, crazy thoughts running through it pummelled me with their ferocity.

Velvet.

I wanted her.

Again.

Already.

Fuck, I'd hardly finished with this orgasm, and I already wanted more.

Before I could say anything, her eyes closed and I knew she was almost asleep. I gently pulled out of her and moved so I could lay her legs on the bed before getting up and dealing with the condom. She moaned softly as I left the bed, but she didn't open her eyes. I watched her for a moment before heading into the bathroom.

Christ, what the fuck had we done?

I disposed of the condom and eyed myself in the mirror. What an idiot I'd been to think that one night with Velvet would be enough. And what the hell was she going to say when she woke up with a hangover and a bad case of regret in the morning?

Fuck.

CHAPTER 9

Mr Brightside - The Killers

VELVET

My mouth was dry and my head ached. I opened my eyes and groaned in pain as the light hit me. My hand flew to my head; the pain was excruciating.

I hadn't had a hangover in a long time, and it came back to me in a rush why I didn't drink to extremes anymore. I slowly sat up and cursed myself as the nausea hit me in waves. Shit, I was going to vomit. I lurched out of the bed, and it was at that moment that I realised I wasn't in my own bed.

I was at Nash's house and I didn't know where the bathroom was. Didn't matter; I'd find it.

Five minutes later I'd found the bathroom and emptied my stomach of it's contents. I dragged myself back to the bed and laid down. The energy it took to vomit wiped me out and sleep claimed me again.

★★★

When I came to, I still felt awful but at least the nausea was gone. As I slowly sat up, I assessed my surroundings. Nash's bedroom was painted in a hushed grey; very masculine. There was no clutter in here, just the bed, bedside tables and a wood chest of drawers. He had one painting on the wall above the bed; some abstract swirl of reds, oranges and black. It didn't make any sense to me, but then again, I figured art was subjective and it must have meant something to him.

As I examined his room, I wondered where he was. The house was silent and I briefly considered that he actually wasn't here. My heart sank at that thought. And then I wondered where the hell that thought had come from.

Shit.

It had just been sex for goodness sake. I may have been drunk, but I vaguely remembered him hesitating to sleep with me, and I also remembered that I'd forced him into it. Well, to say I forced him might have been exaggerating a little; Nash never needed forcing into sex. But what the hell did it mean for our friendship now? If he wasn't here, did it mean he was avoiding me? And why was I upset at the thought that he wasn't here?

Shit.

I pushed the bedspread back, got out of bed and went in search of him. As I padded through the house, I smiled at the simplicity of his surroundings. I liked simplicity and little clutter too. He had the bare basics with only a tiny amount of decoration, and his walls were painted white. I loved the cleanliness of white. I also loved the few plants I saw scattered through his house. It all surprised me.

Nash wasn't here. I looked through the whole house and didn't find him. But I did find a note on the kitchen bench that told me to make myself at home and that he'd gone into work. My heart warmed a little at that but it was still heavy with the worry that he was dodging me.

Deciding that I actually wanted to get the hell out of here, I made my way back to the bedroom and got dressed. Christ, I hadn't made the walk of shame in a long time having given up one night stands awhile ago. I called a cab and waited for them to take me away from the scene of what I hoped wouldn't be the end of my friendship with Nash.

★★★

I stepped out of the shower. My body was clean but the regret still clung to my soul. Why had I been so dumb to sleep with Nash and think it wouldn't affect our friendship. The friendship we'd just patched back together.

I'd texted him just after I left his house to let him know I was gone. That was an hour ago and I still hadn't heard back from him. I didn't expect much, but I at least expected a reply.

Sighing, I got dressed for work. I had to be there in a couple of hours, but first I was going for a coffee with my sister. She'd just broken up with her boyfriend of five years and was struggling to deal with it, so I was making the effort to be there for her. We hadn't always been close but we were now after a lot of hard work on both our behalfs, and I was dedicated to nurturing that relationship.

I checked my phone again as I left the house and shoved it back in my bag in disappointment when I saw there was still no message from Nash.

★★★

"What's wrong with you?" Anna enquired after she took a sip of coffee.

My sister was very perceptive and even though I'd tried to mask

70

my feelings, she'd picked up on them. "I slept with Nash last night."

"Why the hell would you do that?" She knew that I'd fobbed him off for years because I wanted to maintain our friendship rather than risk it by having sex with him.

"I was drunk, horny and mad."

Her forehead crinkled in confusion. "You slept with him because you were mad at him?"

Sighing, I explained, "No, I was mad at James for coming back into my life and screwing with me so I went out and got drunk, and then Nash turned up and I couldn't resist him any longer."

"Yeah, Mum told me that James was back. What a prick."

"I'm so stupid for letting him get to me, but for some reason, I can't help it. He starts talking and it's like I'm right back there, you know?"

Concern was clear in her eyes. "Oh, honey, you should have called me." She placed her hand on mine and squeezed it.

I smiled at her. "Yes, I should have, and I will in future because going out and getting trashed and sleeping with Nash was definitely not the best way to handle it."

She grinned. "Was the sex hot, though?"

I blew out the breath I'd been holding in all day. "Hell, yes. It was the best damn sex I've ever had. I can only imagine how good it would be if I was sober. Nash has some talents, that's for sure."

"God, I knew he'd fuck like a champion," she declared. "You only have to look at him to know he was made for sex."

Remembering the pleasure he'd given me last night sent me into my own little world and Anna had to click her fingers in my face to get my attention back. "Sorry, did you say something?" I asked.

Shaking her head, she muttered, "You like him, don't you?"

"I honestly don't know." My feelings towards Nash were a mess. I loved his friendship, but I couldn't deny the sensations that just thinking about him gave me. Sex with him had been amazing;

we'd connected physically in a way that not many people did. Well, I certainly hadn't experienced that kind of instant connection with many men.

"Damn, Velvet. I think you've gotten yourself into some shit here."

"Understatement of the century, Anna," I said. I could do sex with a guy but I didn't want an emotional attachment. Usually this wasn't a problem with the guys I chose, but caution was screaming at me where Nash was concerned. We already had an emotional bond so I wasn't convinced we'd be able to handle a sexual relationship without complications.

Anna's voice took on a gentle lilt. "Maybe it's time for you to consider opening yourself up to love again, sis."

Fear gripped me. No. I didn't want to head down that path again; I couldn't do it. There was too much chance of pain catching you in it's claws. I'd run so far from it; I wouldn't give it a chance to chase me down again.

"No." I was emphatic.

"It's been five years since James, and you've come a long way, Velvet. I want to see you happy again."

"I'm really fucking happy without a man in my life, Anna."

"No, you're hiding yourself away. I understand why you're doing it, especially after having my own heart torn to shreds, but you need to move on and find a man who will give you the love you deserve."

My chest tightened at the thought of opening myself up to love and pain again. "I've never told you half the stuff that James did to me, and I don't want to get into it now, but I can't put myself through that again. I don't think I'd survive another round of that," I whispered the last sentence as my voice cracked.

"Oh babe," she said, and pulled me close for a hug.

I fought back the tears that threatened to fall, and clung to her.

When I finally pulled away, I apologised, "I'm supposed to be here checking up on you and you're the one looking after me."

"It's what sisters do."

She was right, and I thanked the universe for blessing me with a sister like her.

★★★

Hours later, I was half way through my shift at Indigo when I caught sight of Nash. He'd never replied to my message. He'd also not come and said hello to me, so it annoyed me to see him sitting in his usual spot with two chicks fawning all over him. So many emotions hit me at once; anger, disappointment and jealousy.

Shit. Jealousy of all bloody things to feel. It was the last thing I wanted to feel where Nash was concerned.

He saw me watching him, but he ignored me and carried on with his women. I exited the room as fast as my feet would allow me, and made my way to the staff room. It had been so long since I'd experienced a rush of feelings like this and I didn't know what to do with them. I had the urge to confront him; shit, I wanted to physically attack him he'd upset me so much.

I spent fifteen minutes out the back trying to get my shit together. When I got myself under control, I went back out the front; I had a show to put on in a minute and I was going to give them one hell of a show tonight.

The club pulsed with life as I entered it again, and I took a deep breath and centred myself. The beat of the music washed over me and flowed through my veins, the smell of anticipation hit me and the atmosphere overwhelmed me. This was where I thrived, and I stepped into my skin as I made my way to the stage.

I'd been working on a new pole dance the last few weeks. Nash usually helped me with these; I always showed him first to get this thoughts on it. He'd made me promise that he would always be the first one to see a new dance and was quite territorial about it. Scott had been the first to see one once and Nash had been pissed. He hadn't seen this particular one and the bitch in me couldn't wait to perform it with him in attendance. I knew it was a catty move but I couldn't help myself; he'd hurt me and now I wanted to hurt him.

I took my place at the pole and nodded at the DJ to start the music. My heart pounded in my chest as I began my routine. I looked in Nash's direction and saw he still had the two chicks all over him. They were doing their best to gain his full attention but his eyes were riveted on me. I stared at him for a moment before performing the hell out of my dance. It was the sexiest dance I'd come up with so far and the men loved it; they whistled and yelled out their approval. Little did they know they were in for a treat tonight; I'd decided to end the dance by interacting with the patrons in a way I never did. Scott would be pissed at me, as would Cody. The other strippers were allowed to do whatever the hell they wanted, but I was supposed to remain somewhat of a mystery. I wasn't to encourage touching on stage and if someone wanted to tip me, I was to take it with my hand rather than allowing them access to my g-string. If a patron wanted an up-close-and-personal interaction with me they had to pay well for it, and this policy worked well for the club; they made a lot of money off me.

Tonight, I finished up on the pole and then made my way to the edge of the stage. Making eye contact with one of the men at the front of the stage, I pointed at him and beckoned him closer. I dropped to my knees and thrust my pelvis in his direction, and indicated that he could tip me if he wanted. He greedily laid his hand on my leg and then slid it up my body to place a twenty in my g-string. I smiled at him and then pointed at another guy who did the same. Moving along the stage, I let numerous guys tip me in this manner. They were going wild, and the atmosphere in the club intensified to a point of frenzied excitement. Finally, I stood and seductively walked back to my pole before taking a bow and exiting the stage.

The security guy met me at the back of the stage and escorted me out to the staff room where I grabbed a water and collapsed into a chair. The performance had taken it out of me; perhaps because I'd been so worked up about Nash and had thrown that into the dance.

Just as I was thinking about him, Nash barrelled through the door, a wild look on his face. "What the fuck was that, Velvet?" he roared.

He was exuding anger to an intensity I'd never encountered with him. It should have scared the hell out of me, but instead it turned me on. Fuck, it turned me on to the point where all rational thought flew out the window and all I could think about was his cock inside me.

While I was struggling to push thoughts of his dick aside, he yelled at me again, "Are you going to fuckin' answer me?"

I snapped out of my trance and got back in the conversation. "That was my new dance. Did you like it?" I knew I was playing with fire, and that turned me on too.

"Whether I liked it or not is beside the point. What I want to know is why the hell you broke the rules and let those assholes touch you?"

"It's my job, Nash. I'm a stripper, and strippers get touched. Did you forget that?"

He scowled. "I fuckin' know that, but you don't get touched on the stage."

I pushed my face closer to his. "You mean, I don't get touched where you can see it. If it's away from your eyes and you don't have to deal with it, then you're okay with it."

Shit, where had that come from?

His eyes blazed and he blew out some heavy breaths before saying, "I'm your boss and I say no fuckin' touching on the stage. Are we clear?"

"You can't be serious. You're going to pull the boss card?" I challenged him.

"I am the boss and you will do what I say," he laid down the law.

I glared at him for a moment before saying, "Fuck you, asshole." I turned my back and covered the distance to my locker to grab my bag. After I'd retrieved it, I turned back to him and spat, "And thanks for being a great friend and running off after you screwed me."

Without giving him time to say anything more, I left the club. I hadn't even finished my shift but there was no way I was sticking around to cop more of his crap.

CHAPTER 10

Broken Hearted Girl - Beyonce

NASH

"Nash," the chick whined, "I want your hands on my tits."

Christ, she was a needy bitch. "You'll get my hands when I'm finished with your friend."

She pouted. "Well hurry up because I'm not going to wait all night for you."

It crossed my mind that I could care less if she left.

It also crossed my mind that all I was thinking about while her friend gave me a hand job was Velvet.

Fuck.

I pushed the other girl's hand off my dick and stood. Doing up my jeans, I muttered, "Sorry, girls, but this isn't going to happen tonight."

They started complaining but I wasn't listening anymore. I was going home to try and talk some sense into myself.

It had been four hours since Velvet had walked out on our argument and I hadn't been able to get her out of my head since.

She'd pissed me off and turned me on all in one go. When she'd performed her new dance, the one she hadn't shown me yet, I'd been surprised, but when she'd let those assholes touch her, I'd been fucking ropable. And then when she accused me of not wanting to see other men touch her, I'd started sprouting some shit about being her boss. We both knew I wasn't her damn boss but I'd pushed the point, and for the second time this week I'd had no control over what came out of my mouth.

I had good intentions of going home, but some other force took over on the way and fifteen minutes later, I found myself knocking on Velvet's door.

She took her time, but she eventually answered it. When she realised it was me, she frowned. Her shoulders sagged, and she said, "I don't have it in me to argue with you anymore tonight, Nash."

All the fight left me at the sight of her and the sound of defeat in her voice. Fuck, I'd been a bastard to her, and needed to make this right between us. "I'm not here to fight. I need to apologise."

Defeat gave way to surprise and she stood back, and held the door open for me. I stepped inside and walked down her hallway into her kitchen. I'd been to Velvet's house a couple of times and was always struck by how similar her taste was to mine. We both liked the minimalist look and white walls. She had some colour splashed throughout but it was fairly simple and I liked that too.

I hit the kitchen and spun around to face her. She was watching me warily and I couldn't blame her. "I'm sorry for how I treated you tonight. That shit I said about being your boss was a load of crap so just forget I said it, okay?"

"And?"

"And I shouldn't have said anything about the guys not touching you. That's totally your call." I didn't want them touching her, but I was sorry that I'd had a shot at her about it.

78

"And?"

Christ, she knew how to push me. And she was pushing me into unsafe territory. Who knew where this would end up now. I hesitated for a moment. "And I should have returned your message today."

"Yes, you should have."

I sensed her anger returning and felt the need to douse it before it ignited completely. "Velvet, I shouldn't have slept with you last night when you were drunk. I took advantage and that wasn't fair to you."

The anger that I'd tried to douse, flared at my words. "Oh, for fuck's sake! You didn't take advantage; I wanted that as much as you did. So don't try and get out of this mess by making some bullshit apology."

Her anger fed mine. "It wasn't a bullshit apology," I snapped.

"Why didn't you return my message?"

She asked the one question I didn't want to answer, and my skin crawled with unease. "I was busy."

She threw her hands up and wildly shook her head. "Now, *that's* bullshit and you know it."

"What are you trying to get me to say here, Velvet?" I thundered, "Because I sure as fuck don't think we should be going down this path. Why can't we just leave it where it is and move on?"

Her silence filled the room and she stared at me. "You're right. We fucked and got it out of our system. Let's just move on from that and not look back."

I watched her closely; she wasn't buying what she was saying, but I'd wanted the words she said, so I ran with them. "Good. Agreed."

"Good," she huffed.

Having sorted that, I had the overwhelming desire to escape the tension that was crowding us. "I'll see you around," I muttered, and headed in the direction of her front door. She didn't say anything, but I didn't want her to. I just needed to get the fuck out of here before either of us said something that would send the walls we'd built up crashing down around us.

★★★

VELVET

"HE SAID WHAT?" Roxie exclaimed, clearly flabbergasted.

I loved my hairdresser; not only did she look after my hair expertly, she was great to talk to. "He said he'd see me around, like we were hardly even friends."

"How long ago was that?"

"Five days, and I haven't seen him since." I paused, and thought about it. "Actually that's not completely true; I saw him last night at the club. He was there but he didn't come and say hello."

"Well maybe you should go and say hi the next time you see him there. Shove yourself in front of him, you know. What the fuck's his problem anyway? It was just sex, wasn't it?"

"Yeah, it was supposed to be just sex. I don't know why he's avoiding me now but it really hurts. I've seen him be nice to other women he sleeps with so I feel like shit that he's cut our friendship again. And I could kick myself for going there with him because we had just gotten it back on track."

Roxie assessed me in the way that only she did. She seemed to have a way of knowing what was going on in people's heads, or at least she did with me. "You miss him, don't you?"

The sadness I'd fought for the last couple of days hitched itself to my heart, and I nodded. "Yeah," I whispered.

"What do you want from him?"

"I want him to step up and be my friend. Big deal, we slept together; let's get over it and go back to being friends."

She gave me that look that said 'don't bullshit me'. "You don't really mean that, do you?"

My heart rate picked up with the apprehension that seized me. "I just want our friendship back."

"Yeah, but you want more too, don't you?"

"Nash doesn't do more and neither do I."

Roxie hit me with her trademark directness. "I think you want more from him, and I think you're scared to admit it to yourself, let alone to him."

It was exactly what I'd been thinking about all week. I hadn't been able to figure it out though. "I'm so confused about it all," I admitted, "I don't want to want him, and I'm not sure if I just want sex from him or if I actually do want more. But if I do work out that I'm after a relationship with him, then I'm screwed because he doesn't do them."

She nodded thoughtfully. "No, he doesn't, does he? But maybe it's why he's avoiding you, girl. Maybe he does want something with you and is confused about it too. I think you need to go and talk to him."

I sighed. "Trying to talk to Nash about this is hard work."

"Well shit, girl, the potential sex has to make it worth it, right?" She winked at me.

My body tingled just thinking about that. Hell, she had a point.

★★★

"Can't get enough of the place?" Griff quizzed me, looking up from the paperwork he was doing.

I dumped my bag on the table and sagged into the chair in

front of him. Ignoring his question, I asked, "Why are you doing paperwork? You hate that stuff."

"Cody's busy with staffing problems and Scott asked me to take care of it."

I studied him. Griff was ruggedly sexy and had a commanding presence that you just knew not to fuck with. But if you didn't fuck with him, he was the kind of man who would always be on your side, and I had a deep respect for him. I'd had some of the most amazing and deep conversations with him over the years when he'd let me in; he was a scary guy but he was proof that there was beauty in everyone if you looked hard enough.

Griff was good with silence, and we sat quietly for awhile before he looked up at me and asked, "You after Nash?"

"Huh?" I wasn't sure if he meant tonight or in general.

"Figured you'd come in to see him seems it's your day off and there's no other reason for you to be here. He's out the front somewhere."

"Probably with some skank," I muttered under my breath, jealousy stabbing me with a sharp knife.

"You might be surprised," he murmured, thoughtfully.

"And I might not be."

He put down his pen and gave me his full attention. "You got something going on with him?"

I hesitated for a moment, but then threw caution to the wind. "No. We slept together once, but that's all."

He scowled. "Hell of a way to fuck with a friendship."

"Thanks, Griff. I can always count on you to state the bloody obvious," I grumbled.

"Shit, Velvet, I thought you had your head screwed on better than that. You're a tough bitch on the outside but I know that under all that bullshit, you're just like every other woman."

"What the hell does that mean?"

He leant closer to me. "It means that sex isn't always just sex. For you to give that to a friend, to Nash... fuck, it tells me you want more from him."

Conflicting emotions assaulted me; my stomach was a knot of anxiety at the thought of what he'd said being true. Before I could form a reply, we were interrupted by a voice at the door. "Griff, Cody needs you out the front, brother."

Nash.

I looked up into his eyes. He was talking to Griff but his full concentration was on me. I squirmed under his fierce gaze.

Griff pushed his chair back, and gave me one last piece of advice before leaving, "Keep your fucking legs closed until you work out what the hell you want."

He exited the room, leaving me in a state of inner turmoil. I continued to watch Nash, waiting for him to say something. He didn't take his eyes off me, but he eventually spun around and left without uttering a word.

What the hell?

I jumped up and immediately stalked after him. We were sorting this shit out right now even if I had to tie him to the spot and force him to talk.

He'd made for the front door of the club and I followed him outside before finally catching up to him as he rounded the corner of the building into the carpark.

"Nash!"

He promptly stopped and turned to face me. "Not getting into this with you tonight, Velvet." His voice was savage, and I recoiled.

"When will you get into it with me?" I demanded.

"Do we even have to get into it?"

"You did not just fucking say that, Nash!"

"Yes, I fuckin' did," he threw back at me, hacking into my heart a little more.

He'd knocked the wind out of me and I struggled with where to go from here. "I thought you were different."

"No, Velvet, I'm not. I'm your standard bastard who likes to fuck without further complications. If you thought there was more to this, you were wrong."

My heart ached for my friend; the one I thought was inside him somewhere. I just wanted him back. Instead, he'd disappeared and in his place was this asshole who I didn't want a bar of. "No, I thought you were different because I thought I was your friend. That's all I wanted from you, and you couldn't even give me that."

His eyes flashed with ferocity. "You done?"

"Yes, I'm done. We're done," I spat.

His chest heaved, and he blew out a long breath before saying, "Good."

I watched him turn and leave with the heaviest heart I'd ever had. Not even my ex husband had caused this amount of pain.

CHAPTER 11

Do I Wanna Know - Arctic Monkeys

NASH

I WOKE AFTER A RESTLESS NIGHT. A NIGHT WHERE I'D wrestled with some motherfucking demons. They'd chased me down and knocked my ass flat on the ground, strangling the life out of me. I'd almost hit the point of no return last night. The bottle was begging me to make her my mistress again, and it was taking every fucking ounce of restraint I had not to succumb to her charms.

The one thing that could help me, the release I craved, was the one thing I couldn't make myself do. Sex. Usually I fucked my way out of this black hole, but Velvet had changed all of that. She'd changed everything, and the suffocating pressure I experienced when I thought about her told me that I needed to stay as far from her as I could. The fucking problem was that a need like I'd never known consumed my every waking moment; a need that only she could fill.

Fuck.

My phone buzzed with a text as I was getting ready for the day.

Erika: Thanks very much for assaulting my neighbour.

Me: You're fucking welcome.

Erika: Not what I was aiming for, asshole.

Me: He deserved it.

Erika: I give up.

I shoved my phone in my pocket, choosing to ignore any further messages from her. I'd see her tonight anyway, and had no doubt she'd continue her tirade then. Until then, I had club business that needed taking care of. Griff was meeting me at the clubhouse in half an hour to go over some of it so I pushed everything else to the back of my mind and concentrated on the one part of my life I still felt some control over.

★★★

After dealing with morning traffic I'd finally arrived at the clubhouse only to cop shit off Griff after we finished going over club business.

"You talk to Velvet?" He was giving me the look he reserved for men he wanted to use as his personal punching bag.

"It's none of your business, but yes I did."

"And?"

"What the fuck, Griff? I don't stick my nose in your business."

"My business doesn't include Velvet. That woman is a friend and I look out for my friends, brother. You included."

"You can look out for me by leaving this the hell alone."

"Why are you so hell bent on burying this? I thought you and Velvet were good friends."

"We were."

"Were?"

Fuck.

"Screwing her wrecked the friendship if you must know. Just like I knew it would. Women can't mix the two."

"You sure it's all on her?"

"What the fuck?"

"I saw you knock back two chicks last night. Never seen that before, so I've gotta wonder why. And I can't help but think that Velvet's got something to do with it."

"Got a lot of shit going on, brother. Velvet's the least of my fuckin' concerns," I asserted, more than ready for this conversation to be over.

He contemplated what I'd said and then nodded slowly. "I hope Velvet's still there when you're ready to be honest with yourself. You two would be good for each other."

I felt the desperate need to argue with him about that, but I saw Velvet enter the clubhouse and needed to escape the building more than I needed to argue. "I'll catch you later, man," I muttered as I made my hasty exit.

★★★

I arrived at Mum's for family dinner that night and Carla grinned at me, raining some sunshine down into my shitty day. "Glad you could make it, big brother," she greeted me with a hug.

I wrapped my arms around her and held on for a little longer than necessary. "Wouldn't miss Mum's cooking, babe," I said as I reluctantly let her go.

She eyed me suspiciously. "What's wrong, Nash?"

"Nothing. I'm good," I said a little too enthusiastically.

"You're forgetting who you're talking to. I'm not one of your biker friends who doesn't know you as well as I do; you can't lie to me, so spill."

I rubbed my face. "It's just been one of those months," I admitted.

Her face was a picture of kindness. "I get it," she said, quietly.

I smiled at her, and reached out to squeeze her hand. "Thank you." She knew exactly what was bothering me and I loved her for not forcing me to talk about it.

"Nash," she whispered, "Next month is going to be bad, isn't it?"

My chest constricted. "Yeah."

The worst fucking hell.

Her eyes filled with tears, but she blinked a couple of times and got herself under control. She faltered for a moment before saying, "I'm sorry."

I pulled her to me and hugged her again. We clung to each other for a couple of minutes, neither saying a word, but there was no need for words. Besides, after ten years there were no more words to be said. Words wouldn't bring him back.

Carla moved out of my hold. "You should come into the kitchen. I've got some news to tell everyone." She changed the subject and managed to lighten the mood a little.

"Fuck, I hope you're not going to tell us you're getting married or some shit."

She smacked me on the chest, and poked her tongue at me. "No, smartass, I'm not getting married."

I laughed, and managed to shove some of the shit in my mind to the dark corners again; hidden just enough to be able to function.

She dragged me into the kitchen where the rest of our family was, and they greeted me with the usual Walker hospitality of 'hey, asshole' and 'bout time you got here, dickhead'. I grumbled some shit back at them but my heart was warmed by the love I found in this room. It was a welcome distraction from everything else in my life at the moment.

"So," Carla announced, "I've broken up with Jesse. For good this time."

Relief laid a huge smile on my face; this was the best news I'd had in days. "Thank Christ for that."

"Yeah, well, you were right about him, but don't let that go to your head."

"Shit, never say 'you were right' to Nash," Erika chimed in.

"That's the fucking truth," Jamison agreed, "He'll never let you forget it now."

I raised my hands. "Nope, I promise not to remind you of just how often I'm right," I winked at Carla, "but let the record show, it happens often."

My mother rolled her eyes. "My cocky son. You haven't changed much over the years."

"And yet, you still love me just as much," I joked with her.

"Most days. On the other days, I remind myself that there's a nice guy in there somewhere."

Erika chose this moment to bring up her issues with me. "I'm having one of those days with Nash today; reminding myself he's not all bad."

"You still going on about your neighbour?" I asked.

She put her hands on her hips and glared at me. "Yes, I'm still going on about that. Why did you confront him when I told you not to?"

"You said you'd call the cops; they'd do nothing for you, so I did."

"Well, he came and had a go at me about it last night."

"I'll come and see him again."

"God, no! Just stay out of it, okay? I think we've come to an understanding."

I grinned. "Hate to break it to you, sis, but it looks like I was right again." I held up my fists. "People listen to these."

She rolled her eyes. I laughed and turned to Carla. "So kiddo, what do you want for your birthday?"

She groaned. "Nash, I'm a grown woman, I'm not your kiddo anymore."

I hooked my arm around her neck and dragged her closer to me. "I think if we could just get this one thing agreed upon, it would make my life a lot easier. You'll always be a kid to me and as such you shouldn't date ever again. Okay?"

Jamison started laughing. "I'm with Nash on that one, Carla. If he and I didn't have to deal with the guys that want into your pants, our stress levels would dramatically decrease."

She struggled out of my hold. "I'm only thirteen years younger than you so I'm not sure why that's a huge deal to you."

"Hell, even if there was only three years between us, I'd still have issues with it," I muttered. Carla had given us many reasons over the years to worry about her; Erika too. But Carla seemed to have a knack for finding the biggest dickheads around.

Mum stepped into the conversation again. "Thank God Nash and Jamison worry about you, Carla, I've lost track of the number of times they've had to bail you out, baby."

"And score three to Nash. Right again," I boasted with another huge grin on my face.

Everyone in the room groaned, but I continued to flash my shit-eating grin at them. Family. It was just what I'd needed tonight. And to think I'd almost walked away from them after I served time years ago. Thank fuck Griff had talked some sense into me and led me back to them.

★★★

I walked out of church the next day in a worse mood than I'd walked in. The feeling in the club at the moment was very apprehensive after the fall out between Marcus and J, and Marcus had just cemented his asshole status. Problem was that most of the boys were behind him, leaving the few of us behind J with our dicks swinging in the wind.

"Nash, got a minute?"

I turned to see Marcus walking towards me. "What's up?"

"You know where J has gone?"

"No, that fucker doesn't tell me anything," I lied.

He assessed me for a second. His scrutiny pissed me off; actually, everything about him pissed me off.

"You seen Madison lately?"

"Fuck, Marcus, I don't keep tabs on your daughter. If you wanna see her, you sort that shit out, don't go through me."

His anger threatened to erupt, but he kept it in check. "You need to learn some fuckin' respect. Shit's gonna go down and if you don't pull your head in, things are gonna get real messy, real fuckin' quick."

I stepped closer to him. "Have the fuck at it, asshole, because the way I'm feeling, I could give a flying fuck." My anger burned in me; it was getting harder each passing day to contain it, and Marcus copped a lick of it.

He growled. "Remember you said that."

I watched him walk away; his shoulders were rigid and he strode like he was on a warpath.

"Marcus giving you grief?" Scott caught up with me, a scowl on his face as we watched Marcus talking to some other club members.

"Asked about J and then threatened me. What the hell was up with that meeting?"

Scott shrugged. "Got no idea. He keeps shit to himself these days; doesn't tell me much of what's going on."

"Looks like his intention is to get us back into drugs. Not a good fuckin' move."

"That run he's organised is a bad move. Cops are all over shit at the moment, the last thing we need is to be caught up in that."

"You need to talk to him, brother," I suggested. Marcus had volunteered our guys as protection for a drug run the Adelaide chapter was organising.

Our eyes were drawn to Griff who had just approached Marcus. Marcus gave him a friendly slap on the back and Griff hit him with a smile.

"That looks fuckin' friendly," I mused, "You know what's going on there?" The last I knew, Griff had come around to our way of thinking and was trying to figure out what Marcus was up to.

Scott frowned. "Yeah. No idea what that's all about." He directed his attention back to our conversation. "Problem with this Adelaide deal is that Marcus seems to have convinced everyone else it's a good plan. We're in the minority on this one which doesn't give us many options."

"You heard from J?"

He shook his head. "Not yet. He'll have to come back soon though or Marcus is going to get suspicious."

Our attention was drawn again to Griff. He was laughing at something Marcus had said. That was odd because Griff never laughed at anything.

"Definitely something going on there," I said, feeling mild irritation at Griff.

Scott watched them for another couple of moments. "Yeah."

"Fuck!"

Scott raised his brows at me, questioning my outburst.

"It just feels like if it's not one thing, it's another at the moment." I lifted my hand and rubbed my neck but it did little to alleviate the knots that had formed there. Shit was hitting the fan in all directions and I wasn't sure if I would escape unscathed.

CHAPTER 12

Man I Feel Like A Woman - Shania Twain

VELVET

"CHEERS!" I CLINKED HARLOW'S GLASS AND THREW THE shot down my throat. It burned on the way down but the warm buzz it gave me felt really fucking good. This week had been long and crappy, and I was glad it was over. I'd organised a girls night out at Graggs, a new bar in town. Never having been here before, I wasn't sure what to expect but it was a popular place and the party atmosphere ensured we were having a great time.

Harlow's face flushed with excitement as she ordered more drinks. "This was such a good idea, Velvet!"

Roxie bumped her hip against mine and chimed in, "Fuck, yeah! I haven't had a girl's night out in ages. It's a shame that Madison couldn't be here."

"She's got a good excuse though," Harlow was almost slurring her words. We'd consumed a lot of alcohol in a short amount of time; it was probably time to slow it down because I didn't think she could hold much more.

"What's that?" Roxie asked.

"She's babysitting Nash."

Her words hit me in the gut. I hadn't seen or heard from Nash in six days. Indigo was a lonely place without him, but he'd made his intentions clear, and I was getting on with life.

"Why does Nash need babysitting?" Roxie asked, clearly confused.

"I don't know really, it's just what Scott said when I asked why Nash was going over to Madison's house. It's a bit odd though, isn't it?"

Roxie finished her next drink, and said, "Yeah. I mean, what biker have you ever heard of who needs babysitting?" She eyed me. "You sort your shit out with him?"

I could have killed her. I hadn't told Harlow about Nash and I, but she was looking at me with interest now, waiting for my response as much as Roxie was. "Yes," was all I said.

"And?" Roxie prompted.

"And nothing. He just wanted a bit of fun and now he's done with me." The words physically hurt to say.

Harlow's eyes widened. "You slept with him?"

I shot Roxie a foul look before answering Harlow, "Yes, once."

Harlow looked like she was about to burst with excitement. "I knew you two were totally suited!"

"No, we're not." I sculled my drink; maybe the alcohol would numb the pain that thinking about Nash caused. "Can we please change the subject?"

I must have said that with enough oomph to make them realise I really didn't want to discuss Nash.

Roxie was straight on it. "When do you finish your beauty course? Cause I'm thinking I need a beautician in my salon."

"Shit, that would be awesome. I finish in about a month."

She grinned. "Good. That's settled; we'll get a room set up for you." She beckoned to the bar tender to bring us more drinks while

94

I let the happiness settle in me that she'd made that offer. Nothing in my life had ever come easy, often it felt like I was pushing shit up a hill, but some things were finally falling into place. And this was a huge step in the direction I wanted to go.

"I think we've had enough to drink," I suggested, looking at Harlow who was swaying like there was a bloody cyclone passing through.

Roxie followed my gaze and began laughing. She reached out and grabbed Harlow, trying to steady her. "Doll, it might be time to take you home to lover boy."

Harlow smiled a drunken smile. "Yeah, he'd like that."

Roxie murmured, "Oh, I'm sure he would." She indicated for me to help her get Harlow under control and we made our way outside to find a cab. "Does she always get this drunk this quick?"

"No, she can usually hold her liquor. Maybe she didn't eat much today," I suggested.

Harlow interrupted us. "Was busy at the cafe today, didn't get to eat anything after breakfast," she slurred.

"Scott's going to be pissed at us for letting you drink this much," Roxie said.

"Totally not our fault," I said. I wasn't taking the blame for this if Scott wanted to have a go.

Harlow giggled. "Don't worry about Scott. He's easy to control."

I laughed out loud. "Umm, only for you, Harlow. No-one else gets away with the shit you do where Scott's concerned."

She giggled again just as a guy approached us on the footpath. "Ladies, you ready to go home?"

"That's one of the worst pick up lines I've ever heard," I scoffed. "And that's a damn shame, dude, because you're rocking some serious hotness there." I drank in his muscles, his dark hair, his tats; he had the exact look that did good things to a woman, but he seriously needed to work on his flirting skills.

Nash could teach him a thing or two.

Shit. Random thought number five hundred about Nash for the week; I had to get him out of my system. Maybe this guy could help me after all.

Before I could think about that any further, Harlow trilled, "No, silly, he's the prospect. Scott must have sent him to take us home."

"Either that, or he sent him to keep an eye on you. That's a little too controlling for me," Roxie didn't hide her aversion to men who took charge like Scott did.

Harlow cocked her head. "No, I don't see it that way. Scott likes to make sure I'm safe; I think he only has good intentions when he does stuff like this."

"Yeah, I'm not so convinced." Roxie wasn't a man-hater; she just valued her independence and didn't cope well when her man involved himself in her life like Scott did with Harlow.

The prospect tried to hurry us up. "While I find your conversation about men amusing, ladies, I'd like to get you home so that I can get back to more pleasurable activities." He winked at me as he said this, and his hotness rating skyrocketed.

"I bet you would," Roxie said.

His smirk almost convinced me to throw myself at him but there was some niggling thing in the back of my mind stopping me.

Nash.

I inwardly sighed. Nash sure knew how to capture a woman's attention.

Roxie pushed Harlow into the front seat of the prospect's car and she and I took the back seats. It wasn't a long trip to Scott's house, only about fifteen minutes, and he was waiting outside for us when we pulled up. Harlow stumbled out of her seat into his arms and he grimaced at her drunken state.

He turned his gaze to me and I held up my hands in defence. "Your girl didn't eat today apparently."

He muttered something under his breath but nodded at me. "Thanks for getting her home safe."

Harlow wrapped her arms around his neck and said, "They're good to me, those girls." She hit him with a megawatt smile and you could see the annoyance seep right out of him. Damn, that man was so far gone on his woman. I never thought I'd ever see Scott Cole whipped but it seemed that Harlow had done just that.

"You'll get Velvet and Roxie home, okay?" he directed at the prospect who nodded.

"Thanks," he said, and then he took Harlow inside.

I got out of the car and quickly made my way to the front seat. Doing up my seat belt, I looked at the prospect and asked, "So, you got a name?"

He grinned. "Yeah, darlin', it's Wilder."

"You don't talk much do you?"

"I say what I need to say."

Roxie interjected from the back seat, "Velvet, let the man rest his mouth. He probably has other things planned for it tonight."

I caught his grin. "How long have you been a prospect for?" I continued firing questions at him.

"Coming up to one year."

Damn, he was hard to make conversation with, and not that I wanted to flirt with him, but I figured that would be pointless too. I was sitting next to him with my cleavage on full display and he hadn't even taken a look. Not even a peek. "You're not into women?" I asked. I favoured directness; it usually got you the answer you were looking for rather than fucking around with subtle questions.

He finally ran his eyes over my body before running his hand through his hair. "Baby, you've no idea. But it ain't worth my while to even look at a woman the VP is friends with."

"Thank God for that, because I gotta tell you, it would be a loss to womankind if you were into guys."

He laughed and I lamented the fact I was friends with Scott. We finished the rest of the drive home in silence. He dropped Roxie off first and then me. As I was getting out of the car, I said, "If I ever stop being friends with Scott Cole, I'll be sure to look you up." He grinned and I gave him a wink before going inside. It had been ages since I'd flirted with a man and it felt good. Maybe it was time to get back out there and find some fun.

CHAPTER 13

Everything Has Changed - Taylor Swift & Ed Sheeran

NASH

I DROPPED MY HEAD DOWN INTO MY HANDS. THE question Madison had just asked me was one I didn't want to think about, let alone answer.

"Nash," she said, quietly, "You do feel something for her, don't you?"

The pressure I felt when I thought about Velvet buzzed in my head. It was easier not to think about her, and fuck, I'd tried. Ever since I'd pushed her away, I spent most of my time trying not to think about her. But she consumed my thoughts, day and night. It was worse at night when I was alone, and the darkness encouraged my mind to wander into dangerous territory. Thoughts of the past collided with thoughts about Velvet, and the weight of everything was almost unbearable.

I looked back up at Madison. She was watching me, waiting patiently for me to reply. Finally, I admitted the truth. "Yes, I do."

She smiled. It was a smile full of kindness and love. "Have you ever felt like this about a woman before?"

I sucked in a breath. This was shit I didn't want to go over, but I'd gotten to the point where I knew I had to. I couldn't ignore it any longer. "Once. A very long time ago."

She nodded. "Who was it? Tell me about her."

I'd come here tonight with the intention of talking. Hell, I'd actually asked Madison if I could come over to talk, but now I wanted to get the fuck out of here.

At my silence, Madison spoke again. "Nash, you once told me that people like us need to get this stuff out otherwise we fall back into old habits. You need to talk, and I want to be here for you because you've always been there for me."

I hated it when my words were thrown back at me, even if it was done out of kindness. Ah, fuck it. I opened up. "It was my ex wife, Gabriella. I met her when I was twenty; the first chick I ever did crazy shit for. She fuckin' knew how to push my buttons to get what she wanted and I was a fool for her."

Madison's face was full of surprise. "Wow, I didn't realise you'd been married before."

"It's not a fact I run around advertising, babe."

"So, she screwed you over, huh?"

"In all senses of that word."

"What do you mean?"

My chest was heavy with the anger I'd never resolved where Gabriella was concerned. "She fucked around on me. I found out and we agreed to work on it but then I found out she kept that shit up. And then she screwed our family right over."

Fuck.

My heart was pumping hard and fast in my chest. I stood up and began pacing the room, taking deep breaths to try and calm myself down.

"Are you okay?" Madison came up behind me and placed her

hand on my back.

It never failed to amaze me what the human touch was capable of. Sometimes it hurt and sometimes it loved. Madison's gentle touch was loving and it was exactly what I needed right now. It helped quiet the demons and after a couple of minutes, I had my breathing under control.

I turned to face her. "A man's lucky to have a woman like you in his life, sweet thing."

"I'm always here for you, Nash. It hurts me to see you like this; I wish you would let me help you more."

I pulled her close. "You are helping me, babe. More than you know." I let her go so I could look her in the eyes. "I've never really talked to anyone about this shit. I know I need to but I've gotta get my head ready first."

"I understand. Just remember that I'm always here whenever you need to talk."

"Thanks, darlin'."

The air was thick with the burden of ghosts. This was why I hated digging up shit from the past. We both took a moment to deal with it.

Eventually, Madison smiled at me before asking, "So, what are you going to do about Velvet?"

"I don't know what to do with that," I admitted.

"Okay, let's break it down. You slept together but then you pulled away and were a bastard to her, right?"

"Yeah." My guilt over that was tremendous but I hadn't been able to bring myself to apologise. Being near her made me want her even more.

"You pulled away because you're scared of your feelings for her, right?"

"Fuck, you make me sound like a pussy, Madison."

"Well, let's call a spade a spade, Nash. You men can be real dickheads when you feel something for a woman. And you're being one of the biggest dickheads around at the moment."

"Christ, if I wanted to hear this shit, I would have gone to my sisters, babe."

"Sorry but you do need to hear this shit. For the first time in a long time, you're feeling something and I think it could be good for you. You hide your pain behind that mask you wear, Nash. I know, because I used to do it too. Sex helps numb it but it'll never go away until you deal with it, and I think your soul is ready to deal with whatever pain has been crippling it for all these years."

She was right; I knew she was, but I didn't want to admit it. Shit, life was a lot easier to deal with when you ignored the pain and fucked it all away. Problem was, and she was spot on here, the pain always came back.

"I want her, like I've never wanted anyone."

Smiling, she said, "Good, we're getting somewhere. So, are you willing to open yourself up to it?"

"Can't it just be sex?"

"I swear, it's like pulling teeth with you, Nash. No, I don't think it can be. If it could, you two would already be doing that."

She had a point. "Shit," I muttered.

"Let me ask you something. How many women have you slept with since you and Velvet hooked up?"

Fuck, reckoning day was here. "None."

A huge smile landed on her face. "You've got it bad, Nash Walker, and you don't even know it. You need to get your shit together, apologise to her and man the fuck up, dude."

I scowled at her. "I'm hearing you, babe. I'm fuckin' hearing you."

CHAPTER 14

Who You Love - John Mayer & Katy Perry

VELVET

"GOD DAMN IT!" I YELLED INTO THE AIR AROUND ME. People stared at me but I could care less; it felt good to get it out. My car had just broken down on Brunswick Street of all bloody streets. Breaking down in Monday morning traffic on a busy road was like a special kind of hell as far as I was concerned. Drivers were honking at me and yelling abuse.

"Screw you asshole," I yelled at one guy, "Not sure what the hell you think I can do about it?" I extended my middle finger at him to make sure he got my message.

The fact my phone was out of battery didn't help. I would have to walk to find a payphone.

Shit, what a way to start the day. I reached into the car for my bag, and was searching in it for my purse when I heard the rumble of a bike. Looking up, I squinted my eyes to see Nash pulling up behind me. My heart began beating faster and my skin tingled at the sight of him. He still managed to affect me even after treating me like he had.

He left his bike and walked to me; his face was unreadable, not pleased but not annoyed. "Need a hand?" he asked.

Feeling slightly flustered in his presence, I replied, "No, it's good. I'm just going to call for help. You keep going; I'm sure you're busy."

He frowned, and ignored what I'd said. Lifting his chin at my car, he asked, "What's wrong with it?"

"It's overheating which it's been doing a bit lately." I had a Suzuki Swift hatchback and I loved it but the problem was that it was just getting to that age where things were starting to go wrong with it. I figured my savings account was going to take a hit soon.

"Who are you calling about it? RACQ?"

"Yeah, I'll see if they can tow me home and then I'll call a mechanic."

He frowned again and pulled his phone out. Looking at me, he said, "I've got a friend who can tow it and then I'll take a look at it."

"I can handle this, Nash. You don't have to do that." I couldn't figure out why he was making the offer after the last encounter we'd had.

"Babe, I think you know by now that I don't do anything I don't want to do."

Before I could say anything else, he was on the phone to his friend organising the towing. When he hung up, he said, "He can't get here for another hour or more but he's going to do it and then take your car to my house so I can work on it. In the meantime, I can take you wherever you were going; there's no need for you to wait here. He'll call me when he's on his way and I'll meet him here with the keys."

"So you've just organised all of that without asking me first?"

"Is there a problem with that?"

"I would've liked to have been consulted."

"Shit, Velvet, I'm trying to do you a favour here."

"I realise that, but it's the principal of the thing, Nash."

"What fuckin' principal?"

"A woman likes to be involved in decisions that concern her. That principal."

"I'll remember that the next time I try to help you out but for this time can we just work with what's been organised?" He blew out a frustrated breath.

Shit, a man who listened to me; call me stunned. "Thank you."

Surprise crossed his face and he slowly nodded. "Yeah."

We were silent for a moment, just taking each other in. I broke the silence. "You got a helmet for me?"

"Just one other thing before I get you the helmet."

I tilted my head to the side. "What's that?"

"I've gotta make a stop on the way but it'll just be a quick one."

"Sure," I agreed.

He gave me a tight smile and then walked back to his bike, grabbed his helmet and passed it to me. "Where were you headed?"

"Grocery shopping."

"I can drop you there and then get one of the prospects to pick you up when you're finished," he offered.

God, he was being so much nicer to me than the last time I saw him. "Thanks, that would be great."

"No problem," he said as he mounted his bike and waited for me to get on. A moment later, I settled in behind him and put my hands on his hips. Being this close to him was sending my senses into overdrive. When he grabbed my hands and pulled them around him, it affected me to the point where I wasn't sure I'd be able to stand without assistance when I got off his bike.

He started the bike and we took off. The vibrations as we rode only served to thrill me more. My imagination went wild and I pictured how hot it would be to have sex on a bike; I'd never done it but I bet Nash had. I squeezed my legs against him while I thought about it and leaned closer, hugging him tighter. God damn it, I finally admitted it to myself; I wanted to sleep with him again.

We didn't travel very far, just down Brunswick Street towards the river. He turned into a side street and then pulled into a driveway before switching off his bike. A woman came out of the house we'd pulled up at and smiled broadly at us. She had the same features as Nash, and I decided that she must be his mother. Or at least be related to him somehow.

I followed him off the bike and waited for him to introduce us, but the woman wasn't as patient. "Hello!" she directed at me, excitement coating her words, "I'm Nash's mum, Linda."

I smiled at her. She was so warm; the kind of woman everyone gravitates to, and I couldn't stop myself if I tried. Her arms were outstretched and I moved towards her and into her embrace. "Hi, I'm Velvet," I said. Usually, I'd find it strange that someone I just met wanted to hug me, but this didn't feel weird; it felt like the most natural thing to do.

She continued to hug me. "It's lovely to meet you, Velvet."

When she let me go, I stepped backwards and ran into Nash who'd come up behind me. His hand slid around my waist to steady me. "Careful, sweet thing," he whispered in my ear, his warm breath tickling me. A shiver ran through me, and my nipples came to life. Christ, my whole body came to life when Nash was near me.

Linda's eyes zeroed in on Nash's arm around my waist, and her smile grew if that was even possible. She looked back up at us, and motioned towards the house. "Come in, I'll put the kettle on."

Nash moved his hand around to settle in the small of my back as we followed her. "Mum, we can't stay long. I just dropped in to change those light bulbs that you and Carla can't reach. She mentioned them to me last night."

Linda kept walking down the hall and threw over her shoulder, "It won't take me long to make a cuppa while you change the lights.

Then you can quickly drink it before you leave."

I heard Nash groan behind me, and had to stifle a laugh. His mother had him around her little finger, that was clear from even this small interaction. We hit the kitchen and she turned around and clapped her hands together. "Okay, you go and do the lights, Nash. Velvet can stay here and help me."

Unable to hold it in any longer, I grinned at him. His mother was priceless; she was obviously very happy to see him, and I loved that about her. I never warmed to people this quick but she had a special kind of something that had touched me.

Nash narrowed his eyes on me. "Why are you grinning like an idiot?"

"Your mum has you, doesn't she?"

"She has me where, babe?"

I grinned even harder and leant into him before saying, "I've never seen a woman have any say in your life, Nash, but your mum does, doesn't she?"

A lazy smile formed on his lips. "A man owes a lot to his mother, sweet thing, so yeah, as you say, she has me."

We were caught up in each other until his mother cut in. "Nash, off you go. I want some time with Velvet."

He shook his head in amusement. Before he left he whispered in my ear, "Don't let her talk you into anything, okay?"

"I'm thinking that your mum could talk anyone into anything," I murmured.

"She fuckin' could," he muttered as he left us alone.

Linda watched him go and then she smiled at me again. "Are you a coffee or a tea girl?"

"Coffee, please."

She nodded and then set to work making it. "It's great to finally meet you," she said, surprising the hell out of me. Finally?

"Umm, yeah, you too," I stuttered, not really sure what to say because it wasn't like I knew much about her. Nash didn't often talk about his family. All I knew was that he had a couple of sisters who sometimes did his head in.

"Nash has talked about you a couple of times." She continued to stun me, and I stood speechless because I didn't know what to say to that.

Linda didn't need me to be involved in the conversation to keep going. "Nash hasn't mentioned any other woman since Gabriella so I figured you must mean something to him." She paused and pinned her gaze on me before saying, "Something special that is."

Gabriella? I had no idea who that was; Nash hardly ever talked to me about any of the women in his life. He'd once mentioned a woman trashing his heart, and I considered whether that could be who his mother was talking about.

"Velvet, did you hear what I said?" His mother was watching me carefully.

I did hear what she said but I'd been focusing on the part about Gabriella rather than on the part about me being something special to Nash. "I'm not special to Nash," I eventually said.

Her lips pressed together and she made a funny face at what I'd said. "I beg to differ, honey."

It felt like I was being bombarded from all directions this morning. For a start, Nash had changed towards me and was being nice, and now his mother was throwing ideas out that made no sense to me. And on top of that, I'd learnt something about Nash; he'd had a woman in his life called Gabriella. I would never have picked that; he seemed hell bent on avoiding relationships.

His mother was waiting for me to say something. "We're friends," was all I could muster.

She pulled a face that I assumed meant something like 'sure, if you say so', and then finished making coffees. She brought them to the table and indicated for me to take a seat. "Nash, coffee's ready," she yelled out.

He didn't reply but I figured he would have heard her as she yelled so loud. It reminded me of the way parents yelled out when they had a tribe in the house and needed to be heard.

"So, tell me about yourself, honey. What do you do for work?"

I just about spat my coffee out. That question was always a make or break question for my friendships. A lot of people struggled with the idea that someone would choose to be a stripper. However, I loved my job and had no qualms telling people what I did; it was up to them what they did with the information. And, if they were the kind of person to judge someone based on their profession, I'd rather not have them in my life anyway. "I'm a stripper at Indigo."

She didn't even blink. "How long have you been working at the club?"

"Just over four years now."

"So that's where you met Nash?"

I nodded. "Yeah. He used to sit and talk with me after my shift some nights. He was different to the other guys there."

"What do you mean?"

"Most guys just wanted one thing from me; they assume that if you're a stripper you must be up for anything. Nash never did that." I smiled and then added, "Well, your son is a huge flirt, but he never assumed anything about me and I loved that about him."

"You said that he used to sit with you. Doesn't he do that anymore?"

Damn, his mother didn't miss anything. "No, he's drifted away from me a bit lately."

Her face softened and she looked sad. "It's not just you that he's drifted from lately, honey," she said softly, "He's going through some stuff at the moment and he's taking it out on everyone he loves."

"Oh." What did someone say to that? This visit had been very enlightening but at the same time, I had more questions now than when I'd stepped foot in this house.

"Please give him some time to sort himself out. He'll push you away because that's how Nash deals with his pain, but please promise me you won't let him."

"Linda, I've gotta be honest with you; this has been going on with Nash for awhile now. I've tried to be there for him but he's made it really clear he doesn't want me in his life. I'm not sure what else I can do."

She looked torn, like she wanted to tell me something but wasn't sure if she should. "I'm not sure what he's told you about his life, but I'm guessing not much because my boy likes to keep stuff to himself. Something happened to him a long time ago and the ten year anniversary of that is coming up next month. It was very painful for him and he hasn't fully dealt with it yet. We've tried to push him to do that but he's resisted. I'm watching him unravel at the moment, honey, and I think this year might be the one that finally breaks him. As hard as that is for a mother to watch, he really needs to go through that to move forward. And I'd like him to have as many friends around him to help him through it."

She'd pulled my heartstrings with her little speech; my heart was hurting for him and I didn't even know what had happened. I could only guess that it must have been pretty bad because she was right, Nash was unravelling.

I reached out and squeezed her hand, and nodded. "I'll be there for him."

Relief washed over her. "Thank you."

A mother's love was one of the strongest on earth and it was clear to me that Nash's mother loved him very much. He was lucky to have that.

A couple of minutes later, he came back into the kitchen.

"They're all fixed," he said to his mum.

She pointed at the table. "Sit, have your coffee."

He looked at me. "You in a hurry to get going?"

"Nope, it's all good."

Taking a seat, he asked his mother, "You having any problems with your car at the moment?"

She rolled her eyes. "My car is not as bad as you make it out to be."

"Yeah, it is."

I watched their interaction with fascination. Nash was like a different person around his mother, and I loved what she brought out in him.

"Well, nothing has broken on it for awhile."

He informed me, "Let the record show that when my mother says 'for awhile' in relation to her car, she means for a week or so."

I laughed and Linda pouted, but I could see it was in good humour. "Did you know that Nash is a trained mechanic?" she asked me.

Raising my brows at Nash, I said, "No, I did not know that; he's never told me that snippet of information about himself. I guessed he was good with cars though because he's offered to fix mine."

Now it was her turn to raise her brows. "Really? That's interesting."

I looked between them. "Why?"

Nash was shaking his head and muttering something under his breath that I couldn't quite work out.

Linda answered me. "It's interesting because Nash hates working on cars other than his own these days. He fixes mine out of love but he won't touch anyone else's."

I mentally connected the dots. He hadn't even hesitated to offer to work on mine. I smiled at him, but he just shook his head again.

Nash stood and jerked his head towards the front door, and said to his mum, "We've gotta get going."

Linda followed us out, and gave him a long hug goodbye. I watched them again, liking the way he let her do that. Some guys were funny with displays of affection, but Nash was good with it. He was a lot taller than her and placed a soft kiss on her head before pulling away.

"Love you," she said.

Smiling, he said, "Love you too, Mum. I'll see you on Sunday."

She turned to me and pulled me close for a hug. "Remember what I said," she murmured.

"I will," I promised, and then added, "It was so nice to meet you."

"It was great to meet you too, Velvet," she agreed, and then looking at Nash, she said, "You need to bring Velvet for dinner on Sunday night if she's free."

Because I had made the decision to follow Linda's request and not let Nash push me out of his life, I chimed in, "I'm free."

That made her ecstatic and she clapped her hands together again. "Good, it's settled. I look forward to seeing you on Sunday."

Nash looked like he'd just been ambushed. The best course of action was probably to keep him moving, so I pushed him towards his bike. "Time to go, I need to get my shopping done."

As we walked away from his mother, he muttered, "I've just been played by you and my mother, haven't I?"

I smiled sweetly. "Your mother seems too nice to do something like that."

"None of the women in my life are too nice to do something like that, you included." Warmth settled in my stomach at his words, and I laughed at what he'd said. "Something tells me I'm going to love your family."

"God fuckin' help me."

CHAPTER 15

Can't Stand The Rain - Lady Antebellum

NASH

I PULLED UP OUTSIDE VELVET'S HOUSE AND KILLED THE engine of her car. I'd fixed it, and it'd been the first time in ages that I'd enjoyed working on a car. Now, I was returning it and hoping she had the time to drive me back to my house. Eyeing her driveway, I realised she might not because she had a visitor. Someone who drove a very expensive car.

A couple of minutes later, I knocked on her front door. I could hear shouting coming from inside; a male was yelling at Velvet. Without hesitation, I pushed the door open and stalked towards the voices. I found Velvet and a guy I'd never laid eyes on before in her kitchen. The suit he wore screamed money and I wondered who the hell he was. Regardless of who he was though, I didn't like the way he was treating Velvet.

She was rattled, I could tell that straight away. When she looked at me with eyes that begged me to help her, I didn't hesitate. "What the fuck's going on here?" I demanded while moving in between them, putting Velvet behind me.

The guy glared at me. "This is none of your business so I suggest you leave us to it." He looked me up and down with a 'you're a piece of worthless shit' look.

"Not fuckin' likely," I growled.

"Velvet, kindly tell your friend that we're just concluding a business deal and that there's no need for his help."

"No need, Velvet. But what you can tell me is who the hell he is to you."

She moved so that she was standing next to me. I didn't fail to notice that she positioned herself right next to me so that our bodies were touching; she didn't feel safe with this dickhead. "James is my ex-husband." She supplied the information I was after.

Shit. I wouldn't have picked that; they seemed so different. "You do business deals with all your ex-wives?" I asked him.

"Just the ones who are a little unpredictable."

I'd heard enough. Turning to Velvet, I asked, "What do you want to happen here, babe? You want to finish your discussion with me present or do you want him to leave?"

"I want him to leave." It was almost like she was begging me to get rid of him the way she said it; damn, he'd really shaken her up.

I nodded, and then directed at him, "You heard the lady."

He was fuming; his face was a wild mess of anger, and I didn't want to think about what had gone on between these two during their marriage. I could see what kind of man he was just from five minutes with him. "This isn't finished, Velvet. Not by a long shot. I want that agreement signed and I want it signed in the next week."

I stepped closer to him, and snarled, "That'll be the last time you threaten Velvet. You come near her again and you'll have me to deal with, and that's the last fuckin' thing you want. We clear?"

He played a good game but I didn't miss the flicker of hesitation before he said, "You have no idea who you're dealing with here. Your threats mean nothing to me."

"I don't give a flying fuck who I'm dealing with here. All I care about is Velvet, and I'd suggest you take in what I just told you. I don't fuck around and I don't think twice before I look after those who are mine."

He gave Velvet one last menacing look and then he took my advice and left. I watched him go and after I heard the front door slam shut, I gave my attention back to Velvet. She looked like she was about to break down so I pulled her to me and wrapped her in my arms. A moment later, her body shuddered and she began sobbing. Christ, I'd never seen her like this. Velvet was a tough bitch; nothing ever seemed to get to her, and she didn't take shit from anyone.

I smoothed my hand over her hair and held her tight, letting her get it out. Eventually, she let me go and wiped the tears off her face. "I'm sorry," she stuttered.

"Fuck, you've got nothing to be sorry about, sweet thing."

"I'm sorry you got dragged into this."

"I'm not."

"Well you might be once I tell you who he is and what he's capable of."

"Nope. Like I said to him, I don't give a shit who he is."

"Nash, James has family high up in politics and can make your life hell with the connections he has. He really isn't someone you want on your wrong side."

"Babe, do I strike you as a man who is scared of anyone?"

She took a moment to think about it and then blessed me with a beautiful smile. "No, you don't."

I nodded. "Exactly. And I certainly don't let motherfuckers like him scare me. I don't want you worrying about him anymore; you let me do the worrying."

Her shoulders sagged, and she took a long breath. Then she hit me with a piercing look; one that I knew meant something important was coming. "Nash, what's with the turn around in attitude towards me. Until two days ago, you didn't want anything to do with me, and now you're offering to take on my problems."

Moment of truth. "Madison sorted me out."

"What does that mean?"

Fuck, I hated talking about this shit. But she wasn't the kind of woman to let it go. "I talked to Madison about you; about us, and how badly I treated you. She told me to get my shit together and apologise to you. Seems to be something I'm doing a lot of lately."

"You told Madison we slept together?"

"Yes, and that I fucked it all up by being a bastard to you when I couldn't work out what the hell to do with our friendship after it."

She fell silent so I continued. "Velvet, I don't have a lot of friends like you. It was uncomplicated before we had sex and then it just felt all screwed up. Do you know where I'm coming from with this?"

"Yeah, I felt it too, Nash. But I was happy to forget the sex and just stay friends."

I blew out a long breath and went with complete honesty. "I don't know how to do that when all I can think about now is fucking you again."

Her eyes widened. "Yeah, but you think the same thing about all women. You want to have sex with every woman you meet."

"Not like this; this is something new for me, and I don't know what to do with it." My skin itched with irritation at every word I was uttering; laying yourself out like this was hard to do.

She ran her fingers through her hair and bit her lip. She seemed confused with the whole thing and I didn't blame her; I'd been giving her mixed signals for weeks now. "I'm not sure where you're going with this so I don't really know what to say."

"What do you want between us, Velvet?"

"I want what we had before we slept together."

Maybe I'd left it too long to apologise, but I figured friends was a good place to start from again. "I want that too."

"Good." She smiled but it was forced and I wondered what she was hiding behind it.

"Now that we've got that sorted, tell me what the hell is going on with your ex."

"James is going into politics and wants to pay me to keep my mouth shut if journalists ever come digging for dirt on him. I'll never talk to them but I don't need to be paid to do that. He doesn't believe me and is trying to force me into taking the money."

"You never fail to surprise me, Velvet."

"Why's that?"

"There's so much good inside you but you don't show it often. If people took the time, they'd see it but most people don't fuckin' bother to take the time. They skim the surface of a person and judge the outside layer. I see it in you but every now and then you surprise me with more."

It wasn't often I saw Velvet speechless but she was now. I let her take that in, and then continued, "So he wants you to agree to this within the next week?"

"Yes."

"We'll fuckin' see about that. Don't contact him, okay? Leave it with me."

"Okay, but I'm not sure what you can do about it."

She was still uneasy about this, so to put her at ease, I tried to lighten the mood. Grinning at her, I said, "Most women think my talents lie with my mouth and hands, but I'll share a secret with you; my mind is where it's all at, sweet thing." I tapped my head. "It's a dangerous place up here, and your ex won't know what hit him once I've dealt with him."

It did the trick and she laughed at me. "I believe you when you say it's a dangerous place up there. I'd like to know what the hell goes on in that mind of yours."

Still grinning, I replied, "That makes two of us."

CHAPTER 16

Collide - Kid Rock & Sheryl Crow

VELVET

AFTER A BUSY NIGHT AT WORK, I SANK DOWN INTO THE chair next to Nash and put my feet up on the table in front of us. Smiling at him, I laid my head back, closed my eyes and took a deep breath.

"Long night?" he asked.

Cracking an eye open to look at him, I said, "You've no idea. Assholes were out in full force tonight. Thank God it's Friday; I need two days off."

He scowled. "You should have come and got me to deal with the assholes."

"Nash, I can't rely on you to take care of all the dickheads in my life."

"I'd be fuckin' happy to, babe."

I laughed. "Oh, I'm sure you would love to get those fists out and deal with them all that way."

He grinned. "You know me too well, sweet thing."

"There's a lot I don't know about you, but I do know two

things; you like to get your fists and your cock out at every chance."

He'd just had some of his drink and he almost choked on it at my words. "Fuck, Velvet, you've got a dirty mouth sometimes."

"And is that a problem for you, King of the Dirty?"

His eyes blazed with heat. "No, it's not a fuckin' problem, but damn woman, you have no idea what it does to a man when words like that come out of your pretty little mouth."

My body sizzled with lust. Ever since we'd cleared the air the other day, Nash had gone back to his flirty ways, and I felt like I would explode from the desire he stirred in me. I leant closer to him, and whispered, "It probably does to you what your words do to me, Nash."

He growled, "Christ, Velvet, don't say shit like that unless you're willing to go there again."

I licked my lips. "Maybe I am. Maybe you just need to ask."

"You two look cozy." We were interrupted by J, and Nash shot him a foul look.

"What's up?" Nash asked, his voice and body language clear with his desire for J to hurry up and get the hell out of here.

J raised his brows. "That's a nice fucking way to be greeted after I've been away for awhile."

"We're kinda in the middle of something, asshole."

J smirked. "So I see."

I stepped in. "J, cut to the chase and tell him what you want. I need Nash to take care of something for me."

Nash swung his head to face me. His eyes were glazed with desire, and he muttered, "Fuckin' hell, woman. I'll take that as a yes."

J laughed. "I actually don't want anything; I was just stopping by to say hi before I went home."

Nash stood up, pulling me with him. "Good to see you, man. Say hello to Madison for me."

I saluted him. "Will do." Flashing me a grin, he murmured, "I hope you know what you're getting yourself into there, babe."

"I do this time," I said before being pulled by Nash in his haste to leave. I stumbled a little before righting myself and hurrying to keep up with him. "Nash, where are we going?"

He didn't stop, just kept going in the direction of the front door. "I'm taking you home, and I'm going to convince you that my cock is the best damn cock in the world."

I pulled on his hand to slow him down. He stopped and turned back to face me. "I already know your cock is the best damn cock in the world."

"Well then, I'm going to introduce you to more of it's talents, babe."

"Sorry to slow you down, but I need to get my bag from out back before we go."

"Shit," he grumbled. Motioning towards the staff room, he said, "Let's hurry this shit up then."

Laughing at him, I turned back around and made my way out to the staff room. He followed, his hand glued to my waist. I loved the feel of Nash's hands on me.

As I opened my locker to retrieve my bag, Nash pushed himself up against me. His hands slid around my waist and made their way up my stomach and to my breasts. "I fuckin' love your tits," he whispered in my ear.

Heat shot through me and I moaned. I placed one of my hands over his and held it in place on my boob. "I love your hands on my tits."

He ground himself into my ass, and his free hand moved down to the bottom of my dress. He pulled it up and slid his hand into my panties. I moaned again as his fingers worked their magic on my clit. His other hand continued to knead my breast, tweaking my nipple. When his finger entered me, my body jerked with pleasure and he murmured, "Fuck, you're so wet, sweet thing."

I laid my head back on his shoulder and said, "It's what you do to me."

He hissed with desire, and removed his hands from my body. Slapping me on the ass, he said, "Get your shit, babe, I'm taking you home to fuck you."

★★★

Nash got me back to his place in record time. As he went to switch his bike off, I whispered in his ear, "Don't turn it off. I want you to fuck me on it." I stood and swung myself around to sit in front of him, facing him.

"You sure know how to get a man excited, darlin'," he growled.

His hands moved to grip my ass and his lips dropped to kiss my neck. I arched my neck backwards, giving him full access to whatever he wanted. He kissed his way up to my mouth and then devoured me with a kiss that would melt any woman's panties off. This man knew his stuff, and he was pulling me under a wave of lust that was making it hard for me to think straight. All I could focus on was his musky scent, his hands on my ass, his mouth on mine and his cock that was hard against me, sending my need for him over the edge.

I reached for his zip and slowly pulled it down, letting his cock out to play. He groaned when I grasped him and began moving my hand up and down his hard length. "Feel good?" I asked, softly.

"Like you wouldn't believe." His breath tickled my ear as he spoke and then nibbled on me.

We lost ourselves to the pleasure; I continued to stroke his cock while our mouths and tongues danced together. The vibration of the bike only heightened my desire, and I pushed myself closer, desperate to have him inside me.

He stilled my hand on his dick. "Careful there, sweet thing, I want to come inside you, not in your hand." Reaching behind him, he pulled his wallet out of his back pocket and grabbed a condom out. Grinning, he gave it to me. "You can have the pleasure, babe."

Taking it off him, I said, "You love your cock, don't you?"

"What the fuck's not to love?"

He had a point.

A minute later, I had the condom in place, and he pulled my dress up before positioning me above him. I slid down onto him, and we groaned in unison. He felt amazing, and I started moving in time with him. This wasn't going to take long; between the vibrations and his expertise, I was sure I was about to have one of the quickest orgasms I'd ever had.

"I think I love your cock, too," I breathed out.

"We're doing something wrong if you only think you love it," he said in between thrusts.

I gently bit his lip before sliding my tongue in his mouth and kissing him. Nash tasted of cherry soft drink and I decided it was my new favourite taste.

He groaned into my mouth and pulled away a little. "My lips are always at your service anytime you feel the urge to bite. In fact, my whole body is up for that, baby."

I smiled wickedly at him. "That can be arranged. You just call me whenever you want my teeth on you."

He thrust hard and pulled me tight against him. "I don't think you're understanding me. My schedule is permanently open."

Holy hell, he had a way with words, and I felt them in my core. My toes curled as an orgasm started to take over. My body had come alive under his touch and every nerve ending sizzled with desire.

He knew how to read a woman. "You're close, aren't you, baby?"

I was so close, I couldn't form words so I nodded. He moved his mouth to my ear, and whispered, "Come for me, sweet thing. I want to watch you lose yourself and scream out my name."

His hot breath on my skin and the words he'd said sent me over the edge and I screamed out his name as I closed my eyes and orgasmed.

"Fuck," he muttered and picked up his pace, thrusting in and out as he chased his own orgasm.

His body shuddered a minute or so later, and he stilled as he came. His head dropped down onto my shoulder and I felt his heavy breaths on my skin as he found himself again.

When he lifted his head, he had a lazy smile for me. "Ready for round two?"

I grinned at him. "You need to take care of my other needs first, baby."

He cocked his head to the side. "And what would they be?"

"Well mainly I need a drink, but a woman also likes a bit of sweet talk in between rounds. Do bikers do that shit?"

He chuckled. "I'm all about the sweet talk, darlin'. You should know that about me by now."

"Okay then, take me inside, give me a drink and some sexy talk and then I'm all yours again."

He smacked my ass. "Off, I've got shit to do so I can get my cock back in you."

I obeyed his command and pulled my dress down after I got off his bike. He eyed me and murmured, "That dress is going the wrong way, baby. It needs to go up, not down."

"And the sexy talk begins," I joked.

He switched off his bike and got off before pulling me close. "That's not sexy talk darlin'. Your legs won't be able to hold you up when I begin the sexy talk," he promised.

Good Lord, Nash Walker was something else; my legs were

already going weak just at the thought of his sexy talk.

★★★

I opened my eyes and had to squint to deal with the sun streaming through the window. Shifting in the bed, the hand around my waist tightened and pulled me backwards. My ass hit Nash's erection and he groaned. "See what you do to me, sweet thing," he murmured, sleepily.

Smiling, I said, "Good morning to you, too."

His lips brushed across my shoulder as he swept my hair out of the way. "It's a good morning already."

I turned in his arms and promised, "I can make it better."

His face lit up. "I dare you."

His wish was my command, and I slowly made my way down his body, licking and gently biting as I went. Every time I bit him, he groaned. I guessed that meant he really did like the biting. When I got to my destination, I took a moment to admire Nash's cock. He was blessed; his cock was one of the largest ones I'd ever had the good fortune of meeting.

"He doesn't bite, darlin'," he promised.

I raised my eyes to his. "I'm just admiring the merchandise for a moment."

He moved his arms to rest behind his head on the pillow and stretched his body before asking, "You like what you see?"

"Oh, I do. In fact, maybe I'll just continue to admire it rather than play with it," I teased him.

He wasn't even fazed by my teasing. Grinning, he said, "No worries, sweet thing. I like your eyes on my cock, and besides, it just means that I can admire your tits for a bit longer while I imagine how good your mouth is going to feel wrapped around me."

I sat back on my knees and watched as his eyes dropped to my chest. Nash's gaze on me was almost as good as his hands on me. I massaged my breasts while he watched, and his sharp intake of breath sent heat through me. That was it; I couldn't drag this out any longer. I bent my head and took him in my mouth as far back as I could. His hand landed on my head again and the way he gripped my hair and pushed my head down turned me on even more than I already was. I liked a bit of rough play. My lips and tongue worked his cock into a frenzy, and I massaged his balls with one of my hands. Every now and then I slid his cock out of my mouth so I could suck on his balls, and his groans told me he liked that.

Just as I thought he was getting ready to come, he reached down and pulled me off him. "Babe, I want you to fuck me with your tits." His hungry eyes were dividing their attention between my face and my chest.

"You're a tit man?" I asked.

"Like you wouldn't fuckin' believe, darlin'. I love pussy but I love to watch my dick between a good set of tits and you, sweet thing, have the best set I've ever seen."

He didn't have to tell me twice. Personally, I loved a man who would worship my boobs. I bent them down and took his dick in between them, squeezing as he thrust up and down.

"Fuck," he muttered, his breathing growing ragged.

Our eyes met and held as he fucked my tits to the point of orgasm. He shot his cum over my chest and then lay back on the bed, letting out a loud groan of pleasure. I left him to go in search of something to clean myself up with, and when I came back to the room, he was lying with his arms behind his head again, watching me. I stopped and rested against the doorway, letting him run his eyes over my naked body.

"Christ, Velvet, you've got a body made for sin."

I pushed off from the doorway and walked to the bed. Straddling him, I whispered, "And you've got a mouth that leads to sin." I kissed him, and he sat up, keeping me in place on his lap.

"Opening round for the day was a hit, babe. You ready for more?" he asked while sucking on my neck.

"Always ready for more. And then I'll cook you breakfast," I promised.

His head jerked away from my neck and he stilled, not saying a word.

"What's wrong?" I asked, not sure what I'd said to affect him like that.

"Just been awhile since I've had a woman cook me breakfast," he murmured.

"So it's a good thing, then?"

He smiled. "It's a really good thing, darlin'."

I returned his smile. "Good. Now where were we?"

His hand moved to my breast. "I was about to show your tits some Nash lovin', baby."

"Well don't let me stop you."

His hand rubbed my nipple for a moment and then he lifted me and deposited me on my back in front of him. Moving so he was kneeling over me, he bent his head to my breast and showed me just how good Nash loving was.

★★★

An hour later, we were finished with Nash loving and showered, and I was cooking him breakfast in his kitchen while he sat at the counter and watched me. I was the happiest I'd been in awhile but I still had something I had to clear up. "Nash, what is this?"

He knew exactly what I was getting at. And I had to give it to him that he didn't even hesitate with an answer. "This is us getting our shit together, Velvet."

I had to know whether we were on the same page here. "Tell me exactly what that means to you."

Again, he didn't hesitate. "It means that I feel something for you and I want to explore what that is. I don't know where the hell it will take us but I'm willing to find out if you are."

"I'm willing," I said softly.

"Might be a bumpy road though," he said.

"How so?"

His intense gaze refused to let mine go. "I'm fucked up, baby. I'm trying to work through some shit at the moment, but I need you to know that it might take me some time, and some of it might not be pretty. You think you can handle that?"

His mother's words came back to me and I smiled at him. "I'm a tough bitch, Nash. I've handled your shit so far, haven't I?"

The intensity in his stare softened a little, allowing a small smile to flicker across his lips. "Yeah, you have."

"You need to promise me one thing though. When you need help, you come to me. I'll be here to talk or just to listen, whatever you need. Just don't shut me out. We were friends first and I never want us to lose that."

"I don't make promises I can't keep, Velvet."

His honesty and vulnerability touched my heart and I couldn't fault him for telling me the truth, even if it wasn't what I wanted to hear. "Fair enough. But you know how I feel."

"I do," he said, gruffly.

Silence descended as we both got lost in our thoughts. Nash hadn't given me what I'd asked for, but I felt like he'd given me a whole lot more than he'd given anyone else for a long time. I could run with that; at least until we both worked out what this was going to be between us.

CHAPTER 17

Love's Lookin' Good On You - Lady Antebellum

NASH

"YOU SURE YOU'RE READY FOR THIS? MY FAMILY CAN BE A handful."

Velvet stared at me in the way that says 'you're fuckin' kidding aren't you'. "Nash, you're the biggest handful of all. I think I can cope with your family."

I grinned. "Well get your ass inside then, woman." I smacked her butt and followed her into the madhouse that was my mother's home. Sunday night dinner would be interesting tonight.

Mum lit up at the sight of us. "Velvet, you made it!" I watched in fascination as they embraced. I'd never known Velvet to be so open with someone new in her life. She was very guarded and distrustful of everyone she met. You had to gain her trust and it was hard work most of the time.

"Thank you for having me," Velvet said to mum, and handed her the cake she'd brought. "I had a good friend of mine make us a red velvet cake for dessert."

Mum's eyes shifted to me and she smiled before looking back at

Velvet. "Thanks, sweetheart. The Walkers are big cake eaters."

My mother was sold on Velvet, of that I was sure. And Velvet was just as sold on my mother. It warmed my cold heart. But fuck, heaven help me, the two women in my life getting on? Who knew what shit they'd try and pull on me.

Carla sauntered into the kitchen. "Did someone say cake?" She smiled at Velvet. "Hi, I'm Carla, Nash's little sister, the one he still tries to mother."

Velvet laughed. "Nash sure does have that protective streak in him, doesn't he?"

Carla rolled her eyes. "Oh my God, you have no idea, Velvet! Now where's this cake?"

"Generally comes after dinner, babe, not before," I said, knowing full well that Carla wouldn't hesitate to eat it before dinner.

"A girl makes her own rules in life. Right, Carla?" Velvet winked at my sister and I watched as another Walker woman fell under her spell.

I decided to leave them to it and headed into the living room where Jamison was catching up on the weekend sport. He eyed me as I took a seat. "Your woman with you?" he asked.

My mother had informed everyone I was bringing Velvet tonight, and somehow that had translated into her being my woman. "She's not my woman, man."

"What are you then? Cause you haven't brought a woman home since Gabriella so this seems like something important."

I scrubbed my face as I fought the churning in my gut at this conversation. "I don't know where it's going yet so let's not put a fuckin' label on it, okay."

"Take my advice little brother; work it out as quick as you can because women don't like to be kept waiting. Mum seems to like her so she can't be too bad."

I decided to be totally honest with him. "I'm not sure I'm ready for this. If I was, Velvet would be who I would choose, no doubts there."

"Nash, it's been ten years; you're more than ready for this."

"So I keep being told," I muttered.

Jamison chuckled, but wisely kept his mouth shut.

We were interrupted by Erika who yelled from outside, "Nash, Jamison, need your help!"

A moment later, we found her struggling with a huge pot plant just outside the front door. It was in a heavy terracotta pot and it looked like she was about to drop it.

I quickly grabbed it off her and scowled. "You should have come and gotten us rather than carrying it by yourself."

"I thought I'd be able to manage," she grumbled.

"Shit, Erika, you could have done your back in again."

"Yeah well, I didn't so it's all good."

I got the plant inside as we continued to argue back and forth. We'd spent our whole lives arguing; I was sure it was how we showed our love. When we got to the kitchen, Velvet was on her hands and knees reaching under the fridge for something. Her ass was up in the air facing us and I took a moment to admire it.

"What's going on here?" I eventually asked as she continued to search for whatever it was.

Her head spun around and our eyes met. I raised my brows at her and shifted my eyes to her ass and then back to her face before grinning at her. She shook her head at me but she was smiling. "Your mum took her rings off to do the dishes and one of them fell on the floor and we think it rolled under the fridge so I'm trying to find it."

I leant against the wall and folded my arms over my chest. "Take your time, darlin'."

Erika groaned. "You have a one track mind, Nash."

I smirked. "Velvet doesn't mind, do you babe?"

She ignored me and continued her search while I settled in for the view. I particularly enjoyed it when she tried to extend her arm further because it meant her ass tilted even higher in the air. My dick jerked while I imagined that ass naked with my hands around it.

"Nash!"

I swung my gaze to my mother who was trying to get my attention. "What?"

"Stop ogling Velvet and get everyone a drink, please."

Velvet finally stood up, having retrieved the ring. She passed it to mum and then glared at me.

I held my hands up defensively. "What, babe? A man has to take advantage of certain situations."

She walked over to me, laid her hand on my chest and whispered, "You'll pay for that later."

"Don't make promises unless you intend to keep them, sweet thing."

"You should know by now, Nash, that I'm a woman of my word," she kept her voice low so that only I could hear her.

Christ, this conversation had to come to an end or else I was going to bust a nut in my mother's kitchen. "I look forward to it," I said, and left her to go and get drinks for everyone.

★★★

My family loved Velvet. They fawned all over her during dinner while I sat back and took it all in. It had been a different story with Gabriella; they hadn't liked her from the beginning so this was new to me. It was good; good in a way I never thought would happen in my life. And to say it scared the shit outta me was putting it mildly.

"What do you do for a living, Velvet?" Jamison asked.

She struggled to answer this question which was odd. Velvet

loved what she did, she'd told me numerous times, so I didn't understand why she had that deer in the headlights look on her face. "I'm a stripper at Indigo," she finally said but there was hesitation in her voice.

Perception was one of Jamison's gifts. He leant towards her and asked, "Does it pay your bills, gorgeous?"

She blinked, obviously not expecting what he'd said. "Yes."

He nodded. "Well hold your head high because there's a lot of fucking bludgers out there who bleed the government dry rather than get off their ass and work. You make an honest living and pay your own way; it doesn't matter how you do it."

Erika raised her wine glass. "Cheers to that," she agreed and took a sip while giving Velvet a kind smile.

Velvet's shoulders sagged and she seemed relieved. "Thank you."

I jerked my chin at Jamison and he nodded in response. I'd thank him for that later. For now, I slid my arm around Velvet's shoulders and pulled her close so I could whisper in her ear, "We need to eat dessert really fuckin' quick."

She placed her hand on my leg, close to my dick, and purred, "But, Nash, I think your mum has a story about your childhood to tell me. We can't be rude now." She moved her hand up and down my leg slowly, teasing me.

"I fuckin' knew it," I muttered.

She turned to me in genuine surprise. "What?"

"I knew you two together were a bad idea."

Her head fell back slightly and she laughed, and my dick dug his own grave.

CHAPTER 18

Pornstar Dancing - My Darkest Days

NASH

MONDAY MORNING ROLLED AROUND FAST, AND I DROP-
ped Velvet back at her house after she'd stayed with me last night.
She had treated me to a long night of sex and was worn out this
morning. I couldn't wait to get my hands back on her tonight.

After I dropped her off, I headed over to Blade's warehouse to
meet Scott who was waiting for me there.

I surveyed the warehouse in front of us. "Shit, brother, what
does Blade actually do? This joint is huge," I said to Scott.

"I'm still not sure what he does. He likes to keep shit to himself
and I don't ask."

"You have much to do with him now, after all the shit with
Black Deeds?"

"Not really, and that's the way I like it."

We were greeted at the door by a beefy looking guy who
escorted us up to Blade's office on the second floor. He was on the
phone and motioned for us to take a seat. Blade ended his call and
gave us his attention. "What can I do for you?" The intensity this

guy exuded was off the charts. I wondered if he ever chilled; I highly doubted it. Even at Madison's wedding, he hadn't let his hair down and relaxed.

Scott spoke first. "Nash asked me for some help with a personal matter, and I suggested you might be able to help him."

"With what?"

I answered him, "A friend of mine has an ex-husband who is trying to bully her into an agreement. I've only met him once but he seems like a real piece of work. He has a high public profile so I'm thinking we need to come up with something different to our usual way of dealing with this shit and I figure you could be the man to help us with that."

"Who is it?" He wasn't big on saying more than he had to which I respected.

"James Carr."

His brows shot up. "Fuck."

"You obviously know of him, then," Scott said.

"Know him? I have a long, hard history with that family. They bully people into shit all the time so I can only imagine what he's doing to his ex. I've got dirt on him that would send him to prison for a very long time."

"I just need something to stop him harassing Velvet."

"What's he want from her?" Blade enquired, leaning back in his chair.

"He's going into politics and wants her to sign an agreement that ensures she won't talk publicly about him or their relationship."

"Yeah, I bet she could tell a story or two that would shock that family's adoring public," he mused. "I've heard he's got a violent streak where women are concerned."

Anger pumped through me at the thought of what he'd done to Velvet during their marriage. "I'd believe that after the way I saw him treat Velvet."

Blade nodded thoughtfully. "Leave it with me, Nash. I'll be in touch with some information soon."

I stood up and shook his hand. "Thanks, man, I appreciate it."

Scott and Blade shared an uncomfortable look before nodding at each other. They didn't exchange a word though. I thought after they dealt with Bullet they'd form some kind of truce or brotherly bond or shit, but I guess I was wrong because there was no obvious bond here today.

★★★

Later that night, I watched Velvet perform. Not something new to me. What was new to me though, were the feelings agitating in my gut while I watched her. While I watched other men watch her.

Shit.

I wasn't sure I could sit through it but I knew she'd be upset if I left. So I stayed. Problem was, so did the jealousy and the threat of me acting on it. In the end, I compromised; I spent most of the night in the office out the back. When she finished her shift, she found me on the computer out there.

"Why are you out here?" she asked, clearly surprised.

I leant back in the chair and rubbed the back of my head. "Long story, babe."

"You're not going to tell me, are you?"

"Nope." I shut the computer down and joined her. "You ready to go home? Thought you could stay at mine tonight."

"Just let me get my things."

I watched her walk away. I'd been thinking about her all day. Not only craving her body, but wanting to talk to her, to be with her. I let that sink in and felt the anxiety settle in again. But the anxiety didn't cause nearly as much pressure on my chest as usual.

For the first time in a very long time, I felt like I could work through it.

She returned from the staff room, and placed her hand on my chest. Smiling up at me, she said, "I'm ready to discover more of your hidden talents, Nash Walker."

I bent my head and kissed her, gently biting her lip when I'd finished. "I'm not a man who likes to keep a woman waiting," I murmured, grabbing her hand and leading her out of the club.

★★★

VELVET

NASH HAD BEEN on my mind all day. No other man had ever consumed my thoughts the way he did. To say I was ready for him tonight was putting it mildly.

I couldn't take my eyes off his back as I followed him into his house. He was wearing his standard fitted black tee with jeans, and the way that t-shirt gripped his muscles was mesmerising. They flexed as he walked, and I envisioned running my hands over them.

He kept walking until he hit his bedroom. When he turned to face me, his intense gaze sent my desire for him into overdrive. His voice radiated sex when he commanded, "Take your dress off. Slowly."

I tingled with anticipation, and did as he said. We didn't break eye contact until I had my dress completely off, at which point his eyes dropped to my body. He sucked in a breath at the sight of me in my lingerie. I'd chosen it purposefully for him. It was a bodysuit but there wasn't much to it. The panty was a strip of black sheer material that was connected to the lacy chest material by three pieces of black string on each side. It gave a flash of boob as it didn't cover them completely, and my stomach was bare apart from the strings. My back was bare and my ass was hardly covered by the g-string.

"Turn around," he said, after spending a decent amount of time on the front.

I didn't say a word; just did as he said, and waited for his response.

"Fuck, Velvet."

I waited for him to touch me or start ripping clothes off, but he did nothing. I turned back to face him, and he held out a piece of fabric for me to take. A blindfold. My insides clenched and I gladly took it from him. When he held up a length of rope, my whole body buzzed with desire. He raised his eyebrows questioningly and I nodded my agreement. That rope couldn't be tied fast enough as far as I was concerned. Nash, a blindfold and rope surely had to be every woman's fantasy.

He took a purposeful step towards me and reached behind my neck to undo the clasp of my bodysuit. It fell to reveal my breasts, and his hand curved around one breast, his thumb rubbing my nipple. His other hand slid into my panties, and I moaned when his finger entered me.

"I'm going to make you feel so fuckin' good tonight, sweet thing," he rasped.

He already was. I smiled and reached for his zip, but he pushed my hand away. "As much as I want your hands on me, babe, that'll have to wait. Tonight's all about you." His lips brushed against my ear, and he murmured, "You'll have my cock eventually, but first I'm going to drive you fuckin' wild. Your pussy is going to be so wet for me."

Holy hell, Nash's dirty words already drove me wild. I wrapped my arms around his neck, pushed my body into his and kissed him. Our lips were demanding, urgent. The moment was lost in the need to get closer to each other, to be in each other. His hands sought my ass, my back, and finally, he grasped a handful of my hair and pulled roughly so that my head fell back, breaking our kiss. Wild eyes met mine, and he growled as he bent his mouth to my neck, and sucked it. When his teeth met my flesh, I called out his name, and dug my fingernails into his back.

My fingernails set him off, and he muttered something unintelligible as he let me go, and fell to his knees. He pulled my bodysuit the rest of the way down, lifted my feet and forced it out of the way. I almost lost my balance trying to keep up with his pace. When his mouth latched onto my pussy, I buried my hands in his hair to steady myself. The deep growls coming from his throat as his tongue worked it's magic, shot electricity through me; he had me turned on to the point that my brain was shutting down as I lost myself in the bliss.

Just when I thought he'd brought me to the edge, he stopped what he was doing and stood up. He reached for the blindfold I was still holding, and took it off me. "Time to lose yourself completely, baby," he said, lifting me and walking towards the bed. He deposited me on the bed, and then lifted his shirt over his head and threw it on the floor. Then he reached down to undo his belt; his jeans and boxers hit the floor a moment later.

Nash stood in front of me naked. Beautiful. His well built body was impressive to look at; I'd never tire of the sight. Between the muscles and the ink, he could command my attention without even trying.

"You ready, sweet thing?" he finally asked, after allowing me some time to stare at him.

"More than you know." I had to stop myself from begging him to hurry the hell up with whatever he had planned. Nash could do whatever he wanted to me tonight; I was his to own.

He straddled me and tied the blindfold in place. I shivered as I descended into darkness, and gave myself over to him. "Nash - " I began.

His finger touched my lips, silencing me, and sending another shiver throughout my body at his touch. "Shhh," he said.

I waited for his next move but he didn't do anything. The effort required to lie still without reaching for him, was enormous. My senses were all over the place. Unable to see, I zeroed in on the sound of his ragged breathing and the feel of his bare skin against mine, scorching me.

My anticipation levels grew until I didn't think I could keep it inside anymore. I was about to speak when he finally shifted off the bed, leaving me alone. Not sure what he was doing, I held my breath in an effort to listen to his actions. The sound of his feet on the carpet told me he was still in the room with me. A moment later, I was surprised when music began playing. And stunned when I realised what song he'd put on. Pornstar Dancing by My Darkest Days. The song he'd asked me to use for one of my dances. The dance he often requested I perform.

The driving beat of the music filled the room, and Nash came back to the bed and positioned himself between my legs, distracting me from thoughts of the song and what it meant to him, to us. I waited for him to say something, but he didn't. Instead, he lifted my hand off the bed, and I felt the rope against my skin. He slipped my hand through the knot he'd made and then tied that hand to the bedpost. He repeated this with my other hand, and I lay completely vulnerable to him. Unable to see, unable to escape. Lust coursed through me, and I moaned his name.

He rewarded me with a slow, deep kiss; the kind of kiss that makes your chest tingle with excitement and your tummy swirl with butterflies. His tongue explored my mouth, tangling with mine, and my back arched off the bed as I tried desperately to have more of him. I needed more; I needed it all. Everything he had to give me, I would take. Greedily.

He growled and ended the kiss. Warm breath tickled my neck as he moved his mouth to my ear to whisper, "You like the music?"

"Yes," I breathed out.

He continued to whisper in my ear, "I picture you while I make myself come listening to it."

My pussy clenched at his words and I writhed on the bed. "Fuck, Nash, I need - "

He cut me off again with a finger to my lips. "No talking, unless I say so."

Fuck.

His bossiness turned me on. I needed him to touch me, to fuck me. I was ready, and he wasn't hurrying it along. But I didn't dare utter another word.

The song finished, and Closer by Nine Inch Nails began playing. And then my world exploded around me as Nash began the next phase of pleasuring me. He pushed my legs wider apart and licked my pussy from one end to the other. I waited for his tongue or finger to enter me but neither happened. Instead, my clit came alive with vibrations. It wasn't what I was expecting and I screamed out his name. My hands fought their restraints as I automatically tried to move my hands so I could touch him.

He placed a hand on my stomach. "Don't fight it, baby," he murmured.

I couldn't stop myself. "I need to touch you, Nash."

"You like the bullet? Feel good?"

"I love the bullet, but I want my hands on you too." I was almost begging him.

"Soon," he promised, and then moved the bullet vibrator to tease my nipples. When his tongue hit my pussy at the same time, I couldn't help it, I arched up off the bed again. The pleasure was intense. So good; I never wanted it to stop.

I hooked my legs over his shoulders while he tongued me. He grunted his approval and then began alternating the bullet between my nipples and my clit while mixing in his tongue and his fingers. Nash had just become my new favourite person. I was in sensory overload and the pleasure he was bringing me was pleasure like I'd never known.

When he stopped what he was doing, I could have cried. However, he redeemed himself when he removed my blindfold. I blinked and smiled at him when I found his face above mine. He bent and kissed me hard. His groans of desire filled me, and his hands moved to cradle my face while he continued our kiss. The contradiction in his actions was loud; his kiss was rough and exacting, but his touch was so very gentle. I loved both sides of him.

He ended the kiss but continued to cradle my face. His thumb gently rubbed my cheek and he stared at me. There was no smile, just that intensity I was growing used to. His eyes shifted between mine and he slowly shook his head a couple of times. Pushing away from me, he shifted back to kneel between my legs. I had no idea what was happening but it felt like he'd retreated from me. I needed to touch him; needed to reach him.

"Undo me, Nash," I said.

His gaze flicked to my hands and he only hesitated for a moment before doing as I said. Once he'd undone the rope, he sat on the bed, and I didn't wait another second, I moved to sit in his lap. I wrapped my legs and arms around him, and brushed a kiss over his lips.

"Where did you go?" I whispered.

He blinked; surprised. But he wasn't honest with me. "I'm right here, darlin'."

I slowly shook my head. "No, Nash, you're here physically, but your mind, your soul, left for a moment there."

His eyes widened. He didn't speak straight away, but then he floored me. His arms tightened around me and he said, "I like to fuck, Velvet. And a woman's pleasure is just as important to me as my own. But with you, I care more about your pleasure. And I don't know what the fuck to make of that, baby."

It was my turn to blink. I was speechless so I just smiled at him. His words scared the hell out of me just as much as they made me feel so damn good about myself, about what was happening between us.

"Does that freak you the fuck out like it does me?" he whispered.

A shiver ran down my back. Nash's honesty meant so much to me; I'd never been with a man who wasn't afraid to share his innermost thoughts. I nodded. "Yeah, baby, it does."

His lips crashed down onto mine and we lost ourselves in a kiss that said the words that neither of us could say. It was in that moment that I finally acknowledged just how easily I could fall for this man. And I also gave myself the permission to fall. I didn't know where we would end up, but I knew he was the one to take a chance on.

Nash ended the kiss and murmured, "We need a condom, sweetheart, and then I'm going to fuck you hard. You up for that?"

He had no idea. "I'm always up for that."

Nash didn't need to be told twice; he moved me off him and left me to find what he was looking for. While he was up, he turned the music up louder. He'd made it so loud that I doubted I would be able to hear him talk.

I watched him put the condom on, and then he positioned himself over me, his cock hitting my entrance. My body thrummed, more than ready to have him in me. He'd meant what he said about fucking me hard; a moment later, without warning, he thrust inside me. My eyes squeezed shut at the sensations he caused. I'd waited all day to have him back in me, and he'd teased me to the point of madness. To finally have his cock was like a long sigh of delicious happiness.

He grunted, and pulled out before thrusting hard and fast again. I moaned, and he set a relentless pace of thrusting in and out. My legs gripped so hard onto him to keep up that I knew my muscles would be screaming at me tomorrow.

Between the music that was made for fucking, his grunts of pleasure and his cock giving me what I needed, I knew I wouldn't last long. Nash had managed to captivate every single sense of mine and I was focused solely on reaching my orgasm. However, he stopped what he was doing for a moment and my pussy cried out for him. I didn't have to worry though; he gripped my hips and flipped me over before pulling me up onto my hand and knees. His cock entered me again and I screamed out his name at how good it felt. He resumed his maddening pace, filling me completely with every thrust. I began panting; he'd brought me so close.

Just as I was sure I was about to orgasm, he roared, "Fuck!" He thrust one last time and then groaned as he came. It drove me over the edge and I came with him. My mind exploded with flashes of light, and my body quivered with the intense pleasure he'd given me.

We stayed joined for a couple of minutes. Nash ran his hands over my ass and along my back. "Christ, Velvet, the things you do to a man," he murmured before pulling out of me. The bed shifted as he moved off it and left to dispose of the condom.

I turned and sat on the bed, waiting for him to return. My thoughts were all over the place. And jammed in amongst all those thoughts was the knowledge that Nash and I had just shared more than our bodies. I watched him walk back into the room and knew from the soft look on his face that he felt it too. He turned the music off and came back to the bed. Those muscles of his distracted me again; hell they would always distract me. They'd fucking distract a lesbian, I was convinced of it.

I laid back and he settled on his side next to me on the bed, one leg draped over me. We lay just watching each other for awhile. It felt natural, easy. No words were needed. But eventually, he grinned at me, and asked, "You liked the music?"

His playlist consisted of only those two songs. I wasn't complaining though, they worked for me. I ran my hand through his hair. "I love your playlist although I'm a little surprised you have that song on there."

"The one you dance to?"

"Yeah."

He dipped his lips to mine, and then hit me with the sexy Nash smile I loved; the one that meant he was having devious thoughts. "Sweet thing, you can't be surprised that I get off to thoughts of you. Fuck, any man in his right mind would. You're a man's fuckin' wet dream."

Nash could say the dirtiest thing and yet still make it sound good. "I'll take that as a compliment."

"Good because it was fuckin' meant as one, baby."

I smiled lazily at him. He'd worn me out the last few days and sleep was claiming me. He noticed and kissed me again, before saying, "Go to sleep. I need you rested for tomorrow."

"What's on tomorrow?"

His devious smile returned. "It's your turn to ride me tomorrow night, sweet thing. I'm going to let you do all the work so stop talking and start getting your energy back."

I shut my eyes and began to drift off. "Promises, promises," I murmured.

My stomach fluttered when he whispered, "Baby, that's just the beginning."

I fell asleep to dreams of the pleasure Nash was going to give me; they really were the best kinds of dream known to woman.

CHAPTER 19

Addicted To You - Avicii

NASH

I WALKED INTO THE KITCHEN AND SUCKED IN A BREATH at the sight of Velvet sitting on my kitchen counter cross legged. We'd had a shower together and because she had no clothes at my house, I'd given her one of my t-shirts to wear afterwards. Seeing her in my clothes did shit to me, good shit, and my dick twitched at the sight. The sex with her last night had been out of this fucking world; today was going to be a long day waiting to get back to her.

She was scrolling on her phone and looked up at me.

"You always sit on kitchen benches?" I asked.

"Only the benches of people I really like."

I jerked my chin at her phone. "Don't tell me you're a Facebook addict." I fucking hated that shit.

She held up her phone and flashed it at me, showing me that she wasn't on Facebook. "No, I'm just checking my horoscope for today."

"What the fuck?"

She frowned. "I said, I'm checking my horoscope."

I walked over to where she was sitting. "I heard what you said, but I'm wondering why you follow that shit."

"It's not shit, Nash."

I took her phone out of her hand and read what it said. "Your life may feel like a roller coaster at the moment, Virgo. But you wouldn't have it any other way. Make sure you talk to those close to you about your feelings and communicate clearly what you need from them." I looked at her and shook my head. "You really believe this crap? That could relate to everyone's life, babe."

She snatched her phone back. "Well, I happen to think it relates very well to my life and I also think the advice it gives is good."

Damn, she was hot when she got shitty. I'd have to remember that. I held my hands up. "Fair enough." I leaned in and kissed her before saying, "Christ, you look good in my shirt, sweet thing."

My words did the trick; she gave me a breathtaking smile before flirting with me. "You look pretty damn good in it too but I prefer you with no shirt on." Then she added, "What's for breakfast?"

I unfolded her legs so they fell either side of me. My hands snaked up her legs and under the t-shirt. "Fuck, you've got nothing on underneath this," I muttered as I made the discovery.

She put her hands around my neck, clasping them together. "I was kinda hoping it might entice you to show me again how good your tongue is."

My dick did more than twitch and I cursed the fact I had to go to work today. "Baby, I never need to be enticed to show off my tongue. It fuckin' lives for pussy."

The moan that escaped from her lips got me even harder, and I pulled out of her hold. She frowned. "Where are you going?"

I ran my hand through my hair. "Trust me when I say I want to stay here and fuck you, but I've got club shit to take care of this morning."

Her disappointment was as strong as mine. "Do you get time off at lunch?"

"Fuck, if you're suggesting what I think you're suggesting, I'll fuckin' make time at lunch."

"I'm pretty sure we're on the same page, Nash. I'll be at my place all day; feel free to bring your tongue over. And your cock. Definitely bring your cock." She was grinning at me now and I laughed at her.

"I'll be sure to mention it to him."

"Good. Now, back to my original question. What are you cooking me for breakfast?"

I raised an eyebrow at her. "Isn't that a woman's job, darlin'?"

She raised her eyebrow back at me. "If you think I'm the kind of woman that lives by those outdated ideas, then this ends right now."

I loved it when she fired up, and my dick stirred again. Christ, at the rate we were going, I was going to be hers completely soon. She was going to fucking own me. I needed to slow this shit down a little. "I'm all for equal rights, but I don't cook breakfast for anyone, babe."

"Really?"

"Really."

I waited for her reply. I didn't delude myself; we were in a battle here. A battle to see who held more power at the moment.

She shrugged. "No worries, I'll just have a coffee."

Ah, fuck it.

She'd won.

I made coffee.

★★★

VELVET

SHIT, BUGGER, DAMN.

My morning had gone really well after Nash dropped me at home on his way to the club. I'd finished off some study for my exams that were coming up and then I'd given myself a facial, a pedicure and washed and blow-dried my hair. If Nash was coming over at lunch, I was going to look damn good for him. However, my mother phoned and reminded me I was having lunch with her and Anna. I'd completely forgotten and now had to let Nash know I was cancelling. He hadn't answered my call so I texted him.

Me: Gotta cancel lunch with your tongue. Forgot I had lunch planned with my family. Catch you tonight.

I finished getting ready for lunch and checked my phone before I left. Still no reply. There wasn't much I could do about it so I locked up the house and left. We were meeting for lunch at the Breakfast Creek Hotel and the traffic was a bitch. However, my car was running so well after Nash had worked on it that it made the traffic bearable. Either that, or the fact I was thinking about Nash made it bearable.

The lunch crowd was loud today, and there were people everywhere. I scanned to find Mum and Anna, finally locating them in the corner and then made my way to where they were. Anna grinned at me strangely and Mum gave me a huge smile.

As I sat down, I asked, "What? Why are you two acting weird?"

Anna didn't hesitate to tell me; she was bursting to get it out. "You've been with Nash again, haven't you?"

"How the hell can you tell that?"

She gave me a sly smile. "Well, I couldn't, but it was a good guess." She looked me up and down. "Mind you, you do look very happy and soft."

"What does that mean? The bit about being soft." My sister spoke in riddles half the time; I was forever trying to decipher what she meant.

"Your shoulders aren't as tense as they normally are, and you don't have that look on your face that says 'don't fuck with me cause I'll fuck back'."

Mum laughed and nodded her agreement. "She's right, Velvet. You seem different. Who is this man?"

Before I could answer her, Anna did it for me. "Nash is one of the bikers who own Indigo."

I corrected her. "He doesn't own the club as such; Storm own it."

She waved her hand in the air. "Semantics."

"How long have you been seeing him?" Mum asked.

I sighed, wishing that Anna hadn't said anything. They'd both been pushing me to start dating again for years so I could only imagine the questions I was about to be hit with. I would rather have told Mum in my own time, once I knew where it was heading, if anywhere.

"So, is it dating or just sex?" Anna wanted to know next.

"God! Why do you need to ask so many questions?" She completely exasperated me sometimes. I loved her to death, but her need to know everything drove me insane.

"Why do you always avoid my questions?"

"Aargh!" If I could have screamed, I would have. But I couldn't, and I knew that if I didn't give her an answer, she would just keep asking. I pointed my finger at her and gave her a very serious look. "Alright, I'll answer your question but it's the last one you ask, okay? Otherwise, no more answers."

I waited for her answer and she nodded. "Yes, you answer that and I won't need to know anymore. Except for the size of his - "

"Anna!" I screeched. "Enough! It's not just sex and it's not dating. There, are you happy?"

She looked perplexed. "What kind of answer is that?"

"The most honest one I've got."

Before anyone had a chance to say anything more, my phone buzzed with a text message. I quickly snatched it out of bag hoping it was Nash replying to mine from earlier. I couldn't wipe the smile off my face as I read it.

Nash: Didn't get your message and now I'm at your fucking house with the biggest hard on I've ever had and no pussy to take care of it.

Me: Perhaps you should check your messages more often.

Nash: Fuck.

Me: Poor baby. I miss your tongue.

Nash: Fuck the tongue, sweet thing. Tonight all you're gonna see and feel is my cock.

Me: I'm gonna be in Nash heaven.

Nash: Fuck. No more texts or I'm gonna have to whack off on your front verandah.

I laughed out loud when I read his last text and then put my phone away.

My mother took my hand and squeezed it gently. "I'm happy to see you smile again," she said, softly.

I wasn't sure if it was what she'd said, the tone of it or the emotions I was already feeling today, but my eyes teared up. My heart felt full today; I felt like something had shifted in me.

Something big. And even though I had a sense of anxiety about it, I knew, deep in my soul, that it was a good thing. I knew I had to take this step and let be what may.

"Me too, Mum," I agreed.

I turned to Anna. "Now, enough about me. It's you we should be worried about." I was still concerned for her after her boyfriend dumped her.

"I'm good, sis," she said, but I could hear the sadness in her voice.

Men. Sometimes you could kiss them forever and other times you could just take your glittery, red stilettos and jam them as far up their asses as they'd reach.

CHAPTER 20

Ready To Love Again - Lady Antebellum

NASH

I PULLED MY T-SHIRT ON OVER MY HEAD, NOT TAKING MY eyes off Velvet as she wiggled into her jeans. Not only did she make taking her clothes off an art form, she made putting them on an erotic act also. She finished wiggling into them and did them up before she realised I was watching her.

"Baby, I've never wanted to watch a woman put her clothes on but you've shown me the error of my ways," I declared.

She slipped her top on and then walked over to where I was. Wrapping her arms around my waist, she asked, "So no more taking clothes off?"

I smirked, and ran my hands over her ass. "Let's not get carried away. I've still got my priorities, sweet thing, and seeing this ass naked is at the top of them."

Her smile hit all the right spots. "Okay, just checking. I'd like to keep my man happy."

The minute those words were out of her mouth, there was a shift between us. I fucking liked hearing those words but I sensed she wished they'd never been uttered. It had been a long time since I'd been anyone's man, and with each passing day I was easing more into this relationship, whatever the hell it was. A week ago, it was just sex, now it felt like a lot more.

I pulled her closer before she had a chance to retreat from me. "You make me very happy," I whispered in her ear.

Her body was rigid but at my words, I felt her soften. "Same," she said, and that one word sent warmth through me. Although we'd taken a long time to get here, I felt like we were in the exact right place. Together.

Loosening my hold on her, I stepped back and my eyes drifted down her body. "Babe," I said as I looked back up at her, "don't get me wrong, I appreciate it, but why the hell do women wear the tightest jeans that barely fit them. How the fuck do you breathe in those things?"

She smacked me on the arm. "Why the fuck do women do anything, Nash? To make sure the men in their lives are happy and to make sure their attention stays on them rather than on another woman."

I chuckled having achieved my goal. "Trust me when I say that my attention is firmly on you, sweet thing."

Her eyes narrowed. "You totally said all that to change the topic of the conversation, didn't you?"

Caught out. I grinned. "It may have also been to get you a little shitty. You're fuckin' hot when you're shitty."

She hit my chest this time and pointed at the doorway. "Go. We've got shopping to do."

I did as I was told and she followed me outside. When we reached her car, I put my hand out for her keys. The look she gave me could have brought a weaker man to his knees. "What?" I asked.

"Did you just put your hand out for the keys so you could drive my car?"

"Yeah." I wasn't really sure what the problem was here.

"I don't think so, Nash." She gave me an annoyed look.

"Well we can't take my bike," I said what I thought should have been clear. We were on our way to Ikea to pick up a bookshelf for her and it sure as shit couldn't be transported on a bike.

That just pissed her off even more. "Oh my God, Nash. That's not what I meant."

"What the hell did you mean then?" This conversation had gone south real fucking quick and I was clueless as to why.

"Just because you're the man doesn't mean you get to automatically drive my car. If it was your car, I would assume you'd drive it. I'd never assume that I would. Don't come into my life and think that I'm the woman so I must be relegated to woman jobs." She meant business and I read between the lines. Some asshole had fucked with her and I suspected it was her ex-husband.

I didn't argue, just raised my hands in apology. "I'm sorry, sweetheart. It's all yours." I moved to the passenger door and waited for her to let me in.

She stood staring at me and I waited for her to make the next move. "Shit, Nash Walker, where the hell have you been all my life?" she finally said before walking around to the driver's side.

"Baby, I could say the same thing," I said, softly, more to myself than her, but she caught it and flashed me a smile before getting in the car. Velvet smiling was a sight I could see myself living for; a sight I would trip over myself to make sure I saw often.

★★★

VELVET

I WATCHED AS Nash pulled all the flat packed pieces out of the box and started assembling the cabinet I'd bought. We'd gone to buy a bookshelf and ended up with one of those plus this cabinet that looked tricky to put together. I grabbed the assembly instructions and passed them to him.

He frowned as he took it off me. "Why are you giving me that?"

I gave him a 'you're joking' look. "So you can work out how to put it together."

He shoved the instructions back at me. "I can work out how to put it together without those, sweetheart."

Was he kidding me? I opened them and started reading to make sure what he was doing was actually right. It was a good thing I did because I noticed he was doing something wrong.

I tried to give him the instructions again. "You've got the wrong part there," I insisted.

He stood up and scowled at me. "Velvet, I'm still working out how it goes together. Maybe you should go and do something else while I do this."

"If you'd just read the instructions, you'd work it out faster," I suggested. It annoyed me when men wouldn't read instructions.

The instructions remained in my hands as he glared at me. "I'd work it out a lot fuckin' faster if you'd just let me do it. Without the fuckin' instructions."

I took a deep breath. "Fine, I'm going to leave you to do it on your own." Without waiting for his response, I stalked out of the room. He could really be an ass sometimes.

While he put the furniture together, I took the opportunity to get some study done. I had fallen behind lately due to all the time I'd been spending with Nash. There was only a couple of weeks left on my course so I really needed to buckle down and get it done. I'd have to cut down on my time with him for a little while. And even though I was annoyed at him at the moment, my heart dropped a little at that thought.

I wasn't sure how much time had passed when I heard Nash's voice. Looking up from my books, I found him standing at the door to my study, watching me.

"Sorry, what did you say?" I asked.

He took a step toward me and jerked his head in the direction of my living room. "They're both put together. Do you want to come and make sure I've got them in the right place?"

"Yeah."

I followed him out and found that he had them exactly where I wanted them. "Perfect," I said. "Thank you."

I was still mad at him and there was a divide between us; one I couldn't get past until he'd apologised. The problem was, I wanted him to say sorry without me having to tell him I needed that. And I knew that wasn't going to happen. And that pissed me off even more.

"Okay, babe, spit it out," he said as he crossed his arms over his chest.

"Nash, the fact I have to spit it out really pisses me off."

"I'm not a mind reader. You're going to have to tell me what it is."

"You don't need to be a mind reader for this. You just need to realise that you were an ass to me."

He raked his fingers through his hair. "Fuck, is this about me not taking the instructions off you?"

"Not so much, although that did annoy me. This is because of the way you spoke to me."

He didn't say anything, he just stood there looking confused about the whole thing. Good Lord, men needed it spelt out to them so I did that for him. "Nash, my ex treated me like shit. He didn't hit me or anything like that, but he bullied and belittled me. I won't even contemplate a relationship with a man who does that. Now, I'm not saying you did that at all, but from the start, I'm being

REVIVE

upfront and telling you what I won't put up with. And I won't put up with being spoken to the way you spoke to me."

I watched as he processed that. It didn't take him long and then he moved towards me, lifted his hand to my face and gently rubbed his thumb across my cheek. His eyes were soft; kind. Totally not how I'd expected this to go at all. My tummy did somersaults while I waited for him to speak.

"It's been a long time since I've been in a relationship and I'm kinda rusty, babe. I'm sorry I spoke to you that way. And I'm real fuckin' sorry your ex was such a dickhead."

He'd managed to piss me off twice already today but each time, he hadn't hesitated to fix it. That stunned the hell out of me. Especially after being married to a man who hardly ever apologised for anything.

"Thank you."

The divide between us was gone and his arms circled my waist. His lips met mine in a soft kiss that was so unlike most of his kisses. When he ended it, he murmured, "Fuck, baby, you bring out good shit in me."

This was the Nash I wanted, and the more time I spent with him, the more I wanted him.

159

CHAPTER 21

I'd Come For You - Nickelback

NASH

THE COLD WIND WHIPPED AROUND ME AND THE CHILL from it settled in my bones. June wasn't usually this cold in Brisbane, but this year we were having record low temperatures. I pulled my jacket tighter around me and made the short walk from my bike into Blade's warehouse. He had information for me regarding Velvet's ex and I hoped it would be enough to get the asshole to back off and put her mind at ease. After what she'd told me about her ex this morning, that he'd bullied her, I'd do anything to get him out of her life once and for all. I'd worked out her tough image was a mask she wore for the world. Underneath it, she was vulnerable; not nearly as hard as she projected. And I kinda fucking liked that. It meant she needed me, and I hadn't been needed in a long time. And that felt really fucking good.

"Blade," I greeted him as I entered his office.

He didn't stand, just indicated for me to take a seat. I hadn't worked him out yet but Madison loved him and that was enough for me to go on. He cut straight to the chase. "James has his fingers in a lot of shit. A lot of dirty shit. If that got out, it would be the end of his political career and most likely would harm his father's career too."

"His father is the Minister for Defence, right?"

Blade nodded. "Yes. And James is running for a Federal seat at the next election. He won't want any of this coming to light so this is your best bet to keep him off Velvet's back." He passed me a folder.

"Holy fuck." I whistled as I flicked through the documents in the folder. Blade was right, James would shit himself if this stuff came out. Corrupt deals and prostitutes tended to do that to a politician. Especially married ones who professed to be Christian.

"Holy fuck is right. When you talk with the motherfucker, mention my name. That'll help your cause."

"Thanks, man." I was still reading through the shit in the folder and had no idea how or why Velvet would have mixed herself up with someone like James Worthington.

Blade changed the subject. "Black Deeds giving you any grief these days?"

"Not that I'm aware of. Their new president seems to be keeping them in line."

"Good." He paused before continuing. "I think Marcus has some shit planned; you need to keep your eye on that."

My head jerked up at that. "What do you know?"

"Still confirming information but my contacts tell me he's looking to get back into drug distribution. In a big way."

"Yeah, it's what we suspect too."

"And Scott's on board with that?"

"Fuck no." My voice reverberated around the room.

"Well thank fuck for that. Marcus is an idiot for considering it. Storm does well without the drugs. The attention it will bring you from the cops isn't worth it."

"You're investigating Marcus?" I asked. Blade seemed to be on the ball with everything and everyone so I guessed he was.

"I've always kept an eye on my father." His voice turned cold while talking about Marcus. He paused, thoughtful for a moment before pinning me with a hard gaze. "I have increased my surveillance on Marcus. Recently a name came up that I've never heard of. You ever heard him talk about someone called Blue?"

"No. What was the context?" My interest was piqued and I waited impatiently for him to tell me more.

"All we know is that Marcus is looking for someone by that name. And we believe that the Adelaide President is helping him do that."

My mind was going in a million different directions trying to work out what this could be about. But I came up blank. "I'll pass that information on to Scott," I said, hoping he would know who Blue was. We needed to figure this shit out soon because Marcus was moving fast with his plans.

"Tell Scott to contact me if he wants in on this and I'll keep him up to date."

I frowned at what he'd said. "You two don't talk?"

Blade fixed that hard gaze on me again. "We're not close, no. My brother is stubborn where I'm concerned. Seems to be a trait he shares with our father." His tone pricked my skin with it's barbs.

He didn't wait for me to say anything before he stood and made it clear I was to leave. I held up the folder he'd given me. "Thanks for this," I said, and then turned and left his office.

Blade and his odd relationship with Scott was soon forgotten as I contemplated sorting Velvet's ex-husband out. My fists were itching to have their way with him, but I knew I had to tread carefully. His connections meant I had to approach this from a different angle than I usually approached assholes. Fuck though, I could go a round with him and be a very happy man.

★★★

A couple of hours later, after dealing with Storm business, I walked into James's office ready to do battle with him. His secretary was reluctant to let me in but when he'd opened the door to find me waiting, he hadn't wasted any time letting me in.

"To what do I owe the pleasure?" he drawled as he sat behind his desk. The arrogance was dripping from him and I squeezed my fists to settle them.

I threw the folder Blade had given me on his table and nodded at it. "Take a look, asshole."

His brows raised. Patronising. Again, I reminded myself to ask Velvet what attracted her to him.

He opened the folder and I watched the flicker of surprise cross his face. After he'd flicked through some of it, he looked up at me. A cold stare emanated from his eyes, and he attempted to call my bluff. Throwing the folder back across the desk at me, he said, "You've wasted your time coming here, Mr Walker, if you think any of this worries me."

He'd looked into me. Interesting. "I think that if any of that doesn't worry you, you're a bigger dickhead than I gave you credit for."

He contemplated my words. "Where did Velvet drag you from? Actually, don't bother answering that. You're exactly the type of man that is about right for her."

I fought the desire to introduce him to my fists. "Where the fuck did she drag *you* from? It's beyond me what she saw in you."

"I can assure you that I had a lot more to offer her than you do. I can see exactly what she sees in you; she sees her father."

What the fuck? I didn't want to get into that with him so I left it alone. "She's a lot fuckin' better off without a man who screws around on his wife with prostitutes."

A harsh laugh escaped his lips. "And you've never cheated on a woman? I find that hard to believe; you bikers are neanderthals."

I didn't answer him because I would have to admit an indiscretion. Guilt sliced through me at that thought and then the pain hit; the pain I'd managed to bury lately.

Fuck.

He kept at me. "Thought so. Velvet's found what she deserves." He stopped talking but then looked at me thoughtfully. "You do know that she's damaged goods, don't you?"

I'd heard enough from this motherfucker. "I don't want to hear any-fuckin'-thing else you have to say about Velvet." I picked up the folder and threw it back at him. Pointing at it, I said, "That shit will become public knowledge if you don't back the fuck off her. She's not going to talk about you to the media but she's also not going to sign your dirty deal." I turned to leave, but then faced him again, and added, "Blade has more shit on you than what's in that folder so don't fuck around with this. Let Velvet know you're dropping it otherwise I'll be back."

There was more than a flicker of surprise when I mentioned Blade's name; there was fear, and that made me a happy fucker.

CHAPTER 22

Thunder - Jessie J

VELVET

I EASED INTO THE CHAIR AND LET MY BODY RELAX. IT had been a busy week of work and study, and I was exhausted. Sex with Nash had also taken it out of me; he was insatiable. I'd actually told him I needed a night off from him last night and as much as I'd missed him, the sleep I managed to get had been worth it.

My Saturday had been a lazy one so far. I'd slept for most of the day, having only gotten out of bed at two in the afternoon. Nash came over and woke me up, and although I could see the desire in his eyes, he hadn't pushed for sex. Instead, he made me coffee and waited patiently while I showered and dressed. Madison had invited us for dinner; she said she had a surprise for us which made me nervous. I wasn't a fan of surprises. It also kind of felt weird to be going to dinner with Nash. This was the first time we were going to something together, and although we'd spoken about us working towards something, our relationship wasn't clearly defined. The idea of turning up to an event together where our friends would be was a little intimidating. I wasn't ready for all the questions they'd be sure to have.

"You alright, sweet thing?" Nash's voice dragged me out of my restful haze. He was standing behind me and was gently massaging my neck and shoulders. I could grow used to this kind of attention.

I sighed deeply. "Nash, has anyone ever told you how amazing your massages are?"

He didn't answer me and his hands slowed down. "No," he said before adding quietly, "I've never given massages to anyone else."

My heart rate sped up, and my body tingled. Nash shared pieces of his heart with the most simplest statements. I wondered if he realised what they meant to me. "Well I'm telling you that your hands are magic."

He chuckled and then I felt his warm breath next to my ear as he whispered, "I've been told that before, sweetheart, but it means more coming from you."

And I tingled again.

His hands kept working their magic and I closed my eyes, letting his touch ease the tension out of my body. I was sure we could have happily stayed in our own little bubble, however Madison interrupted, dragging us out of it.

"You two going to come inside and join us?" The way she asked made it sound like she almost expected us to say no.

Nash gave my shoulders one last squeeze before taking his hands off me. I missed his touch instantly. "What's this surprise you've got?" he asked her.

She grinned. "She'll be here soon."

"She?"

Madison winked at him and nodded. "Yes, she. I think you'll love the surprise."

My mind was racing trying to figure out who and what Madison was talking about. Nash appeared to be doing the same. I gave him a questioning look but he shrugged his shoulders and said, "Got no idea, babe."

We followed Madison inside. Her house was buzzing with people; Scott and Harlow were here with Lisa, J's sister, Brooke was here with Crystal, and Griff was here too.

Brooke gave me a warm smile. "Hi, Velvet. It's good to see you again." We'd met at J and Madison's wedding, and had spent a lot of the night chatting. She was lovely and I was really happy to see her again.

"Hey, Brooke. You too. How's that hot fireman treating you?" When I'd met her, she had just started dating a fireman. The photo of him on her phone she'd shown me was hot and I could only imagine what he looked like in real life because photos taken with mobile phones didn't do anyone justice.

She blushed. "He's good. I just dropped him at work, otherwise he would be here tonight."

"I think I'm going to have to meet this man. Anyone who can make you blush the way you just did must be a man worth knowing." I winked at her.

Nash's hand slid over my ass and he pulled me close. "You don't have any free time to meet another man, sweet thing," he murmured.

Brooke watched us with interest; clearly surprised. "Yeah, I don't think I'll introduce them, Nash. Velvet's stunning, and I think she'd steal his attention." It was her turn to wink at me now.

Nash growled, and his grip on my ass tightened. "She's busy for the rest of the fuckin' year," he said, and I had to stifle a laugh at his possessive attitude. Definitely not the Nash I was used to, but damn it made me glow.

Harlow joined the conversation. "Nash, you're not going all territorial, are you?"

I wasn't sure how he would handle this now, but he surprised me yet again by saying, "Yeah, babe, I think I am. And if anyone's got shit to say about it, I don't give a fuck."

He'd managed to surprise Harlow too. She sighed, a dreamy look in her eyes. God help us; Harlow was a born romantic. "I knew it would just take a good woman to make you change your ways."

Harlow had a way of making you feel good about yourself. Calling me a good woman touched me in unexpected ways. I'd struggled with my self worth growing up and marrying a man who took every opportunity to tell me how worthless I was, hit me even harder. Over the last couple of years, I had dealt with a lot of my issues and was a much stronger woman, but there were days where I questioned myself. Being told I was a good woman by another woman meant a lot.

Nash was amused. "Let's not get too excited, Harlow. A woman won't make me change my ways completely."

She grinned at him. "And we wouldn't want that, Nash. But I have a feeling that Velvet's going to change you in all the right ways."

I was growing uncomfortable with this conversation now. Changing a man was never a goal of mine, and I disliked women who fell in love with the idea of a man only to then spend the rest of their lives trying to change him to be what they wanted. Also, Nash and I were still getting to know each other; I didn't want to make this out to be more than what it was yet.

I smiled at Harlow, and then looked up at Nash. "I'm going to go and help Madison in the kitchen."

He nodded, and let me go.

A moment later, I breathed a sigh of relief when I hit the kitchen and found Madison on her own. She looked up at me, and caught the look on my face. Frowning, she enquired, "You okay?"

"Yeah. It was just getting a little intense in there with Harlow and Nash. I needed some space."

"What? Are they arguing?"

"No. Harlow's going on about me changing Nash in all the right ways or some shit. I love her, but damn, she's a hardcore romantic, isn't she?"

Madison laughed. "Yeah, she really is. And to think she ended up with a biker like Scott; the least romantic man you could find."

"It's certainly a strange combination, but it works for them, doesn't it."

"Possibly he tames the romantic side of her, tames those unrealistic expectations she might have, and she brings out the tiny bit of romance he has in him." She shrugged. "I've really got no idea, but I'm glad they found each other."

We fell silent, lost in our own thoughts. I was contemplating Harlow and Scott; it had certainly shocked the hell out of me when he'd pursued her, but she had been the best thing for him. And he had changed in subtle ways. Perhaps that was what Harlow had meant; people change each other without even meaning to.

I was snapped out of my thoughts when Madison passed me a pumpkin and some potatoes. "You can be in charge of getting those ready."

I took them off her. "What's for dinner?"

"Roast lamb and vegies. And I'm making cheesecake for dessert."

"Did I hear the word cheesecake?" J asked as he joined us.

"Yeah, baby, I'm making that chocolate one you like," Madison told him, giving him a huge smile.

He dropped a quick kiss on her lips before taking a swig of his beer. "That's why I married you, woman." He grinned at her. "That and your other assets."

"Yeah, yeah, J. We all know why you really married me."

"And why's that?" He leant against the kitchen counter, waiting for her answer, still grinning like an idiot.

"Because you're a very smart man who knew I was the best

thing to ever happen to him."

He pushed off the counter and leant his face down to give her a longer, deeper kiss. "Can't argue with that, baby," he murmured before adding, "Your surprise guest has arrived, by the way."

"Oh my God, why didn't you say something?" Madison shrieked, slapping him away from her, and running out to the lounge room.

I was intrigued to see who it was so I followed her out. The sight that greeted me punched me in the chest, and threatened to suck all the happiness out of me.

Serena.

Madison's best friend, Serena, was in the lounge room. And she was all over Nash. And Nash wasn't doing anything to stop her. In fact, he had his arms around her, his hands dangerously close to her ass. He was listening intently while she whispered something in his ear. Whatever she said was funny, and he roared with laughter just before she moved her face away from his and laughed with him. My gaze zeroed in on her hand that was placed across his chest; almost in a possessive manner.

Madison reached them and pulled Serena out of Nash's arms so she could hug her. "You finally made it!" she exclaimed.

"Yeah, chica, I finally got here," Serena replied, squeezing Madison back.

They finally let each other go, and Serena passed her car keys to Nash. "Can you bring my bags in, sexy?" she asked him, and I was stunned when he grinned at her and nodded. I watched him walk outside, my heart icing over.

I knew it was a stupid reaction, but I couldn't control it. Jealousy tore through me at the sight of them together. I'd seen them together at Madison's wedding and presumed they hooked up afterwards. The chemistry between them was clear for all to see.

"How long you staying for?" Nash asked as he came back in

with two bags. "Your car is fuckin' loaded, babe. Looks like you're moving in."

Serena and Madison blasted megawatt smiles in unison. "I *am* moving in!" Serena announced delivering another blow to me.

Nash's face lit up, and J grumbled, "Fucking hell, why did I ever agree to this?"

Serena poked her tongue at him. "Oh hush, biker boy." Then she looked at Nash, and said, "Maybe I'll move in with Nash instead. He wouldn't whine like a school girl about having me."

Laughter erupted from everyone; everyone except me. I stilled, waiting to see where this would all end up. Nash's eyes found mine, and my heart began beating faster in anticipation of what he would say or do. I hated this; it was exactly why I didn't do relationships. The not knowing where you stood with someone sucked. This afternoon, I thought I knew where we were at, but now that was all up in the air as far as I was concerned. And that it all rested with Nash paralysed me.

My gut churned with the jealousy I desperately didn't want to feel while I waited for Nash to make his move. He smiled at me before saying something to Serena. She listened intently to what he said. His gaze was focused on me while he spoke and when he'd finished talking, her gaze followed his until she found me. She smiled, and then smacked him on the back, propelling him in my direction.

He didn't need much propelling though, he was striding towards me with determination. When he reached me, he grabbed me by the arm and pulled me along as he kept walking into the kitchen.

"Talk to me, sweet thing. What's going through that mind of yours?" he asked when we were alone.

Nerves gripped me. I didn't want to admit my jealousy to him. God, we'd only been sleeping together for a week, and it wasn't like we'd made any promises to each other. In fact, I was sure Nash came with a warning that read 'no promises will ever be made to any woman'. And even though he'd told me he felt something for me, I wasn't delusional; men were fickle creatures and he could change his mind at any moment.

Here he was though, looking at me with what looked like worry, and he managed to coax the truth out of me. "It's not pretty, Nash. You sure you want to know?"

He chuckled. "Baby, none of the shit in my mind is ever pretty. I can cope with ugly; we're old friends."

I blew out a breath, and pushed through my fear. He could do what he would with it; at least I'd know where I stood and there would be no more worrying and wondering. "It's obvious that you and Serena shared something at J's wedding, and still have some kind of connection. I won't bullshit you; I was jealous when I saw her all over you."

"Fuck, Velvet, you amaze me."

I frowned. "Is that a good thing or a bad thing?"

He smiled, and traced his thumb over my cheek. "It's a really fuckin' good thing, sweetheart."

Impatience circled me. "Okay, so I'm glad it's a really fuckin' good thing, but can you tell me why?"

"I haven't dated a lot of women - " he stopped when I fixed him with a 'you're kidding' look. "Baby, I won't lie, I've slept with a fuckload of women, but I haven't dated many. The few I dated, were jealous bitches and never failed to accuse me of shit and argue with me every fuckin' time they were jealous. We spent more of our time together arguing instead of loving, so for you to have a rational conversation with me about it fuckin' amazes me."

"So, continuing this rational conversation, where are you at with Serena?"

Nash looked pissed, and I figured I'd said something wrong.

He threw me off when he asked, "He really did a number on you, didn't he?"

I instinctively knew that he was referring to James. "Why do you say that?"

"Because I told you last week that I wanted to see where this went for us, that I feel something for you. But at the first hurdle, you assume I'm out. I've watched my mother and sister get dragged down by men, watched them struggle with doubt about themselves. That doubt was put there by those men, and I see that same doubt in you, baby. And I fuckin' hate it."

I had to stop my mouth from falling open. Seriously, this man was shocking the shit out of me. Repeatedly. I'd never met a man so in tune with my feelings; a man so perceptive, and willing to get it all out there in the open. Maybe there really was a chance at something here.

"Yes, he did a number on me," I admitted. "He shredded my self belief and then he kicked me out with nothing to my name, and even less to my self worth. I've spent years building myself back up, Nash, and I honestly thought I was over it, but being with you has brought my insecurities out."

"I can see that, and I want to fix it. I don't want you to have any doubt about this shit. As far as Serena is concerned, yeah we had sex, but that's all it was. She and I are too alike to ever work, and to be completely honest, I'm not interested. And I doubt she is either. We kept in touch but just as friends so you have to trust me on that one. Can you do that?"

I trusted Nash implicitly. I had no idea why, but I did. "Yes, I trust you." My voice was certain. I wanted to give that to him; I sensed he needed that.

"Thank you. Now, about those insecurities of yours... I'm not interested in anyone else. I only want you, Velvet. I haven't been interested in a relationship with anyone for ten years, baby, so when

I tell you that I want one with you, that should tell you how serious I am about this."

My belly fluttered. I tried to speak, but nothing came out. He'd completely flabbergasted me. He knew it, and curled his arm around my waist, and pulled me close. His lips swept across mine softly before he asked, "Are we on the same page, sweet thing?"

Still at a loss for words, I whispered, "Yes."

It was enough for him. He smiled and nodded. "Thank fuck for that."

★★★

Later that night, after he'd blown my world with his mad sex skills, I curled up next to him in his bed. I snuggled into his chest and he put his arm around me, letting his fingers trail up and down my back.

"Can I ask you something?" he said, a serious tone to his voice.

"You can ask me anything," I said because I was fast getting to the point where I would trust him with everything.

"Are you close to your father?"

Shit, that question had come out of left field. "No, I don't have anything to do with him."

"Tell me about him, sweetheart." His fingers continued to caress my skin, loving me with their touch; making me feel safe with him.

"He's a cheating, lying criminal who never cared about my mother or me and my sister." In my mind, that covered everything he needed to know about my father.

Nash wanted to know more though. "He cheated on your mother?"

"Repeatedly. One of my earliest memories is of my father with another woman on our couch. Turned out she was a friend of my mothers, and stayed over one night after a party. My father screwed her while my mother was asleep upstairs."

"Are they still together?"

"God, no! She left him when he went to prison the first time about ten years ago."

Nash was taking this all in, and I loved that he was interested to know about my family. "Where is he now, babe?"

"He's in prison again. This time he'll be in there for awhile because he got mixed up in some bank robberies and they assaulted some of the security guards." My jaw hurt from clenching it and the first stirrings of a headache surfaced. Talking about my father always upset me.

"So, it's just been you, your mother and sister for awhile now?"

I bit my lip, not wanting to answer this question. But I had to be honest with him; he'd been honest with me about his stuff so far, it was only fair. "I walked away from my family when I was twenty. Growing up, I'd been embarrassed by them. Kids at school used to pick on me about my white trash family because it was common knowledge what a lowlife my father was. When I got the marks at school to be offered a scholarship to university, I took it and ran."

Most people were stunned when they discovered I'd studied at uni, but Nash didn't blink at it. He simply asked, "What did you study?"

"Law."

"You're a lawyer?"

I made a habit not to carry bitterness about my past actions, but this was the one area in my life I struggled not to be bitter about. "No, I never finished the degree. I fell in love and gave it all up."

He was incredulous. "You gave it up for James?"

"Yes. He was everything I never was, and he wooed me with all that glitters." It was painful to admit that I'd fallen for him and what

I thought a life with him would mean.

"I just don't see it, babe. He's an asshole. And the Velvet I know doesn't give a shit about money." He was struggling to believe me, and I liked that. I liked that he didn't see me as that person because she was shallow, empty woman.

"Nash, I've changed a lot since then, but back when I met James, I would have done anything to escape my background. I thought that I could change everything about me and my life, and it would make me happy. When he asked me to be his wife, I honestly thought he was everything I'd ever wanted. And I didn't have to think twice when he suggested I give up my studies to concentrate on building a family with him. I'm just lucky that my mum and sister welcomed me back with open arms when I finally walked away from him."

Something shifted across Nash's face and I felt his body tense. His voice was gruff when he asked me, "You wanted kids with him?"

My heart ached dredging this up. "Yes," I whispered, "It was all I ever wanted. The idea of creating my own family that I could love and give everything to that I never had, that was what kept me going some days."

Nash stopped caressing my back. His hand stilled as he asked, "What happened, sweetheart?"

I swallowed, the tightness in my throat making it hard. I raised my eyes to look at his face. The concern I found there reached out and touched me lovingly. In that moment, I fell a little more. "I fell pregnant pretty much straight away but I miscarried. And James kept getting me pregnant only to lose the baby each time. Falling pregnant was never hard, but I just couldn't carry a baby to term. With every baby lost, James became more of an asshole and chipped away a little more of my self belief each day. Until the day he decided I was useless to him, and he erased me from his life." My voice caught and I held back a sob. It wasn't the memories of James that threatened tears; I mourned my lost babies. When the one thing you want in life is given but then ripped from you, over and over, it causes wounds that never truly heal.

Nash moved to lay over me. He held himself just above me, his powerful frame rigid, his muscles flexing. His eyes held mine for a moment, and then he shifted to lie on his side, resting on his elbow. He reached out and cradled my cheek with his hand, letting his thumb rub gently over my skin. "In my experience, it's the ones we love the most who have the ability to crush us. They have the fuckin' ability to rip our hearts out and shred them until we're left broken and hopeless. And then life has a way of trampling us even more when we're down. I'm in fuckin' awe of you, baby. You took that shit that happened to you, all of it, and you said to fuck with it. And you've built your life into something good. In fuckin' spite of all those assholes."

My heart constricted. Nash saw me clearly. He saw all the pain I'd experienced, all the obstacles I'd faced, the struggle of my life. And he saw what I'd done with all of that.

He got me.

The first tear escaped and he brushed it away. When the subsequent tears fell, he leant down and kissed them away. I couldn't stop them; it was years worth of tears that I'd been holding in. They just kept flowing. And Nash let them. He sat with my pain in a way that no-one in my life ever had before.

I opened my mouth to say something, but he gently laid a finger over my lips. "Shhh, baby, there's no need for words. Just let it all out," he whispered.

I did what he said, and sobbed quietly in his arms. He watched me, not flinching from it, and when I started to settle, he shifted again on the bed to lie on his back. His arm rested over my shoulders and he settled me close to him.

"Go to sleep, darlin', tomorrow's a new day, and I'm gonna

make you breakfast and take you for a long ride. Best way to blow some of the shit out of your head as far as I'm concerned."

Some of the heaviness in my heart had shifted; opening myself up and sharing my pain with Nash had freed me. Sleep would claim me soon, but until then my thoughts were focused on him. He cared deeply; I sensed it in my soul. I'd caught glimpses of it in him over the years, but he'd kept it well hidden. Nash was so broken that he didn't allow himself to share the love he had to give, and he didn't allow anyone in to give him the love he needed. I wanted to give him what he'd just given me. I wanted to help him unshackle himself from the pain holding him back.

CHAPTER 23

Who I Am With You - Chris Young

NASH

VELVET BLASTED ME WITH A SMILE THAT STOLE ME. She'd already stolen my body. Now she stole my fucking heart. Truth be told, she'd stolen it last night when she bared her soul to me. The moment she reached deep inside and laid herself out for me was the moment she had it; the moment she finally owned me. I'd known it was coming, I just thought it would take a lot fucking longer.

And I was okay with it. I was more than fucking okay with it. Call me a pussy, I didn't give a fuck. This woman was going to revive me; I was sure of it.

She eyed me with a questioning look. "I didn't think you made anyone breakfast, Nash Walker."

I grinned at her. "Turns out I was wrong. Now sit your ass down, woman. You're about to have your mind blown by my food."

"Your talents extend to cooking?"

"Baby, you ain't seen nothing yet. My talents are many and varied."

"Well bring it on, dude. Hit me."

I'd made eggs benedict for her, and her eyes widened in appreciation when I placed it in front of her.

"A biker who can cook?" she mused as she began eating. Her face lit up after her first bite. "Oh my God, Nash, you can actually cook!"

I laughed. "You've met my mother, sweet thing. She's not the kind of woman to send her boys out into the world without cooking skills."

"I love your mother," she declared.

"Not something I hadn't worked out, baby."

After we'd finished eating, she made her way to the sink. Eyeing me, she said, "I'll wash, you can dry."

"The plates can dry without my help." No fucking way was I drying dishes. I had a dish rack for that shit.

She smacked me on the chest with the tea towel and pinned me with a dirty look. "I bet that's not something your mother taught you."

"My mother taught me to be efficient with my time, and drying dishes is not a good use of my time." This debate was amusing me, if only to see her getting worked up.

"You know what my mother taught me, Nash?" she asked as she planted a hand on her hip.

"What, darlin'?"

"That a man who doesn't do as he's told, doesn't get sex for the rest of that day."

"Bull-fuckin'-shit." I burst out laughing as I said this.

She raised her eyebrows at me, challenging me. "You want to take a chance on it? Or do you just want to dry the damn dishes?"

I had to give her credit. She was standing her ground, a straight face in place, and I had no doubt that she would withhold sex if she so chose to prove a point.

I put my hand out. "Give me the fuckin' tea towel," I muttered, snatching it off her.

"Thank you," she said, smiling at me while she filled the sink.

"Just to be clear, babe, tonight there's gonna be sex. A lot of fuckin' sex."

"Yeah, baby," she said in that breathy, sexy voice of hers.

I shook my head. "I've been fuckin' played again, haven't I?"

She didn't answer me, just smiled broadly at me.

I watched her in silence while she filled the sink. Velvet was a woman I could spend hours looking at and never tire of the view. But I was interrupted this time by a chuckle in the hallway. I turned and grinned at who I found standing watching us.

Kick.

"Hey, brother," I said, walking towards him.

"Nash, long time no see." We hugged, slapping each other on the back. He pulled away and smirked at me. "I see you've finally found a woman to tame the asshole out of you."

Velvet laughed. "I'm under no illusions. Nash does have his good points though, so I'm sticking around for those."

Kick put his hands up. "I don't want to hear anymore, darlin'. I'll take your word on that." He put his hand out to her and introduced himself, "The name's Kick."

She shook his hand. "Good to meet you. I'm Velvet."

Recognition dawned on Kick's face; I'd obviously mentioned her to him before. "Real good to meet you, darlin'."

"What brings you to town?" I asked him.

"Club business." It was clear he didn't want to discuss it in front of Velvet.

I nodded. "How long you staying? I presume you're staying here."

"Yeah, brother. I don't know how long yet." He jerked his head in the direction of the bedroom he usually crashed in and I nodded.

"I'm gonna crash for a few hours, man."

"Sure. We're going for a ride. Be back later this afternoon so I'll catch you then."

He focused on Velvet. "See you later, darlin'."

She smiled. "Bye."

Once he'd left us, she asked me, "Kick's Storm, right? But not Brisbane?"

"Yeah, he's Sydney chapter. We go back about eight years. He's always had my back."

Nodding, she said, "Okay, dishes and then I wanna cuddle up to the back of you on your bike."

I curled my hand around her neck, and brushed my lips against hers. "Fuck, the things you say, baby."

She rested her hand on my ass, and whispered, "The things I say have got nothing on the words that come out of your mouth."

I grinned.

She was right.

★★★

I watched Velvet walk back into the bedroom, my eyes taking in the t-shirt of mine she was wearing. I'd just fucked her after she gave me a mind shattering blow job, and I was wondering why the hell she'd put clothes back on after cleaning up in the bathroom.

"What's with the shirt, babe?"

She crawled onto the bed, positioning herself half on me and half on the bed. I put my arm around her and rested my hand on her ass, pulling the shirt up so I could feel skin.

"You've got a visitor in the house, Nash. I don't want to be roaming around naked if I get up during the night."

I chuckled. "Kick wouldn't mind."

"I'm just going to ignore you said that. Or better still, how about I take it off and go visit him in his room. You reckon he'd like that? And you'd be okay with that?"

"Fuck. Okay, woman, you win. I see your fuckin' point," I grumbled.

She fell quiet for a moment, before asking, "How did you meet Kick?"

"I met him in prison."

She moved so that she was lying almost on her stomach with her arms resting on my chest. Her eyes met mine; questioning. This wasn't something I ever spoke about; it was all new to her. "Because you were open about that, I'm going to assume you're okay with talking about it but if not, just tell me to back off. What were you in prison for?"

I ran my hand over her hair as I answered her; I liked the constant contact with her when she was near. It helped calm my demons; the demons that pushed to the surface when I thought about this time in my life. "For assault."

Her eyes were kind; she held no judgment. "How long were you there?"

"Two years."

Silence surrounded us as she took it in, her eyes never leaving mine. She seemed to be weighing something up. Finally, she asked, "Nash, have you ever talked about this with anyone?"

"Yeah, babe." I fought the rising anxiety, and focused on her in an effort to quiet it.

She chewed her lip and then wiggled her way up my body a little bit so that our faces were closer. Her warm breath settled on my skin as we stared at each other. When she reached her hand up to run her fingers through my hair, my anxiety calmed and I blew out a breath.

She saw me relax and smiled. "You okay, now?" she whispered.

It was in that moment, I realised Velvet knew what she was

doing. I nodded. "You know?"

"That you're suffering from anxiety?"

"Yeah," I said, softly. Time slowed. My focus was entirely on Velvet; I saw only her. It was like the maddening assault of emotions and feelings quieted, and receded, allowing me full control over my attention for the first time in a long time.

"My mum suffered from it for years. I recognised the symptoms. Have you had it treated?"

"Yeah, baby," I admitted, and then added, "You're the only person I've told though, besides my doctor."

"Your family don't know?"

"I'm sure they realise, but it's not something we talk about. They've tried to get me to, but talking about it brings up shit I don't want to deal with."

She continued to run her fingers through my hair.

Soft.

Calming.

Loving.

Exactly what I needed.

"I'm here for you, whatever you need. Tell me you hear me when I say that," she said, her piercing gaze demanding so much from me.

Fuck.

I hesitated, but she didn't let me off. She held my gaze, and I knew she wasn't budging an inch. I had to give her what she'd asked for. And I knew it was going to be both my undoing and my healing.

Fuck.

Slowly, I nodded. "Yes, I hear you."

Her hand moved to my face, her fingers tracing soft patterns on my cheek. Never in my life had I been with a woman who was so caring; who didn't ask me for anything in return. Velvet just loved.

She'd loved me as a friend for so long now and I hadn't truly acknowledged that for what it was. It was way past time to do that.

I took her hand in mine. "Thank you."

She smiled. "You're welcome."

I shook my head. She didn't know what I was thanking her for. "No, baby. I'm thanking you for what you've already done for me, not for what you're offering to do now."

Confusion flickered over her face. "What have I already done for you, Nash?"

"You've been a friend to me. And I was a bastard to you on more than one occasion. I don't fuckin' deserve you but I'm gonna take you and everything you're offering."

She swallowed hard, and her eyes teared up.

"Shit, sweet thing, I didn't want to make you cry," I murmured.

Smiling through her tears, she said, "They're happy tears, baby."

"Happy for what?"

"You reminded me that I'm worthy of love. James took that belief from me and I've struggled ever since to feel worthy again. And you do deserve me, Nash. I see your pain. I know there's more, and I know you'll share it with me eventually, but whatever has happened to make you think you don't deserve love, it's not true."

Fuck me, she was an angel. I wasn't sure I'd ever deserve her. I rolled us over so I was lying over her. Bending my lips to hers, I murmured, "You're mine now, Velvet."

Our lips joined in a slow, gentle kiss. A kiss that stirred long buried desires. Life had thrown a lot of fucking curve balls, and hadn't turned out the way I'd planned. And although I'd never have the one thing I'd always truly desired, I knew that having Velvet would help me deal with the loss of that dream. Fuck knew, it was time to finally deal with that; ten years was long enough to hold onto that heartache.

CHAPTER 24

Brave - Sara Bareilles

VELVET

MINE.

That's what I was thinking as I watched Nash walk to his bike. He was mine. He'd given himself to me last night, making me happier than I could ever remember.

I watched him leave, and then went inside, out of the cold wind. Mondays were my least favourite day of the week, and today was no exception. The only shining part of the day was that I woke up to Nash loving. And afterward, he'd made me toast and coffee. We hadn't made plans to see each other tonight because it looked like he might be busy with Kick. So, I had a long day of study, work and no more Nash loving ahead of me. Yeah, Monday could kiss my ass.

Bella rubbed herself against my legs, happy to see me. I picked her up and pet her. "Sorry, baby, I've been neglecting you lately, haven't I?"

She purred at my touch.

"Nash has kinda been taking up all my time. You'd understand if you were a woman," I said as I placed her back on the ground and fed her.

Once she was happy, I made my way into the study, ready to tackle the mountain of work I had to get through today. However, just as I was about to take a seat, there was a knock at my front door so I headed back out there to see who it was.

James stood on my verandah, a contemptuous look on his face.

"What do you want now?" I asked, joining him on the verandah rather than letting him inside. Surprisingly, the old feelings of inadequacy I usually felt around James did not surface.

"May I come in?"

"No, James, Say what you need to say and then you can go. There's no need to go inside for that."

His brow arched. "As you prefer. I've come to tell you that I'm withdrawing my offer."

I scoffed. "Nash came to see you, didn't he?"

Annoyance covered his features. "You need to tell your lapdog that if any of what we discussed surfaces, his club won't know what hit it."

I cocked my head to the side. "First of all, Nash isn't anyone's lapdog. I have no control over anything he does. And second, I'm guessing that whatever dirt he has on you must be huge for you to come here today. Which means that if any of it were to get out, you wouldn't have the power to hurt him or his club." God, it felt so damn good to say this to him. My heart was beating with excitement to finally have the courage to take him on. And to feel no fear.

He scowled. "I'm deadly serious, Velvet, when I say that you don't want to take me on. And you don't want to talk to anyone about me, us or our marriage. You thought you got screwed in our divorce? You'd be fucking decimated over this if you pursued it." The vein in his neck pulsed and his nostrils flared as he spat out his threat.

"See, that's what you never understood, James. You already fucking decimated me. You ripped me to pieces and left me ruined. Back then I had no-one to help me; I had to face all my monsters by myself. And I did. It took me years, but I put myself back together, stronger than before you found me. So, knock yourself out because I know I have what it takes to survive. And this time around, I have someone who cares about me to back me up."

His eyes narrowed on me. "This biker really has you, doesn't he?"

I had no idea where he was going with this now. "Yes, he does, if you must know."

"You know his past? That he was in jail for years for beating a man up?"

"James, I know Nash. I know his heart. And yes, I'm aware of his past. But let me tell you, Nash has a reason for everything he does. And his reasons aren't dirty like your reasons. I'll take a flawed man who does things out of love or honour over a man who does stuff for his own personal gain."

He glared at me. The cold wind whipped around us, biting me with its iciness. This was the end of us; finally. I could feel it in my bones and the weight I'd been carrying for years lifted.

The last words he delivered failed to hit me in the way he intended. "I have no idea what I ever saw in you, Velvet."

I smiled as I tasted freedom. "That's because you never opened your eyes, James."

He blinked; confused. I turned and opened my front door to go back inside. But he had one last thing to ask. "You won't talk about us, will you?"

I gave him my attention one last time. "It's good to see you beg, asshole. But I'm the bigger person, and no, I have no intention of ever talking about us. I won't waste my breath on you." With that, I walked away, letting the door slam behind me. Adrenaline was pumping through me. I could hardly contain my happiness, and felt the need to talk to Nash. He didn't answer his phone though so I sent him a text.

Me: Fingernails on your back.

I didn't hear back from him and although that disappointed me, I grinned to myself knowing that the text would affect him. I'd eventually hear back from him.

Leaving my phone in the kitchen so I wouldn't be distracted, I headed into the study and began the hours of work I had to do in order to pass my exams. I was so engrossed in it that I didn't realise how much time had passed until I heard someone banging on my front door.

"God, who now?" I muttered to myself as I padded out there.

I opened the door to find Nash filling the doorframe, his muscular arms leaning on either side of it, an intense gaze directed at me. "You can't fuckin' send me a text like that and then ignore the fuck out of me, woman."

God, yes.

My core clenched, and desire consumed me. I stepped back, and he powered through the door, one arm scooping my waist and the other one curling around my neck. He shut the door with his foot, and turned to push me against the wall. His lips crashed down onto mine, and he let out a low growl as he kissed the hell out of my lips. A delicious warmth flowed through me; this man possessed the ability to send me from zero to a hundred in seconds. He could do whatever he wanted and I would take it all. Anything. Everything. He didn't even need to ask.

His hands moved down to cup my ass and lift me. I wrapped my arms and legs around him, holding tight. I'd never let go of him; not now, not ever. He was mine, and that knowledge thrilled me.

He dragged his lips from mine, moving his head so he could look down at me. Butterflies swirled in my tummy when his eyes landed on my chest. His breathing had grown ragged, and I realised just how worked up my text had gotten him.

"Are you going to fuck me, Nash, or are you just going to look at me?"

His gaze swung straight back to mine. It scorched me with the passion it held. The desire he felt was clear to see. In response to my question he raised his brow in a 'what the fuck do you think' manner. "After that text you sent, it's going to be quick. And you're not going to complain, sweet thing. You fuckin' asked for this."

I smiled sweetly at him, and tightened my arms and legs around him. "Baby, there's something you might not have worked out about me yet." I paused as I moved my mouth next to his ear so I could whisper, "I like it hard, fast and rough."

As I moved my face away, I caught the clench of his jaw. "You're gonna get your fuckin' wish," he rasped.

He didn't waste time. One minute I was up against the wall, the next I was standing and he was ripping my clothes off. In the frenzy, I fumbled with his belt. My fingers weren't cooperating and he pushed them out of the way, undoing his belt and pants faster than I could blink. He pushed his pants down, and spun me around to face the wall.

Warm breath tickled my neck as he positioned my arms up against the wall, and murmured, "I love looking at your ass while I fuck your pussy." He slapped my bare ass, and my hunger for him intensified. "You like that?" he breathed into my ear.

I pushed my ass back, into him. "Yeah, Nash, I like that. Do it again."

He growled, and slapped me again. My body thrummed. The deepest parts of me woke under his touch, and cried out for more. When he ran his hand over my bare skin, I shivered.

"Baby, why the fuck did we wait so long for this?" he begged to know.

I had no good answer for that question; the waiting seemed pointless now. "No more waiting, Nash. Hurry up and fuck me."

He didn't need any further coaxing. "Give me a second, darlin'. We need a condom."

"We really need to sort something out about that," I complained, hating to wait for him.

"Yeah, babe, we do," he agreed, and then, having the condom in place, he whispered in my ear, "Ready?"

I tingled all over; Nash's breath, body and dirty mouth had me way past ready. "Yes."

His cock entered me; rough, hard and fast. Just the way I'd asked for. His hands gripped my waist and he held me in place while he fucked me exactly how he'd promised me he would.

"Babe, touch yourself," he grunted.

My clit was screaming out for attention so I did what he said. The pleasure caused by my fingers collided with the pleasure he was giving me, and I moaned.

Nash enjoyed the sound of pleasure, and groaned. "Shit, I'm gonna fuckin' come soon. You and your fuckin' texts..." He stopped talking and thrust hard one last time before stilling. "Fuck," he groaned again before letting his head fall onto my shoulders.

I was so close to my orgasm, and I knew Nash would get me there faster. "Nash, I need your fingers."

He knew exactly what I needed, and he took over from me. His mouth kissed my neck before whispering, "You want my fingers to fuck your cunt, baby?"

I moaned at the thought, and nodded, unable to get words out. He pulled out of me and inserted his fingers while continuing to rub my clit with his thumb. The pleasure was intense; divine. He slid an arm around my waist and pulled me back. I leaned into him, dropping my head back onto his shoulder.

"So good..." I moaned, and lost myself to the orgasm that was taking over.

He bent a little so he could push his fingers deeper, and that sent me over the edge. I screamed out his name, and accepted all the pleasure he gave. While I recovered, he moved his hands and scooped my hair off my shoulder so he could lay gentle kisses along it. Nash doing gentle right after rough almost killed me.

"Babe, as much as I'm enjoying this, I have to get back to the club," he said.

"So, you just came over for a quickie?" I didn't care; I was just giving him grief to rile him up. Nash all bothered was a turn on.

He slapped me on the ass, softly this time. "Had no fuckin' choice, sweetheart. You send me a text like that again, you better be ready to spread your legs."

I laughed. "I knew it would affect you, I just didn't realise how much."

He turned me around to face him, and planted a kiss on my lips. "Velvet, I'm not sure you realise just how much *you* affect me, let alone your fuckin' text messages."

I smiled. "I do now." I paused, and then added, "James came to see me this morning."

He stilled, and a scowl covered his face. "What did that asshole want?"

"You went to see him."

He nodded once. "I did. So I'm fuckin' hoping you've got good news for me otherwise I'll be paying him another visit."

"He won't be bothering me again. Thank you for that."

He caressed my cheek. "Any time, sweet thing."

I bit my lip. I needed to tell someone what this meant to me, but I wasn't sure anyone would get it. "Nash, this is huge to me. I feel like, for the first time in years, I can do anything; be anything. I didn't realise just how much he was holding me back. It probably sounds stupid - "

He cut me off. "Nothing you say sounds stupid, Velvet. I might be an asshole, but I get what you're saying. I get *you*. I've watched my sister go through life not feeling worthy, and it breaks my fuckin' heart to see the shit she accepts from men. I'm over the fuckin' moon to know that you can move past that dickhead and believe in yourself again."

I wrapped my arms around his neck and kissed him, long and hard. My heart threatened to explode out of my chest. When it ended, I said, "You're not really an asshole, Nash Walker." Then I grinned, and added, "Well, maybe just a little bit asshole, but life would be boring if you weren't."

It was his turn to grin now. "Babe, I'm glad we've established once and for all that I'm a little bit asshole, but can we get dressed now. I'm standing here with my pants around my legs looking at your tits and ass, and if you don't put some clothes on soon, I'm not gonna make it back to the clubhouse. And I'll never hear the fuckin' end of it from Scott."

I pouted. "I'd be worth it though. Right?"

He sighed. "You've no idea, sweet thing. No fuckin' idea."

CHAPTER 25

Her Jealousy - Gin Blossoms

NASH

"Let me get this straight, you're saying that you believe Marcus was responsible for that bust on your club ten years ago?" Scott said, clearly astonished.

Kick nodded, rubbing his jaw. "Yeah, brother, that's what we think."

I was struggling to keep up with the conversation; my thoughts kept going back to this afternoon with Velvet. She consumed my thoughts constantly; thank Christ she didn't know just how much.

I focused back on what was being said. Kick had asked me to organise a chat with Scott tonight and was now revealing the reason for his visit to Brisbane.

Scott really was incredulous; surprising, because at this point I'd believe anything of Marcus. He asked Kick, "Can you just go over that again for me?"

Kick gave me one of his impatient looks; he was one of the most impatient bastards I'd ever met. He was also one of the most loyal and honest, so yeah, I believed what he was telling us now.

Looking back at Scott, he repeated himself, "Our cop friends have been talking recently about that drug bust ten years ago, the one that put our VP and two other members inside, and the word is that Marcus snitched on our club in order to save himself from something. No idea what that was though. This was back when your club was running drugs too. My VP wants confirmation it was Marcus before he moves on this. And if he gets that confirmation, it won't be pretty for your father."

I didn't doubt what he'd just said about the consequences for Marcus if they discovered this to be true. The Sydney chapter was the Mother Chapter of Storm and their President and VP were violent motherfuckers who even Kick did his best not to piss off, and Kick wasn't the kind of man to worry about anyone.

"Any of this ringing bells for you, VP?" I asked.

Scott slowly shook his head, obviously still processing it. "No, but I'll be looking into it, that's for damn sure."

Kick frowned, and asked, "You think it's wrong?"

"No, brother." He gave me an enquiring look, and I read what he was asking. I nodded to indicate it was safe to talk to Kick about Marcus. Turning back to Kick, he said, "A few of us are currently looking into Marcus's activities. Seems he's trying to steer us back into drugs and has hooked us up with Adelaide for a foot in the door."

"You don't want back in the drugs?" Kick asked.

"Fuck, no. We don't need it to survive, and we don't need the attention."

"Yeah, I hear you," Kick agreed.

"What's your plan?" Scott asked him.

"I've got some coppers up here to talk to; see if they know anything. Other than that, I don't think there's any club members who would know much. Unless you think there's someone worth talking to?"

I remembered what Blade had said the other day. "You ever hear of someone called Blue?"

Scott swung his head in my direction. "No, why?"

"Haven't had a chance to tell you yet, but Blade said he's upped his surveillance on Marcus and they've come across that name. Said that Marcus is looking for someone called Blue."

"Who's Blade?" Kick asked.

"Marcus's son, my half brother, but he's not tied up with Storm. He's got his own thing going on."

I eyed Scott. "Might be worth Kick's while to go have a chat with him."

Scott nodded. "Yeah, brother. You want to hook that up?"

"Sure," I agreed.

Scott stood. "Anything else?" he asked Kick. "

"Nope. Thanks for your time, man."

"No problem, Kick. Just keep me in the loop. Yeah?"

"Will do. And like I said, the repercussions for Marcus won't be good if he was involved."

"Yeah, I'm hearing you," Scott said, his concentration far away; probably sifting through his mind to find anything that might relate to this.

He left and when I heard the front door slam shut, I said to Kick, "Fuck, man."

"Yeah, brother, fuck is about right. I've never liked Marcus but I like Scott; it'll be a lot for him to deal with if his father did this."

I considered it. "Mostly, I think he'll be okay with whatever happens. Marcus has fucked him and their family around, and Scott has nothing to do with him anymore."

"That's good. I believe Marcus is guilty; it's just a matter of proving it. Once we have proof, my VP will move fast. You think Scott will step up to Presidency if this goes the way I think it will?"

"Yeah."

"And who would take on VP?"

I didn't hesitate. To me, it was a no-brainer. "Griff."

He nodded, and then grinned at me. "We going hunting tonight, or are you pussy-whipped these days?"

I thought about Velvet, and returned his grin. "No hunting for me anymore, brother."

"Figured as much. What's the story there? I thought you'd sworn off relationships."

"Yeah, you and me both. Velvet and I kinda happened by accident but I think it was inevitable."

"She know about Gabriella and Aaron?"

"No." The anxiety surfaced but it was bearable; I focused on my breathing to keep it under control.

"When do you plan on telling her? Before the end of June?"

I rubbed the back of my neck. "Shit, Kick. I don't fuckin' know."

"Christ, Nash. It's been what, ten years this year? That's a long fucking time to carry this shit with you and not move on. Seems to me you could do with a woman to help you through it."

He was right. I knew he fucking was. I'd been dealing with this very thought the last couple of days. The closer Velvet and I got, the more I wanted to open up to her. "You're a pushy fucker, you know that?"

His face remained serious. "Yeah, and you need someone like me to push you, otherwise you're going to end up alone and miserable. You'll be chasing pussy in your fuckin' wheelchair if you don't find someone to settle down with."

I laughed at that thought. "They'd be fuckin' lucky to have me, asshole. My cock will still be in hot demand when I'm in a wheelchair."

He lost the serious face and grinned at me while shaking his head. "Shit, you never shut up about your cock, do you? Just tell me you'll talk to her, brother. It's time."

I raked my hand through my hair, and agreed, reluctantly. "Yeah, I'm gonna fuckin' talk to her."

Kick stood. He had that determined look in his eyes, the one that told me he was on the prowl. "I'm gonna hit your club. You coming?"

I jumped up, fucking tripping over myself to leave. Velvet was working tonight, and although we hadn't made plans to see each other, I'd known that wouldn't happen. I needed her. Kick just looked at me and gave me that 'you're so gone' look. I scowled, and muttered, "Not a fuckin' word, brother."

★★★

VELVET

IF ANYMORE ASSHOLES spoke to me tonight, I swore I was going to rip their fucking nuts off. Seriously, it must have been full moon or something, because Indigo was full of them tonight. Their filthy mouths and grabby hands seemed to be all I could hear and feel. I sighed. Maybe it was because I was missing Nash, maybe that was making it worse. His presence had a way of calming me. Having him in my life made it better, and certainly having him around while I was at work made it easier to deal when assholes got in my face.

This job was really starting to lose its appeal. I'd always enjoyed it, but lately I didn't look forward to coming to work like I used to. Even the attention from men that I once craved, no longer held any interest for me. I didn't want it; I just wanted Nash' attention.

"Velvet, take a break, babe. I don't want to see you for at least forty-five minutes. You've been working your ass off tonight," Cody said as he walked past me to the bar.

I could have hugged him. "Done," I replied and immediately headed out to the staff room before he changed his mind.

The first thing I did was kick my shoes off, the second thing I did was pour myself a bourbon, and the third thing I did was knock that drink back in half a minute flat. Then I thought, fuck it, and poured myself another drink.

It was after two drinks in quick succession that Wilder sauntered in. I admired his muscles. Damn, he was built, and the shirt he was wearing did nothing to hide those muscles. He wasn't quite as big as Nash, but I didn't know one woman who would knock him back if he was on offer.

He laid a sexy smile on me, a smile that would have gotten him laid if I wasn't with Nash. "You seen Scott?" he asked. All credit to him, his eyes didn't stray from my face. Wilder was serious about not messing with a friend of the VP's.

The alcohol had loosened my tongue and I pursued a conversation with him even though he'd made it clear he wasn't keen on chatting with me. "I'm trying to work you out, Wilder," I said as I walked towards him.

"Don't try too hard, darlin'. Not much here to see."

"I'd beg to differ. I don't think I've ever met a man who didn't make eye contact with my chest. I know you said you're avoiding the VP's friends but for you to honour that even when he's not around tells me a lot about you. And that intrigues me."

No words came out of his mouth; it seemed he was doing battle in his mind with what to say or do. His eyes flashed a warning, and when he spoke, his voice was like a delicious cocktail of danger and desire. "Gorgeous, I'm fighting like fuck not to look at your chest. I've seen that sweet body of yours and it's a body I could spend days admiring. I'm no different to any other man where that's concerned."

His sexy voice slid right through me. It was a good thing I believed in total faithfulness when I was with a man, because if I didn't, I'd be more than tempted by him. "No, there's something decidedly different about you. And I like it."

He sucked in a breath, and ran his fingers through his hair. "Fuck, you're a dangerous woman."

I was about to tell him where Scott was when a menacing presence filled the room.

"Wilder." Nash's formidable voice boomed around us.

I turned to look at him and found him glaring at Wilder.

"Nash." Wilder met his glare; his shoulders tensing.

"What the fuck's going on here?" Nash demanded to know.

I figured I needed to step in; if it hadn't been for me, Wilder wouldn't be in this position. "Nothing's going on, Nash," I said, walking to him. The need to touch him, to let him know he had nothing to worry about was overwhelming.

His glare landed on me; he was furious, and it scared me, but it didn't stop me. "Stay out of this, Velvet," he warned, those beautiful green eyes of his full of anger.

I moved into his space and placed my hand on his chest. "Wilder wasn't doing anything," I said, softly.

Nash's chest heaved. He removed my hand and repeated himself, "I said, stay out of it." His eyes didn't leave mine and his voice was dangerously low.

I wasn't sure what had caused him to have such an extreme reaction but it hurt to have him talk to me like that. I took a step back, away from him. He watched me for another moment, and then turned back to Wilder.

Wilder was looking between me and Nash, and when he finally figured out what was going on, he held his hands up. "Fuck, Nash, I didn't realise she was your old lady."

I felt it necessary to clarify that. "No, I'm not Nash's old lady."

Nash swung his head to face me again, fuming, before fixing his glare back on Wilder, and declaring, "Yeah, well now you know she is."

Wilder looked pissed, and although I figured that was directed at me, he didn't dare look in my direction. Instead, he said to Nash, "Sorry, man. There was nothing going on though. I just asked her if she knew where Scott was."

They were talking about me like I wasn't even in the room, and that annoyed me. Now we were all pissed. Tuning out their conversation, I sat and put my shoes back on having decided I would get back to work. Once they were on, I looked up to find Nash still abusing Wilder. His eyes, however, were firmly on me. I stood, checked my makeup and hair, and then attempted to get past them to leave the room. They could continue their argument without me.

Nash watched me walk towards him, and reached for me as I tried to keep going. His grip was firm on my wrist, and I glared at him to let me go. He stopped talking to Wilder so he could give me his full attention. Wilder used the opportunity to leave and Nash didn't argue; he just kept staring at me.

I tried to pull out of his hold but he was too strong for me. "Nash, you need to let me go so I can go back to work."

"They can wait." He was still fuming.

"There's no need. We're finished here." My voice was tight, harsh. I needed to put some distance between us right now; I was worried what I would say in the heat of the moment.

"We're not finished here, Velvet." The way he said my name made my skin crawl. There was no soft in it, only hard and angry.

I tried to pull my arm free again, and this time he let me go, but his body language was clear; he had no intention of letting me walk out of the room.

"Okay then, say what you need to say so that I can get back to work."

"I don't want you talking to Wilder, or any of the other guys for that matter."

My eyes widened. I couldn't believe what I was hearing. "You're kidding, right?" But even as I said it, I knew he wasn't.

"No, I'm not fuckin' kidding," he thundered.

My body tensed, and my heart began pounding in my chest. This was the Nash I didn't like. I spoke calmly, deliberately. "If you're not kidding, we have a problem, Nash."

"We do have a problem, babe. I won't put up with you flirting with any of the boys."

It was like a kick in the guts; he didn't trust me. The accusation was barely concealed in the tone he'd taken with me. "You're saying you don't trust me?"

"I'm saying that if you don't flirt, then there won't be a problem," he said, firmly.

This was Nash laying down the law; laying down his law. And I didn't like it. Not one little bit. "Well, I'd say we will have a problem then." I stood my ground; there was no going back now.

His face clouded over. He'd obviously expected he could tell me what to do without any argument from me. "What the fuck does that mean?"

"It means that I am not the kind of woman you can order around. What the hell happened to us having a rational conversation about this? You know, like the one we had about my insecurities. The one where you said you hated women who automatically suspected you of cheating? Because it sure as hell feels like it's one rule for you and another for me."

"Velvet, you're twisting my words. I never said I didn't trust you. I simply said I don't want you flirting. Can you manage that?

"Fuck you, Nash!" I yelled, finally losing my cool. "Yes, I can manage not to fucking flirt but what you don't get is that I won't be *told* to do anything. You can *ask* me to do anything but the minute you just make a ruling and call it done, that's not fucking on."

He stood there, taking in what I'd said, eyes flashing anger, and his face hard. The tension clung to the air while we remained silent, having said what we both wanted. *Checkmate.*

My heart felt like it was going to explode out of my chest I was so angry. And hurt. He'd really fucking hurt me. I decided to finally put that space between us I wanted to before. "I'm getting back to work now," I told him. My tone made it clear there would be no argument.

He blew out an angry breath, and stepped aside to let me through.

Neither of us said another word, and the pain I felt in my chest as I walked away reminded me why I avoided getting close to men.

CHAPTER 26

The Great Escape - Pink

VELVET

I PUSHED THE DOONA OFF ME, GOT OUT OF BED AND traipsed into the kitchen to get a drink. Bella followed me and almost made me trip when she insisted on getting in my way. I bent down and picked her up. "Baby, don't make me fall over. I've had a shitty night as it is. I don't need to add a broken leg to my list of things I'd rather forget."

When we hit the kitchen, I placed her back on the ground and made a cup of tea. Nash would not leave my thoughts; I'd been tossing and turning for hours. I checked the time. Just after four am.

Shit.

I hadn't heard from him after our argument, and my stomach felt sick over it. Although I was angry at him, I wanted to work it out. I hated the silence that fights caused between people. And the doubting. I fucking hated the doubting.

Shit.

I drank my tea while mentally sifting through the jobs I had to get through in the morning. My reasoning was that if I was busy thinking about that, I wouldn't be busy thinking about Nash.

I was so wrong.

"Fuck it, give up, cause you're never gonna stop thinking about him," I muttered to myself as I washed my mug up. "Shit, now you're even talking to yourself."

I was deep in thought when there was an almighty bashing on my front door. At least that's where I thought it was coming from. A couple of moments later, I peered through the curtain to see Nash standing on my verandah.

I opened the door to find him waiting for me with an intense look on his face. He didn't wait for an invitation to come inside; just barged straight in and stalked to my kitchen where the light was on. I didn't particularly want to talk to him while he was in this kind of mood so I took my time following him.

When I got to the kitchen, I didn't give him a chance to say anything; I spoke first. "If you've come to keep arguing, I'm not interested. I don't want to fight anymore, Nash."

"I do trust you, Velvet," he started, his voice rough, not at all what I was expecting. The anger I thought he was projecting was something else instead. There was almost a brokenness to it; to him. My heart listened closely while he kept talking, because I was sure he was about to crack himself wide open for me. "I'm fucked up though, where this shit's concerned, and I find it hard to trust."

His voice cracked on his last word, and he stopped talking. His eyes frantically sought mine; searching for what, I wasn't sure, but I sensed his desperate need for me to wait patiently for him to get this all out.

So, I waited.

His hand pushed through his hair, and he blew out a long breath. "I was married. Her name was Gabriella. We met when I was twenty, back when I didn't have a clue. I would have done anything for her. I married her and planned a long fuckin' life with her, but she threw it all away when she cheated on me. And not just once." He placed his hands on his hips, and bent slightly forward, expelling more long breaths. It was like he couldn't catch his breath; almost like he'd just run a fast race and was struggling. I realised that's exactly what was happening; he definitely was struggling for breath.

I placed my hand on his back, and said, "Nash, you need to focus on your breathing. Count your breaths."

He did as I said, and began taking longer breaths. I counted them in my head as he took them, more out of habit than anything. Memories of my mother's experience with this flooded my mind. I hated watching him go through this just as much as I'd hated watching her. Watching someone struggle through anxiety made you feel useless and desperate; desperate to be able to take it all from them and carry their burden. But you fucking couldn't and that was the bitch of it all.

The house was silent apart from Nash's breathing. I welcomed the silence; it allowed me the space to think. My anger dulled as the pain spilled from him. It was in this moment I realised how broken he was. He hadn't done the work to move past this hurt, and I wondered how long he'd been carrying it.

He was starting to get his breathing under control, and straightened. His eyes found mine. They were wary.

I gave him a small smile, and reached for his hand. "How long ago was this?" I asked, softly.

His chest heaved again, but he maintained his breathing. "Ten years ago."

I didn't want to rush him, so I squeezed his hand, and waited for a moment before saying, "Tell me about her, Nash."

He stared at me, and all I could see was his damaged soul. But his eyes were reaching for me; he needed me. I gently guided him to sit at the table, and prodded him to talk again. "What was Gabriella like?"

His hands fidgeted on the table, and he stared at them for awhile before finally opening up. "She was fun, spontaneous, up for anything. She was everything I wasn't back then." He paused, and looked at me. I was stunned by what he'd just said, and he must have been able to read that on my face. "You might find it hard to believe, but back then, I was the responsible one. Growing up, I had to be. My father left when I was twelve, and my mother was pregnant with Carla. Jamison and I helped run the house and raise the girls during our teens while Mum was working two jobs making ends meet. I left school when I was fifteen to take on a mechanic apprenticeship to help her with the bills. So yeah, I had to be responsible and organised. When I met Gabriella, I was working as a mechanic, and desperately wanted her to be a part of my life. She made me feel alive again after all the shit I had to deal with at home."

"What do you mean by that?" I asked, wanting to keep him talking, and wanting to know more about his life.

"Dad never had anything to do with us after he left; not one fuckin' word. Still hasn't to this day. Erika was ten when he left, and Carla never knew him." His eyes blazed with anger now. "He fucked them up. Erika got into all kinds of shit; boys, alcohol, drugs, skipping school. You name it, she fuckin' did it. All she wanted was a father who fuckin' cared. God help him if I ever find him."

"So you were helping your Mum deal with all this?"

"Yeah, Jamison and I tried to help. We spent nights trying to track Erika down, nights trying to keep her away from the parties, nights at the fuckin' hospital while they dealt with the shit she'd put in her body. Mum was wrecked; physically and mentally." He stopped, and pierced me with his gaze. "The whole thing was fucked up."

"You wouldn't know it now; your family was amazing when I met them."

He gave me a tight smile. "It's been a long fuckin' road to get there."

My heart was hurting for what he'd been through; for what he'd missed out on in life. "And Gabriella?"

His words cracked my heart a little bit more. "I fell hard for her; hard and fast. I'd fucked around with a lot of chicks before her, but she was different. She made me want more. I chased the shit out of her. She was all I wanted, and I felt like the luckiest bastard alive when she said she would marry me. Problem was, she didn't have a fuckin' clue what loyalty was."

"How long were you married for?"

This question seemed to rattle him, but he kept talking. "I was with her for five years, three of those we were married."

He stopped talking and I sensed a change in him. It was like he'd put the wall back up and wasn't going to talk anymore. Suddenly, he stood, and began pacing the room.

I stood and moved towards him. "Nash, what - "

He cut me off, his voice rough again. "Velvet, I can't do this with you if we don't have total honesty. I'm not saying you haven't been honest with me; I'm just telling you what I need. And I'm not trying to control you when I tell you I don't want you flirting with the boys. What I am telling you though, is that I can't be in a relationship with someone who does that."

The vulnerability in his words touched me. Nash had a way of doing that in the most unexpected moments. He laid his heart out for me, and I had no intention of trampling it. I would happily give him what he needed, and although I regretted the fight we'd had to have to get to this point, I was also grateful for it because it had forced him to open up.

I nodded. "I hear you, Nash. And I understand what you're saying."

The look he pinned me with revealed his need. "Can you give that to me?" He expelled a ragged breath, and I watched as his shoulders slumped a little.

I was close enough now to touch him, and I placed my hand on his cheek. Softly. Lovingly. I whispered, "Yes, I can give you that, baby."

His chest heaved once again, and he curled an arm around my waist. Pulling me into his arms, he pressed a long kiss to my forehead before tightening his hold on me. I lost track of how long we stayed like that. It was time we needed to reconnect after everything that had been said.

When we finally pulled apart, he murmured, "I'm sorry, baby."

I looked up into his eyes. The anger was gone, but there was still something there. I wasn't completely sure, but I sensed he had more to tell. He'd shut down towards the end there, but I wasn't going to push him anymore tonight. I whispered, "Me too."

He bent his lips to mine, and kissed me. It was a gentle kiss, but I felt his desire tangled in with the softness. I felt his need too; it matched mine. Our lips and tongues slowly explored each other; there was no rushing, no wild frenzy. There was urgency though. Our bodies pressed together, and we clung to each other while we drew the kiss out. I didn't want it to end; Nash was whispering sweet nothings through this kiss. And for a man who didn't do hearts and flowers, I knew it meant something.

When his lips left mine to trail kisses along my jaw and down my neck, I tilted my head to the side to accept everything he wanted to give me. His hands moved to the bottom of my t-shirt and he slowly removed it, his eyes firmly focused on my chest. He dropped my shirt on the floor and bent his mouth to my nipple. When his tongue circled it and he began sucking, I moaned, and moved my hand to the back of his head to hold him there. He lavished attention on both my breasts, causing my whole body to light up with desire.

When he'd finished, he looked up at me, and murmured, "I'm a lucky man, sweet thing."

"We're both lucky, Nash," I said.

"Fuck, I need to get you under me, baby," he growled.

He didn't wait for a response, he scooped me up into his arms and walked us into my bedroom. My body sung with desire and anticipation in a way it never had for anyone else. He placed me on the bed, and I watched as he removed his clothes. His muscles always drove me wild, especially when they flexed while he undressed.

Once his clothes were off, he grabbed a condom out of his wallet and put it on, watching me while he did this. My tummy fluttered as he watched me; Nash's attention on me always had this effect. It only intensified when he joined me on the bed and removed my panties. And when his tongue licked my clit a second later, my eyes squeezed shut as I let the pleasure take over. I was no longer in control of my of body; Nash had complete control now.

Strong hands slid under my ass, gripping me while he kissed my pussy. His soft kisses slowly turned demanding, and he began licking and sucking, working both of us up. The growls coming from him were as much a turn on as his mouth. Knowing he wanted me as much as I wanted him caused both my body and my heart to pulse in ecstasy.

He brought me to the edge. I was writhing under him, my hand clawing at his hair, and when I cried out his name, he pulled his mouth away and let go of me. His glazed stare sent a shiver of lust through my body, and I reached for him. "I need you in me, now," I begged.

Nash wasn't a man who needed to be told twice. He moved

fast, positioning himself over me. But he didn't enter me straight away. Instead, he rubbed his thumb along my jaw, watching me with that intensity that was all Nash. "I want you, Velvet," he rasped.

I stroked his arm, my touch gentle, and whispered, "I'm all yours, Nash." My legs wrapped around him as I said this, trying to hurry him.

He shook his head. "No, baby, I want you in my life, not just in my bed. I don't want to fuck around with this anymore." He moved his face closer, his eyes burning into mine, his voice rough and demanding when he said, "I need to know that you're mine."

Time slowed, and my entire world became Nash in that moment. I saw only him, felt only him, heard only him. He was asking me for everything, and I was going to give it to him. After years of pushing men away, pushing my need to be loved away, I was finally going to let it in. I moved my hands to hold his face, and I nodded. "I'm yours Nash, only yours."

A look crossed his face; relief perhaps. And then he pushed inside me. Slowly, all the way. He didn't pull out, just let himself settle in me. "Fuck, baby, I love being inside you," he groaned.

I tightened my legs around him, and squeezed his cock. He hissed, and pulled out. I waited for him to thrust in again but he didn't. He stilled, and dipped his head to kiss me. It was another gentle kiss. Nash was showing me a softness I'd never seen from him before; it was a side to him I could get used to. But I knew it wasn't something I would see very often, so I soaked it all in, letting his gentleness wash over me. I let him love me in this moment. It was too early in our relationship for words of love, and besides, I figured Nash wasn't the kind of man to make declarations like that easily, but I knew in my soul that this was his way of cherishing me.

As his lips left mine, he thrust inside me again. This time, he began a slow rhythm of thrusting in and out. I let him set the pace, enjoying the sensations his slow movements were giving me.

"Nash," I moaned his name as I felt my orgasm building.

He was holding himself above me, watching me while he moved us towards our release. At the sound of his name, he grunted, and thrust harder. "Fuck," he muttered, a look of determination on his face. "I fuckin' love it when you say my name."

I heard him, but I didn't have it in me to say anything. My mind could only focus on the pleasure he was giving me. Instead of using words, I used my body to show him what I was feeling. I clung to him tighter, and dug my fingernails into his back.

My nails set him off like they always did. He pulled out of me and then thrust hard and fast; the slow was gone, and the Nash I craved was back. Picking up his pace, he fucked me with a relentless intensity. I shut my eyes as I spiralled into the orgasm I'd been chasing. When I finally came, I squeezed my arms, legs, and pussy; taking every last drop of bliss he was giving me.

And then he came. He rammed into me one last time, and roared, "Fuck!" Losing himself in it, his legs and back tensed as he stilled. His head dropped and I moved my hands to hold the back of his neck, gently stroking him there. I loved this time after he came; I felt so close to him in that moment.

Once he'd recovered, he pushed off me, and left to dispose of the condom. I curled up on my side while I waited for him to return. Sleep was already claiming me, and I closed my eyes, savouring the thrill from everything Nash had just given me.

The bed dipped, and I opened my eyes to find him settling in next to me. I ran my gaze over his powerful body, and unable to help myself, reached out and touched his chest. He laid on his back and reached for me, positioning his arm underneath my head and tucked me into his side.

Kissing me on my head, he whispered, "Go to sleep, baby."

I smiled, but he didn't see it. I hoped he could sense it though.

My last thought before I fell into a deep and peaceful slumber was that the journey ahead didn't matter, so long as I had Nash by my side.

CHAPTER 27

Broken - Seether

NASH

FUCK, I WAS A GREEDY BASTARD.

I'd just had Velvet's mouth and pussy around my cock, and as I watched her walk into the bathroom, I decided I wanted her again.

Now.

But, fuck it, I had to be at Mum's house in twenty minutes to do some jobs for her. And that wouldn't leave me enough time to take Velvet the number of ways I wanted her. I wasn't sure there'd be enough time during the rest of my life to get my fill of her.

Guilt hit me when I thought of the way I'd treated her last night. Thank fuck she'd let me explain myself, and had a heart as big as she did to accept me and my faults. I'd really fucking meant it when I told her I was a lucky man. I wasn't sure there were many other women out there as good as her.

My thoughts were interrupted by a text message.

Gabriella: I need to see you.

Me: No.

Gabriella: Fuck Nash we need to talk.

Me: I've got nothing to say to you.

Gabriella: Well I've got shit to say to you and I'm coming there.

Fuck.

My chest tightened at the thought of seeing her. I had to put a stop to this so I dialled her number.

"Nash," she answered in her breathy voice. My heart thumped in my chest at the sound of it. Christ, even after all these years, she was able to affect me; able to bring out the anger in me fast.

"Don't fuckin' come here, Gabriella. I'm warning you, if you do, you won't like what you find," I threatened.

"Have you dealt with this, Nash?"

My anger exploded out of me. "I fuckin' deal with this shit every goddamn day of my life. Don't fuckin' ask me that crap."

She was silent for a moment. "I meant, have you found a way to move on, to be able to live with it."

Sweat broke out on my forehead, even though it was freezing today. I realised what she was asking me, but she was the last person on Earth I wanted to be having this conversation with. "I'm not getting into this with you. Don't come here." My words were delivered furiously, and I stabbed at my phone to hang up.

Fuck.

Over the last couple of weeks, I'd felt like I was moving towards a place where I'd be able to finally work through the shit in my head. Having Velvet in my life was helping me with that; she calmed me. But the thought of Gabriella turning up, the day before the anniversary, fucking blew it all to pieces.

I heard the shower turn off, and decided I needed to get out of here. I had to put some distance between me and Velvet while I processed this, otherwise I knew I'd fuck up all the good we had going now. My temper was walking a tightrope today, and I didn't want to take it out on her.

"Baby, I've gotta head over to Mum's now," I yelled out as I put my boots on.

"Wait, don't go just yet. I need to kiss you goodbye," she called out.

My dick jerked. Christ, when Velvet did sweet, my whole body responded. I joined her in the bathroom a moment later, sucking in a breath at the sight of her naked in front of the mirror. I moved behind her, pressing my hard dick against her ass, and slid my hand around her waist. My lips brushed her shoulder as I made eye contact with her in the mirror. The room was still steamy from her shower so I reached out to wipe the mirror so I could see her clearly.

"Jesus, woman, you're fuckin' glorious. And if I had the time, I'd fuck you and show you exactly what you do to me."

Her head fell back against me, and she moaned, "Baby, it wouldn't take you long to make me come. I'm permanently wet for you." As she said it, she took my hand from her waist and guided it down to her pussy. "Let me borrow your fingers, just for a minute," she added, and almost made me blow in my pants.

I breathed into her ear, "You fuckin' own my fingers, sweet thing. I hope you know that."

She wasn't lying when she said she was wet, and I easily slid two fingers in. I reached deep, and was rewarded with another sweet moan from her lips. All the shit I was dealing with was momentarily forgotten as I lost myself in her. Giving her pleasure could become my full-time job as far as I was concerned. I'd become a fucking workaholic.

"Nash!" she screamed when I moved my free hand to her breast and began tweaking her nipple.

I bent a little and worked harder on her pussy, giving her clit some special attention. My cock was screaming to get inside her, and although I had intended on just making her come with my fingers, I knew I was going to fuck her now. "Change of plans, babe," I murmured, and pulled away from her so I could get a condom.

Her eyes met mine in the mirror and she hit me with her sexy smile that would always bring me to my knees. Her tongue flicked out to lick her lips, and she said, "I hope those plans involve your cock."

Fuck, she was killing me today. I went in search of a condom, and quickly got it in place. When I got back to her, she was bending forward, ass out, and staring at me in the mirror with a look that told me to hurry the fuck up.

I stepped behind her, never taking my eyes off hers, and pulled her pussy back onto my dick. My arm wrapped around her waist, and I thrust until I was balls deep. "This is going to be really fuckin' fast, Velvet. You ready?"

She squeezed my dick with her pussy, and begged, "Hard, Nash. Fuck me hard."

I pulled out and then gave her what she wanted. Who the fuck was I to argue? I pounded into her, and the sounds of my balls slapping against her and our groans filled the room. When she began rubbing her clit, it sent me over the edge. I came on a hard thrust, losing myself for a moment to the sensations surging through me.

Velvet's pussy clenched around my dick a second later, and she orgasmed. I watched her in the mirror as she came; she was fucking beautiful. The way her eyes squeezed shut really turned me on, and I ran my teeth along her shoulder, gently biting every now and then. Her eyes flew open, and she smiled at me.

When I lifted my head, she moved her hand to force me back

down. I grinned at her. "You like my teeth on you?" I asked, as I nipped her again.

"Yeah, baby, I love your teeth, your mouth, your hands, your cock. I could go on, but I think you get the picture."

I gently slapped her on the ass, and muttered, "I get the picture, babe. Tonight, I think you should show me just how much you love my cock."

I pulled out of her, dealt with the condom, and did my jeans up before coming back to her. She'd turned around to face me, and I had to drag my gaze away from her body. Her arms came up around my neck, and she whispered, "Have a good day, and I promise to show your whole body some love tonight."

I pressed a kiss to her lips. "You're spending the day with Harlow and Madison, yeah?"

Her face lit up. "Yeah, girl's day out."

I smacked her ass again. "Okay, babe, I've gotta get out of here. I'm already running late and if I stay here any longer, I might be tempted not to go at all."

She pushed me towards the door. "Go. I don't want your mother mad at me for keeping you."

I shook my head. "I don't think it's possible for her to be mad at you, darlin'. She never fuckin' shuts up about you."

The smile that landed on Velvet's lips was beautiful. It was the kind of smile I hoped to put there for the rest of her life.

★★★

I arrived at Mum's fifteen minutes later, and braced myself for her complaints about me being late. But she didn't give me any grief. She simply asked, "How's Velvet?"

"I'd say she's having a great day," I said, before asking her, "What's wrong with your car? Carla said it wasn't working."

We were in her kitchen and I could see her brain working overtime. I really hadn't wanted to come today because I knew she would bring up what was happening tomorrow. But Carla had called and insisted I take a look at Mum's car. She hadn't been specific as to what was wrong with it though, and I was fast getting the sense there was nothing wrong with it.

She pointed at the table. "Sit. I'll make us a coffee before you have a look at it."

I fought with the annoyance that consumed me. "I don't want coffee, Mum. Just tell me what's wrong and I'll fix it."

She gave me a pointed look, and then admitted, "There's nothing wrong with my car, Nash. I just wanted some time with you."

I rubbed the back of my neck. "Shit," I muttered, but I didn't sit down. I had no intention of staying for the conversation I knew was coming.

She surprised the fuck out of me with her next words. "Gabriella called me the other day."

"What the hell? What did she want?"

"She wants to come and see you. To talk about it. I don't think she's coping, and I told her you weren't either."

The blinding rage I'd managed to keep at bay the last couple of weeks roared to life. My ears pounded with it, and my vision blurred. "*She* isn't fuckin' coping? Fuck, if it wasn't for her, none of this shit would have ever happened. I'm not seeing her; I won't. And I'd appreciate it if you didn't talk to her about me," I thundered.

Mum remained calm, but her voice took on the firm tone she hardly ever used. "Nash, I'm worried about you. Your anger is getting worse, and I'm worried you're going to end up back where you were when you went to jail."

"I'm dealing with this, okay? And I'm not going back to jail."

She kept going, but her voice softened. "I hope not, because I don't want you to go through that again. I don't want any of our family to go through that again. You don't know what it's like for us to watch you do this to yourself; what it was like for us to watch you go to prison." Her voice cracked, and then she continued, her eyes begging me to hear her, "Do you know how hard it is for a parent to watch their child go through what you did? And then to watch their child spend the next ten years struggling with the weight of it?"

My heart pumped furiously in my chest. I tried to control my temper. Tried not to explode at my mother, but I couldn't stop myself. The pain took over. "No, I wouldn't know because I don't have a fuckin' child," I spat at her.

Fuck!

My skin crawled with hurt, anger, pain. The need to rip it all off was overwhelming, but I didn't know how to do that. I'd never worked it out. The only things that eased it were fighting and fucking. But even I knew that I'd come to a point where they weren't working anymore.

She let me hurl my hurt at her. She didn't flinch; rather, she welcomed it. "I know you don't want to see Gabriella, and I understand that. But I truly think it would be good for you. It might start to give you some closure."

I stood there, wearing my brokenness like an old, familiar coat, and I admitted one of my greatest fears to my mother. "I can't see her, can't be in the same room as her. If we got into this in person, I'm worried what I would do." I took a deep breath before I delivered the rest in a rough, distressed voice. "I'm worried my anger would make me do something none of us could come back from."

Mum's hand flew to her throat as she gasped. "You're worried you would kill her?"

I nodded, the despair I'd been living with for ten years rising to the surface. "Yes, a life for a life."

She was worried; I knew she was. It almost made me wish I hadn't told her, but a part of me felt relieved to get it out there. "Nash - " she began.

I cut her off. "I'm not going to see her so there won't be a problem. And now that you know why, I'm hoping you'll stop trying to push me."

She nodded, and was about to say something when my phone buzzed with a text message.

Scott: You and Kick free to meet with Blade today?

Me: When?

Scott: As soon as possible.

Me: Yeah, I'll round Kick up.

I eyed Mum. "I've got club business to take care of. You gonna be okay?"

She reached out to hug me, and then murmured, "I'll never stop worrying about you, baby. I just hope you can stop bottling this up. Maybe Velvet can help you."

I gave her a tight smile, and tried to reassure her. "She's helping."

"Good." She shooed me with her hands. "Go. Take care of your work. And talk to Velvet. Promise me that at least."

I couldn't make promises I wasn't sure I could keep. "I'll tell her you said hi."

I left her to go in search of Kick. The weight I'd been carrying felt a little lighter, and I contemplated talking to Velvet tonight; contemplated telling her what I hadn't told her last night. I'd finally be laying myself bare to her, and I wasn't sure anymore if that scared the shit out of me or made me feel the kind of hope I hadn't felt in a long time.

★★★

Blade met Kick and I at Scott's house. Scott had called in Griff and J for this meeting as well, and the mood was sombre. We were fairly sure that Marcus was still spreading lies about Scott to other club members so there was a sense of urgency to this.

Blade listened silently while Kick shared with him what he'd already told Scott and I. I watched Blade; his face was a blank mask. He hid his emotions completely. I'd never met someone as unreadable as him. Griff came close, but perhaps because I'd gotten to know him, I could read him better than Blade.

When Kick finished talking, Blade asked, "Are you in with any cops up here? To ask if they know anything about this."

"Yeah, I spoke with some of them today, but they knew nothing. Said they'd look into it for me, but I'm not holding my breath." Kick looked at Scott, and said, "I spoke with two of your older members today, the two who I know will keep this quiet. They knew nothing either, although one of them said that in the year this happened, there was some club rivalry up here with Black Deeds. And that Marcus had some cops in his pocket who helped him deal with any problems that came from that. I don't know if that ties in at all with the shit in Sydney, but if you've got anyway to look into it, that'd be helpful."

Scott nodded. "Yeah, brother. We'll take a look into it."

Blade also agreed. "I'll get my guys onto it as well."

Scott looked at Blade. "Anything else come up about this guy Marcus is looking for?"

"Blue? No, nothing yet," Blade replied.

"Fuck," Scott muttered. "I've been racking my brain trying to figure that out, and haven't come up with anything either."

I eyed Griff and J. "You two come up with anything?"

"Nothing," Griff said, quietly. He'd been acting strange all week, and even today he was off. I made a mental note to talk to him when I get a chance; to make sure he was alright.

"I called some of the boys in Adelaide to see if they knew anything. Not one fucker seems to have a fucking clue," J said, clearly frustrated.

Kick listened to everyone, and then informed us, "You were right about Marcus wanting back in on the drugs. Our supplier told us that Marcus approached him yesterday. He told the supplier he's got some loose ends in the club to tie up, and then he'll be good to go."

Not what any of us wanted to hear.

"Thanks for that info, Kick," Scott said. I noticed the stress that was clear on his face. This was taking its toll on him, and he'd grown moodier than usual over the last week.

Kick made to leave. He eyed me. "Nash, I'm gonna head home now, brother. Thanks for the bed."

I slapped him on the back. "It was good to see you, man."

He jerked his chin at everyone, and then left us to discuss our plan going forward.

Blade was the first to speak. "This isn't going to be as easy as I first assumed. I've got some of the best guys around working on this, and they're not finding anything. Marcus is smarter than I gave him credit for."

Scott nodded. "Yeah, I'm realising the same thing. I'd really like to know who the fuck this Blue guy is. If Marcus is looking for him, there's a damn good reason."

Blade opened his mouth to speak, but we were interrupted when Madison barged into the house, followed closely by Harlow and Velvet.

J stood as soon as he saw Madison. "What's wrong, baby?"

She pushed her way through us, and pointed at Harlow. "She's sick, and we were close so I brought her here."

Harlow was holding her hand over her mouth and bolted into the bathroom. Scott followed her.

Velvet made her way to me, and I pulled her close, and asked, "What's wrong with Harlow?"

"She started vomiting, no warning, just hung her head out of the car window, the poor thing."

"So, girl's day is off?"

She grinned at me. "Maybe. You got a better option for me?"

"Fuck, yes, I've got a better option for you, sweet thing. I'm always full of better options."

She whispered in my ear, "So long as it involves your favourite body part, I'm down."

I slid my hand over her ass, pulling her even closer to me. "Oh, you'll be going down alright, darlin'."

She moaned, softly. No-one else in the room would have heard it, but I did. And it hit me right in the dick. I looked over at Griff. "We finished here?" I asked.

He nodded. "Yeah, not much more to discuss at this point."

Thank fuck for that. "I'm out of here then, brother."

Velvet gave me a strange look.

"What?" I asked.

"I need to check with Madison first, to make sure she's okay with calling it off."

"Well, hurry that the fuck up, baby," I muttered.

I watched her ass sway as she made her way to Madison. She had those tight fucking jeans on again today, and I couldn't wait to get her home and get them off her.

"What are you thinking?" she asked when she came back to me.

I smirked. "I was just thinking I'd be doing you a service by taking those jeans off."

She raised a brow. "Oh, really? And how's that?"

"They're so fuckin' tight, so I'd be helping you breathe properly again."

"What would I do without you, Nash Walker? You're just too good to me."

Chuckling, I agreed, "I really am. Now get your ass out to my bike so I can make good on my promise to help you breathe again."

★★★

I watched Velvet sleep later that night. We'd ended up spending the rest of the day and night together. I'd introduced her to more of my talents in her bed, the shower, and on her dining table. She'd fallen asleep just before eleven pm, and I was left alone with my thoughts. Not a good place to be; not tonight.

I'd tried to talk to Velvet tonight, but the words got trapped and I couldn't force them out. She'd known, too. And the thing I fucking loved about her; she didn't push the point. It was like she instinctively knew that I needed the time and space to sort my shit out. And with each day together, I knew I'd get there. I had that much faith in us.

I brushed a soft kiss across her forehead before laying back on the bed. I placed my hands behind my neck, and settled in for a long night. There would be no sleep tonight; I was fairly sure of that. All there would be were memories. I did it every year; dredged up the memories that should have been the beginning of many more. But we'd fucked it all up. There were no more memories to be had. And all that was left were the ghosts that haunted me.

CHAPTER 28

Storm - Lifehouse

VELVET

I ROLLED OVER AND REACHED FOR NASH. THE BED WAS empty though. Sitting up, I listened to see if I could hear him in the house. Nothing.

My feet hit the ground a moment later, and I went in search of him. He'd been off last night, and I was concerned. I found him in the kitchen, leaning against the bench with a coffee in his hand. He turned when he heard me, and I sucked in a breath at the sight of his face.

He looked ravaged.

I started to walk towards him, but he placed his coffee mug down and took a step away from me. I stopped, not sure what was happening. It was big though, whatever it was.

He spoke first. "I've got some club stuff to take care of today, so I'll be busy all day." His voice was off; ragged almost.

"Okay," I said, carefully.

He didn't move though, just stood watching me, warily. I wanted to go to him, to comfort him. But I knew he wouldn't allow that so I didn't move. I waited for him, for his next move.

Taking a step in my direction, he said, "I don't know when I'll be finished, so we shouldn't make any plans for tonight." He took a breath before adding, "I'll call you tomorrow."

That was like a slap in the face, but I knew deep down he hadn't meant it the way it came out. I also knew he needed me to let him go. I nodded. "Okay."

He blinked, like he hadn't expected that to be so easy. "Okay," he said, and left without a kiss goodbye. I watched him go, my heart heavy. The worst part was, I had no idea why.

★★★

A couple of hours later, I was dressed and at a loose end. Nash was on my mind; I couldn't think about anything else. I'd sent him a text message but he hadn't replied. There was something very wrong with him; I knew it in my gut. And being the kind of woman I was, I couldn't not check in on him, so I grabbed my car keys, and made the short drive to the Storm clubhouse.

His bike was out the front, and I entered the clubhouse with a small amount of hesitation. I didn't want him to think I was checking up on him; there was a difference between checking up and checking in, and it was the latter I was doing.

The first thing I noticed was that the clubhouse was pretty empty. Sunday morning; I guess most of the boys were having a quiet day at home. The second thing I noticed, or rather, heard, was yelling coming from the bar area. And it was Nash's voice that I heard. And, holy shit, I'd never heard him so mad.

I hurried in the direction of the yelling, coming to a halt only when I found him. He was yelling at a woman, and his focus was so intently on her that he didn't see me. I could see both their faces from where I was standing, and she had tears streaming down hers.

Nash, on the other hand, looked like he was about to explode. He towered over her, and his voice thundered out abuse. I struggled to make out what he was yelling; I was actually more concerned for the woman at this point. He looked like he wanted to kill her.

Finally, I decided to step in, for her safety mostly. "Nash," I said, as I moved toward him.

His head spun around to face me, and he stopped yelling. But it was like he didn't even recognise me. Wild eyes frantically searched my face, as if he was trying to place me.

The woman took the opportunity to yell at Nash now that he'd stopped yelling at her. "I lost him too, Nash; not just you. I've struggled just as much as you - "

He whipped his head back around to face her, and cut her off. "I don't give a fuck about you and what you lost. If you hadn't fucked your way through your friends, none of this would have happened," he roared.

Gabriella.

Shit.

She stunned me with what she yelled back at him. "I wasn't the only one who fucked up, Nash. You couldn't keep your dick in your pants either."

Wow. Hadn't seen that coming.

Her words seemed to jar him. And from his reaction, I knew what she'd said was true. I could also tell he felt tremendous guilt about something; perhaps about cheating on her, I wasn't sure.

He pushed his hand through his hair. It looked like he was doing battle in his mind about something. And then, suddenly, he turned and punched the wall near where they were standing.

"Fuck!" he yelled, and punched the wall again. The force of his punches put two huge holes in the wall, and I could see he was going to punch it again.

"Nash!" I yelled at him.

He twisted to look at me. This time, I'd managed to get through to him; recognition crossed his face. But he was in a wild state, and I didn't think I had any hope of calming him. Shit, I wished that Scott or one of the boys were here. I pulled my phone out with the intent to call Scott, but Nash was on the move.

He didn't give Gabriella another moment's attention, and he didn't say anything to me. Instead, he stalked out of the clubhouse, and to his bike. I rushed after him, yelling out his name, but by the time I caught up with him, he was already on his bike. He looked at me for a long moment before roaring off.

Shit.

I knew he needed me, but with no idea where he'd go, I was stuck. My phone was still in my hand, and I figured it was definitely time to ask for Scott's help. I called him, but he didn't answer. I tried again a couple more times. Still no luck. Bloody hell, why wasn't he answering his phone?

Gabriella hadn't come outside, and although I felt like perhaps I should have gone to make sure she was okay, I wanted to find Nash more. And I had an idea; his mother might know where he went. So, I put his ex out of my mind and drove to Linda's house, hoping like hell she was home.

Fifteen minutes later, I pulled into her driveway, and was relieved when she answered her door. The minute she saw me, she knew something was wrong and ushered me inside.

"Is he okay?" she almost whispered.

"No. He just had a huge argument with Gabriella at the clubhouse, and then he took off. He's in a very bad state, Linda, and I have no clue where he would have gone. Do you?"

Her eyes filled with tears, and her hand covered her mouth for a moment. "He'll be at the cemetery."

"What?" I couldn't fathom why she'd said that.

She reached out and squeezed my hand. "You need to go to the

Mount Gravatt Cemetery; that's where he'll be."

There was an urgency to her voice, and the way she said it made me believe she was right. I decided not to stand there and ask questions.

"Okay," I said, softly.

She didn't say anything else; she simply nodded at me, trusting me to look after her son. I felt the weight of that, and hoped I could give him what he needed.

★★★

Thank fuck it was a Sunday. The traffic wasn't too bad. I did speed a little though, but fuck it, I had a good reason. On my way there, my mobile started ringing. Normally, I wouldn't be bothered answering it, but I figured it might be Scott or even Nash, so I pulled over and answered it.

Nash.

"Nash, where are you?" I begged him to tell me.

There was no sound on the other end, except for his ragged breathing. When he spoke, his strangled voice shredded my heart a little bit. "Velvet... I need you," he pleaded.

"I'm on my way, baby. Where are you?" I fought tears. Nash was drowning in his pain, and all I wanted to do was put my arms around him, and hold him.

"The cemetery..." He choked on his words, but I had the information I needed.

"Okay, I'll be there in about ten minutes," I promised.

He hung up without saying anything else, and I planted my foot on the pedal.

★★★

I found him fairly quickly when I arrived at the cemetery. He was on his knees, hunched in front of a gravestone. It was an overcast, cold day, and he cut a forlorn figure in the distance. I hurried to where he was, out of breath by the time I got there. He heard me just as I got to him, and he turned his head to look at me.

The look of pure agony on his face threatened to rip my heart apart. The Nash hunched on the ground in front of me was not the Nash I knew. And yet, he was. This was the missing piece to Nash; the piece of the puzzle that had been missing for so long. I'd grown to love this man, but I'd often struggled to connect the two sides to him that he showed me.

I knelt next to him. I didn't touch him, didn't say anything. It was up to him now to do what he needed to do.

His anguished voice sliced through me. "He would have been thirteen this year."

A sob escaped my lips. Oh, God. I hadn't wanted it to be true, but it was.

"Aaron. That was his name." His voice cracked, and he stopped talking. His pained stare locked onto mine. He needed me like never before.

I gently touched his arm. "What happened, baby?"

His chest rose and fell unevenly, and he expelled a long breath before finally giving me the missing piece of his story. "She cheated on me, over and fuckin' over, but I wouldn't have my son grow up without two parents so I tried to make it work. Fuck, the shit I put up with from her; that bitch should never have been a mother. Then, I fucked it all up myself. I'd been drinking, and her best friend threw herself at me, and I thought 'to hell with it'. I wanted to make her fuckin' hurt." His wild eyes searched mine, frantically. "It was once. I only did it once. She found out, and went mental. Said she was gonna leave me and take Aaron, and never let me see him again. I was furious; no-one was taking my son from me. But she managed to get him into the car and she left. And that was the last time I saw my son."

Nash had been ravaged by his grief, and my heart bled for him, for everything he'd lost. I moved closer to him, and placed my hand on his back, gently rubbing up and down. My touch seemed to calm him a little; enough to carry on.

"She crashed the car that day, and he died." He breathed a long, deep breath in, and then blew it out. "And it's my fuckin' fault." His eyes squeezed shut, and he began sobbing.

I couldn't control my own tears, and they fell freely, too. My arms went around him, and he clung to me. Heaving sobs wracked his body, and he buried his face against my chest. I placed my hand on his head, and stroked his hair. It was hard to see Nash like this. He was such a powerful force; to see him devastated like this, ruined in this way, was difficult.

I had to be strong for him though. Nash was at the point where he couldn't take it for a second longer. He couldn't deal with the pain that had haunted him for the last ten years; he needed me to help him through this.

After I'd let him get his grief out, and I felt his shudders subside, I whispered, "It's not your fault, Nash."

He slowly lifted his head to look at me with pained eyes. "It is, Velvet. If I hadn't slept with her friend, she wouldn't have taken him that day, and they wouldn't have crashed."

My heart was already hurting for his loss, but now it constricted in pain at the guilt he'd been carrying with him. Ten years was a long time to blame yourself for something that, ultimately, was out of your hands. I wiped the tears from his face, and said, "Yes, everything you did led you all to that day, but it wasn't *your* choice for Gabriella to take your son, and it wasn't *your* driving that was involved in that accident. You can't blame yourself for the actions of other people."

He was listening to everything I said, but I wasn't sure if it was getting through so I tried another tack. "Nash, think about your mother, and your family. You guys had it hard, really fucking hard, because your father left. He walked out and left your mother pregnant, and with no money or support. He also left three other kids behind for her to raise on her own. It was a long, hard road for her, and for all of you. His leaving caused your life to be changed forever. Was it your mother's fault he left?"

"No!" He seemed incensed that I would even suggest that which was exactly what I was hoping for.

"No, it wasn't. None of us have control over another person's actions. We might think we do, but when all is said and done, people will do whatever the hell they choose to do. Regardless of the situation, and regardless of whatever events cause that situation, the only control we have is over ourselves. If you'd had your way, Aaron would never have been in that car that day, and he would still be alive." I took a breath. My heart was racing; I needed him to hear me, and understand that what I was saying was right. "It's time for you to stop laying the blame for this at your own feet, baby. Your guilt is eating you alive."

He stilled, and I knew he'd heard me. Really heard me. I just hoped it was enough to get him through the first hurdle. He had a lot of work ahead of him to sort through his pain, but his first step was going to be letting go of his guilt.

His chest heaved one last time, and slowly, his breathing returned to normal. We were on our knees, still clinging to each other. He held on for a couple more moments before letting me go. "I miss him. Every day, I fuckin' miss him."

I nodded. "I know, baby." I reached for his hand, and held it.

He looked down at our hands, and squeezed mine before looking back at me. "I need you, Velvet. I've never needed anyone like I need you. If I'm gonna get through this, you have to be by my side."

I curled my hand around his neck, and pulled his lips to mine. The kiss I gave him wasn't passionate or sexy; it was a kiss full of love that told him I'd be right where he needed me. Our lips gently tangled, and our souls joined; we would do this together. When we pulled apart, I promised him, "I'll be with you every step of the way, Nash."

His relief was evident, and he murmured, "Thank fuck."

CHAPTER 29

Love's Poster Child - Keith Urban

NASH

Two weeks later

I LEANT BACK IN MY CHAIR, AND LAUGHED AT THE JOKE Carla had just told everyone. My arm was draped across the back of Velvet's chair, and I moved it to her shoulders, and pulled her to me so I could plant a kiss on her forehead.

Surprise flickered across her face. "What was that for?"

"Because I can."

Our eyes danced with each other, and I grew hard when I saw the desire in hers.

My brother broke the trance we were in. 'Hey, do you two ever leave each other alone? Cause I've seen you three times in the last two weeks, and you're always all over each other."

I grinned at him. "Not if I can fuckin' help it."

He returned my grin. "Lucky fucker," he muttered.

I looked around the table, and counted my fucking blessings. My family, and Velvet had all gathered to celebrate Carla's birthday at Mum's. Erika, Mum and Velvet had spent the afternoon cooking while Jamison and I had taken Carla skydiving. It was something she'd always wanted to do so we'd finally agreed to it. Jumping out of a plane wasn't something on my bucket list, but I had to admit, it was pretty fucking exhilarating. It was maybe even something I would happily do again.

Mum started to clear the table, and Velvet hopped up straight away to help her. They exchanged smiles, and I thanked the universe for giving me two women as amazing as these two.

Carla started bouncing in her chair, clapping her hands together.

I jerked my chin at her. "What the hell's got you so happy, babe?"

"It's present time, Nash! What did you get me?"

I groaned. My sister was all about the presents; always had been. I pitied the poor fucker who ended up with her; if he didn't get it right every birthday and Christmas, his life wouldn't be worth living. "Settle down, darlin'. You'll find out in a minute."

Velvet looked at me and smiled; she'd helped me choose a present for Carla which meant this year, I was on a fucking winner. I'd have to milk this for everything it was worth; get as much out of Carla while she was still loving me for the present. I flicked a smile back at Velvet, and when she turned back to help Mum, I let my eyes drop to her ass. Christ, I really was a lucky fucker; Jamison was dead on the money.

Erika jumped in and helped clear the table while Jamison and I kept Carla occupied. When they'd finished, we all moved into the living room for present opening. Carla was almost bursting out of her skin in excitement.

"Bloody hell, Carla. Anyone would think you were still twelve, the way you're going on," Jamison grumbled.

She glared at him. "There's nothing wrong with showing your happiness, Jamison."

I stepped in before these two started a fight. Passing my present to her, I said, "Happy birthday, babe. You're gonna fuckin' love this present."

Her excitement levels skyrocketed. "Really?" she asked, as she started ripping into the wrapping paper.

A second later, her entire face lit up, and the biggest smile I'd ever seen on her face took over. "Oh my God! I love it!" she squealed.

I curled an arm around Velvet's shoulders and pulled her close, murmuring in her ear, "Remind me to show you my appreciation later on, yeah?"

She blasted her sexy smile at me, and breathed into my ear, "Don't you worry, baby, I'll be reminding you for a long time."

"What did he get you?" Erika asked.

Carla, still beaming, held it up. "It's a GHD Air hairdryer."

Jamison frowned. "A G-what?"

I nodded at him. "Exactly, brother. All you need to know is that it's a fuckin' expensive hairdryer that's guaranteed to make all the women in your life love you if you give them one."

Carla grinned and pointed at me. "What he said."

Jamison groaned. "Fuck, your present should have gone last, Nash. I've got no hope now."

Eyeing Velvet, I murmured, "There's some serious Nash loving in this for you, sweet thing."

Her hand moved to my leg. "I'm counting on it, baby."

★★★

The next morning, Velvet was running around like a mad woman. She had her final exam for her beauty course today, and was worried about passing.

I walked into the kitchen where she was studying her notes.

Moving behind her, I snaked my arm around her waist and leant my chin on her shoulder. I tried not to let her tits distract me, but a man can only achieve so much, and a second later my eyes were glued to her chest.

She reached a hand back and ran it through my hair. "Nash, stop looking at my boobs, and finish getting ready. You're dropping me off this morning and I don't want to be late."

"How do you know I was looking at your boobs, sweet thing?" I asked, without taking my eyes off them. My addiction to her tits was getting out of hand, but I was helpless to control it.

She sighed, and the rise and fall of her chest only turned me on more. "I know what you're looking at because you're always looking at the same thing."

"Any man in their right mind would be doing the exact same thing as I am right now." I straightened, and turned her in my arms so I could see her face. "Talking of men looking at you, did you talk to Scott about finishing up at Indigo?"

"Yeah, my last shift is next week."

I breathed a sigh of relief. "Thank Christ for that, babe. I can't take much more of those assholes leering at you."

She reached up and cupped my cheek. "I know, baby, but it's not much longer now."

"And then you're starting at Roxie's?"

Her eyes lit up; I knew she was looking forward to this. "Yes, on the Monday after I finish at Indigo, so it's all worked out really well. She's set a room up for me to rent off her, and she's got ladies booked in already."

I loved seeing her happy. I brushed a kiss over her lips, and murmured, "We've come a long way, haven't we?"

Nodding, she asked me, "Have you thought anymore about going to see Gabriella?"

Velvet and my family all thought I needed to go and talk to

Gabriella, for closure or some fucking thing. I wasn't so sure, and was stalling on it. "Babe, it's only been two weeks since I last saw her. I'm still fuckin' angry at her, and that's not gonna go away anytime soon. Let me get through this shit in my head, deal with that first, and then I'll think about going to see her."

"Okay. You're probably right. At least you'll consider it; that's all I really wanted you to do at this point."

I pulled her to me. "How the hell did I get so lucky?"

"Why? What do you mean?"

"I mean, you don't fuckin' nag me, you don't bitch about shit to me, you haven't tried to change me, and you cope with my addiction to your tits and pussy. How did I get that lucky, woman?"

She grinned. "Oh, there's still time, baby. I can do all that stuff if you want."

I grinned back at her. Two could play this game. "Okay, how about we work on curbing my addiction first? Get that one out of the way before you start in on the nagging and bitching."

She pulled my face down to hers. "I'll make you a deal, Nash Walker. You keep that addiction for the rest of your life, and I promise not to start with the nagging and bitching."

"Done," I agreed, and smacked her on the ass. "Now, get your shit together, and let's get you to your exam."

★★★

After I dropped Velvet off at her exam, I headed to the clubhouse. The last two weeks since Kick left had been tense. Marcus was rounding his troops up so to speak, making all sorts of promises to the boys who agreed to Storm moving back into drugs. There were only a handful of us left who were against it, and if he called for a vote, we'd be outnumbered.

From the moment I entered the clubhouse, I knew something

was off. And when I found Scott in the bar area, he confirmed it. "Dad's gonna make his move in the next couple of days, brother."

I sat at the table with him. He was in the corner by himself, with his morning coffee. I drowned out the noise of the other guys talking and laughing, and gave Scott my full attention. "Who told you that?"

"Wilder. Dad's taken a liking to him, and is using him for all sorts of shit."

I liked Wilder, even after my run in with him, but I was wondering what was in it for him to be playing both sides. "Can we trust Wilder? Why's he giving you that information?"

Scott leaned forward so he could drop his voice. "You remember how Wilder became a prospect?"

I searched my memory, but came up with nothing. "No."

"I brought him in. And I did it intentionally. It was after I found out about Dad. I had a gut feeling that shit was going to go south, and then I met Wilder. He'd been screwed over by Dad, and was looking for payback. I figured it would be useful to us to have a member I could be sure of if shit ever hit the fan, so I sponsored him."

"Fuck, it could have gone the other way; could have backfired on you."

He nodded. "Yeah, brother, it could have. I was willing to take that risk though, and I'm glad I fucking did. Wilder's proved himself, and I'm pretty sure he's going to be patched soon."

"Any news on Blue?"

"No, still coming up empty on that one. You heard anything from Kick?"

"They're convinced Marcus is their man, but because of his ties to Adelaide and some of the other chapters, are reluctant to move without proof. Marcus has been busy making friends; seems he's got allies everywhere."

"Fuck," Scott muttered.

"How the hell did he screw Wilder over?" I asked.

"He - " he began, but stopped talking because Marcus was headed straight for us.

"Nash, Scott," he greeted us, clearly not pleased to see us.

"Marcus," I said, jerking my chin at him, but Scott didn't say a word.

He scowled at Scott before saying, "Church tomorrow. Don't be late. We've got a lot of shit to discuss."

I nodded, and he left, as quickly as he came. Mind you, it couldn't be soon enough as far as I was concerned. Giving my attention back to Scott, I shared my thoughts. "Not looking forward to tomorrow, brother. Christ knows what surprises he's got in store for us."

Scott was deep in thought, and slowly nodded as he took in what I'd said. "I hear you, man. I fucking hear you."

★★★

A few hours later, I parked my bike and waited for Velvet to come out of her exam. She'd told me she would catch a lift with a friend, but I'd had the urge to see her, so here I was. While I waited, I reflected on the last two weeks. The day at the cemetery had been life changing for me. Opening up to her had changed everything; it had scattered the demons in my soul far and wide. Some still lingered, and I knew it would take time to clear them out completely, but I could breathe again. The weight of regret and guilt had lifted, and the pain had dulled a little. It would never go away, not fully, but it was becoming bearable. Having Velvet in my life helped. I wasn't a talker, but having her to go home to, to laugh with, just to be with, helped get me through. And she gave me hope. For the first time since Aaron's death, I wanted to make plans; plans for my life, plans that included someone else.

I heard her laughter, and looked up to find her walking towards me with a huge smile on her face. She threw herself into my arms. "What are you doing here, baby?"

Fuck, I liked it when she called me baby. I wrapped my arms around her, letting my hand glide down her back and onto her ass. "Thought I'd pick you up, take you back to my place and fuck you," I growled, both of my hands on her ass now.

"You say the sweetest things," she purred.

"I told you I'm all about the sweet talk, darlin'."

Her eyes glazed over, and a smile slowly made its way onto her face. "Yeah, you did, and I've learnt that when Nash Walker says something, he means it."

"I do. And on that note, you need to get your sweet ass on the back of my bike so I can make good on my promise."

She didn't waste any time. Yeah, Velvet was addicted to me as much as I was to her.

CHAPTER 29

This Means War - Nickelback

VELVET

DARK GLASSES COVERED MY EYES AS I WALKED INTO Roxie's salon early the next morning. She took one look at me and burst out laughing. "That man of yours wearing you out, hon?"

I took my glasses off and slumped in a chair. "Like you wouldn't believe."

Madison started laughing. "I knew it would take a strong woman to crack Nash, but I'd never factored in that it would take someone with a lot of stamina to keep up with him."

"You need to make me coffee, woman," I begged Roxie.

"Make your own damn coffee," she said with a shake of her head. "I'm thinking you actually might need some Redbull or something like that." Then, looking at Madison, she suggested, "I think you should tell Nash to get his shit together and stock his fridge with energy drinks for his woman."

I dragged myself out of the chair. "Fine, I'll make my own coffee," I grumbled as I trudged to the back room. "Don't come running to me when you're down and out though, babe. I'll remember you letting me down in my hour of need."

They both laughed, and I had to smile. As tired as I was, I was more than happy to be worn out from Nash loving. I thought about him while I made coffee, and by the time I got back to my chair, I was grinning.

Madison narrowed her eyes at me. "You perked up. What gives?"

"I was just thinking about how happy I am with Nash. I never in a million years would have picked that I'd end up with him, but I'm glad I did."

Madison smiled at me, warmly. "I'm glad you did too. There's something special about Nash, and I love that you are helping him deal with his pain. He seems so much happier these days."

"Yeah, he is," I agreed.

Roxie cut in. "What are we doing with your hair today, Velvet? You want a colour or just a cut?"

"A colour and cut, but just trim the ends. Nash would hate it if I cut any of the length."

Roxie rolled her eyes. "Ummm, where's the real Velvet? She doesn't let any man tell her what to do."

I laughed. "He hasn't told me not to cut it, and trust me, I'd never listen if he did. But, let's just say my man likes to pull my hair, and I kinda like it, so there's no way in hell I'm cutting it."

"Of course he does. My bad," she muttered, and went out the back to get the colour ready for my hair.

"I'm so happy for you and Nash. You both deserve happiness," Madison said.

"Thanks, babe." I sighed, and added, "God knows, Nash really does after everything he's been through."

She nodded. "Yeah, my heart breaks for what he's gone through. I can't even begin to imagine losing a child."

My pain surfaced. I could imagine, but not fully. It had been devastating enough to lose babies before they were born; the thought of losing a child that had lived and breathed, caused actual physical pain.

I didn't want to have this conversation so I sat in silence. Madison must have felt it too because she didn't say anything further. When Harlow stepped through the door of the salon, I was happy for the distraction.

Standing to greet her, I said, "Thank God, you brought cake with you."

She put the cake down on the counter, and gave us both a hug. "I brought you half and half, Velvet. We've got celebrating to do."

I frowned. "What are we celebrating?"

"You passing your exams," she said as if I'd asked the dumbest question on the planet.

I grinned at her. "I love you. Yes, let's celebrate that because I'm pretty sure I did. And when I find out for certain next week, we can celebrate again."

"Yes!" Harlow exclaimed. "I like the way you think, honey."

"What kind of cake did you bring?"

"Hummingbird and caramel mud."

"Oh my God, woman, you're gonna kill me. I love those."

She smiled, and said, simply, "I know."

Roxie came out with the hair dye ready to go. She greeted Harlow, "I just heard the words caramel mud. Your hair cut is on me today because I fucking love caramel mud."

Madison laughed. "I think you should be thanking me, Roxie. I mean, if it wasn't for me, you wouldn't know these two. Which means you wouldn't be getting cake and you wouldn't have a beautician starting here soon."

Roxie's trademark sarcasm was in full force today. "You want a medal, babe? I'm sure I could round one up for you."

Madison poked her tongue at Roxie and we all burst out

laughing.

These women made my life so much better just by being in it. I'd never been big on friends; I'd resisted opening myself up to women as much as I had to men. But sometimes in life, people managed to work their way into your heart. It happened slowly, until one day you realised how big a part they played in your happiness, and just how lost you'd be if they weren't there.

★★★

NASH

CHURCH.

I had a sense of foreboding about today, and it unsettled me.

Taking my seat at the table, I looked around to gauge the mood of the room. Marcus was emanating control. Fuck, he looked like he was ready to take on the world. And like he knew he would fucking win if he did.

Smug bastard.

This wasn't going to be good.

Scott sat next to Marcus, a fierce look on his face, his body tense.

And, Griff, our Sergeant-at-Arms, was on Marcus's other side. He too, looked ready to go to battle.

The room filled quickly, and Marcus called the meeting to order. He ran through the usual business, fairly routine stuff. I sat back and watched it unfold, wondering when his agenda for today would be realised, because he sure as fuck had one. There was a nervous energy in the room; watchful eyes everywhere were taking it all in.

Everyone knew that something was going down today.

Fuck.

When it finally happened, I sat in stunned silence, not believing my eyes or my ears.

Marcus asked if anyone had business to bring to the table. I looked around to see who it would be; I figured Marcus had someone primed for this.

I wasn't the only one looking around the table. Anticipation pervaded the room. The tension our club had been under the past couple of months had stretched us and placed us in a precarious position. Like a house of cards, all it would take would be one knock, and everything we'd worked hard to achieve would be threatened.

Griff stood.

I watched him, waiting to see what he had to say. I had no idea what he was doing; this hadn't been discussed at any of our meetings. He pushed his shoulders back and adopted an aggressive stance. His jaw was set and there was a determined look on his face. When he spoke, his voice was hard and cold. "I call an officer challenge for the Vice Presidency. Scott has lost confidence in the President, and I don't believe he can or will do his job properly."

What the fuck?

I sat up straight in my chair, my shoulders tensing. What the hell was Griff doing?

I flicked my gaze to Scott. His face registered shock, but he said nothing. Anger and disbelief seeped out of him.

I sucked in a breath at the magnitude of this challenge.

Griff.

I'd never seen it coming. And Scott obviously hadn't either. I looked at J; he was as stunned and angry as I was.

Griff had fucking played us for fools.

He'd double crossed all of us.

And, Marcus sat there with a satisfied smile on his face that made me want to hurt every last motherfucker who was with him on this. I wanted blood. I fucking wanted Marcus to bleed for everything he'd ever done to his family, and to his club.

And, I knew that one day we would have his blood for this. Scott, J, and I would fucking make sure of it.

What happened next was a blur to me. One of the other members seconded the motion, and Marcus called a vote for next week's Church.

Scott pushed his chair back and stood. Fury rolled off him. His eyes bore into Griff, and he spat out, "I want a vote on this today; I don't want to wait another fucking week for it."

"Griff?" Marcus asked.

Griff nodded his approval, and the vote began. It was happening so fast; it felt like we were on a freight train hurtling towards destruction.

Marcus voted yay, and got the voting started. I watched in horror as nearly every member voted with Marcus.

Scott was out.

Griff was in.

The gavel came down, and the decision was reached.

Loyalties had been discarded.

Trust had been broken.

Family had been screwed over.

And I knew Storm would never be the same.

EPILOGUE

My Sacrifice - Creed

NASH

Three months later

I TOOK THE THREE STEPS UP TO THE DOOR WITH hesitation. And, I hesitated again before knocking. Coming here today was essential, but I still felt trepidation.

Gabriella opened the door. She didn't smile, but her face revealed her relief at seeing me. "Nash." She didn't say anything else, and I knew it was up to me to find the closure I was searching for.

"I've come to tell you I'm moving on. The shit that happened will always stay with me, but I can't hold on to my anger about it any longer." The words wrestled their way out of me. They had to be said, and I had to follow through, but I still struggled to even look at her. I wondered how the hell I would ever manage to let my anger go. And then, I remembered Velvet, and my anxiety settled to a manageable level.

"Thank you for coming," she said.

"I didn't come for you; I came for me, Gabriella. I've finally realised I had no control over what you did that day. All these years, I've held onto you, and let you project your feelings onto me. I'm done. And I'm finally letting you go. I'll deal with my shit, and you deal with yours. Don't text me or ring me anymore."

Surprise, and then anger crossed her face. "You came here to say that to me? We need to talk about Aaron; about what happened."

I shook my head. "There's nothing more for us to say to each other. And what I actually came to say to you was goodbye."

"No! You don't get to decide that," she ranted, her anger taking over.

"I do get to decide that. And I have decided that." I paused, before saying, "Goodbye, Gabriella."

Without giving her a chance to say anything else, I turned and made the short walk back to Velvet's car. She was watching me through the window, a concerned look on her face. "You okay?" she asked as soon as I was back in the car.

I gave her a tight smile. "Let's just say, I'm getting there. This shit is never gonna be easy though." I blew out a long breath. "You need to drive before she comes down here," I said. I knew Gabriella, and I knew her temper. It was as quick to flare up as mine, and she would come down to give me a piece of her mind; I was sure of it.

Velvet nodded, and did as I'd said. We drove in silence for awhile. I stared out the window, my mind drifting. The last couple of months had been fucking hard. Between dealing with my shit, and then club shit, I was exhausted. Mentally at least. And yet, there was light in amongst all that.

I turned to Velvet. "Thanks for coming today."

She glanced at me quickly before looking back to the road. "I wouldn't be anywhere else, baby."

She was my light; the sweet in my life.

I reached out to brush my hand over her cheek. "I love you, sweet thing."

It was the first time I'd told her, and I didn't know how she would handle it. I shouldn't have been concerned.

Turning again, she smiled at me.

And then she gave me everything when she said, "I love you too, Nash."

TO MY READERS

Thank you for reading Revive. I hope you enjoyed Nash & Velvet. While I was writing this book I was a little concerned that Nash wouldn't live up to your expectations - that he wouldn't quite be who you thought he was. Nash has always been the fun, flirty, sexy biker in the Storm men. I always knew what his backstory was, but when I got into writing it, he was even more broken than I thought. And angry. The way he fought his feelings for Velvet really brought out the asshole in him, and that's when I started to get concerned. However, he is who he is, and I stayed true to that.

Writing this story turned out to be a very personal experience for me in that it touched on aspects of my own journey in life. I wrote some parts in tears because they stirred up emotions & feelings about stuff I've been through and am going through currently. But, through that, I realised just how much writing the Storm MC series has, and is changing my life. And, for that, I really need to thank you for reading my books and supporting me.

Thank you!
Nina xx

"Your largest fear carries your greatest growth."
(I don't know who wrote this quote to give them credit.)

ACKNOWLEDGEMENTS

"A friend is one who overlooks your broken fence and admires the flowers in your garden."

I need to thank a lot of people so if you're reading this, settle in ;)

Eliahn, thank you. I know you think I love my Mac more than you but truly I don't. Thank you for letting me do my thing. And for trying to organise me - God knows, I need it!

Kathleen, you're #2 this time around babe. Thank you for everything, baby doll ;) You know how awesome I think you are (just re-read your birthday card if you forget!). The next year is going to be epic! I can't wait to see what you do, and I can't freaking wait until we see the world together next year!!

My family & friends - thanks for your support, love and encouragement. I'm sorry I don't say it more often, but I'm always thinking it. Love you all xx

Melanie Sassymum & Elle Raven - I really would be lost without you two amazing women! Thank you SO much for everything you've done to help me with Revive. You girls are always there for me, even at 2am in the morning! I never expect you to drop everything for me but you always do, and I truly appreciate it. I'm so excited for you both, and am right behind you as you chase your dreams! *"A girl should be two things: who and what she wants." ~ Coco Chanel* (Here's to being who we want and doing what we want!) xxx

Jani Kay - *sigh* *sigh *sigh* Fuck, fuckity, fuck! I don't know how to put into words what I am feeling as I sit here thinking of you. Or how to condense it. Some people show up in your life completely unexpectedly, and give you so much of themselves without asking anything in return. That, my love, is you. I really fucking wished you lived in QLD! Thank you for absolutely everything, babe. I am so excited for what's ahead with you and me! xx

Louisa M - Thank you, thank you, thank you! This cover ROCKS!! I have had so many readers, bloggers and authors contact me to say they love it. I am so very grateful to have you as my cover designer and also to have you in my life. I remember meeting you on a street team last year and thinking how beautiful your teasers were - I never imagined that this year, we'd be working together! And, wow, the Slay cover is just as gorgeous!! xx

To my #STORMCHASERS - I fucking love you. LOVE YOU! Just in case that didn't sink in... YOU GIRLS ARE FUCKING AWESOME! And you've taken it to a whole new level the past few weeks. I have so much to look forward to each day - The #DAILYFIX, Christina's Quotes, Paula's Countdown. The support you all give me is beyond amazing. Thank you for everything you do for me. PS Here's to #fingerling ;)

Bloggers - I have a special place in my heart for bloggers. You ladies do so much for authors and it's all done out of a love for books and wanting to share the characters you love with other readers. It's all done for nothing, and I am so sorry I don't take enough time to tell you more often what it means to me, but it means the world. Please don't hesitate to contact me if I can ever help you in any way. I love to donate to giveaways and am always open to take part in character interviews or spotlights, or takeovers or anything that you want to do (well, pretty much anything ;)) so just email me at _authorninalevine@gmail.com_ if you need something.

Christina G (Mrs Walker) - I will always remember the day you started messaging me. I felt a connection with you straight away and knew I had to have you in my readers's group so that I could chat with you more often. I never knew our friendship would grow how it has. I love chatting boys, books, music and husbands with you ;) Thank you so very much for all the support you have shown me. xxx PS I really, truly hope that I did your man proud. *"Unexpected intrusions of beauty. This is what life is."* ¯ *Anonymous*

This indie author world is amazing! I've met some gorgeous authors (some in person and some online who I can't wait to meet in person!). I'd like to give a shout out to some of these ladies. You all inspire, encourage and support me in ways you will never know. Thank you so much! - Chelle Bliss (that Gandy prank was fun, huh?!), Lili Saint Germain, Rachel Brookes, River Savage, Kirsty Dallas, Monica James, Lilliana Anderson, Lyra Parish, Pepper Winters, Lila Rose, AC Bextor, Ava Manello, KT Fisher, Jennifer Ryder, Carmen Jenner, Nina D'Angelo, Max Henry, Dee Kelly, Emma Fitzgerald, Emma Hart.

REVIVE PLAYLIST

Revive was heavily influenced by music. I listen to music constantly while writing. You may have noticed that I listed a song at the beginning of each chapter - those songs helped inspire those chapters. Here's a list of all the songs that inspired Nash & Velvet's story.

All my playlists are on Spotify if you'd like to follow them.

Walk of Shame ~ Pink
Scream ~ Usher (this song was on repeat for all the sex scenes ;))
Addicted To You ~ Avicii
Wild Ones ~ Flo Rida
Bad Influence ~ Pink
Raise Your Glass ~ Pink
F**kin Perfect ~ Pink
Slut Like You ~ Pink
Total Eclipse of the Heart ~ Bonnie Tyler
Livin' La Vida Loca ~ Ricky Martin
Need You Now ~ Lady Antebellum
Lookin' For A Good Time ~ Lady Antebellum
Angels ~ Robbie Williams
This Is Who I Am ~ Vanessa Amorosi
I Wanna Dance With Somebody (Whitney Houston)
Crazy In Love ~ Beyonce
Broken-Hearted Girl ~ Beyonce
All I Want Is You ~ U2
I'm The Only One ~ Melissa Etheridge

Piece Of My Heart ~ Melissa Etheridge
Cream ~ Prince
Kiss ~ Prince
Get Off ~ Prince
The Great Escape ~ Pink
Bleeding Love ~ Leona Lewis
Man! I Feel Like A Woman ~ Shania Twain
Undressed ~ Kim Cesarion
Who You Love ~ John Mayer & Katy Perry
Everything Has Changed ~ Taylor Swift & Ed Sheeran
The King of Wishful Thinking ~ Go West
Last Kiss ~ Taylor Swift
Out of Reach ~ Gabrielle
Collide ~ Kid Rock & Sheryl Crow
Sad ~ Maroon 5
Big Girls Don't Cry ~ Fergie
Just A Fool ~ Christina Aguilera & Blake Shelton
The Last Time ~ Taylor Swift
Low - feat T-Pain ~ Flo Rida
Replay ~ Zendaya
Stay With Me ~ Sam Smith
Need You Tonight ~ INXS
Better Man ~ Lady Antebellum
Do I Wanna Know ~ Arctic Monkeys
Hey Jealousy ~ Gin Blossoms
Mr. Brightside ~ The Killers
Never Be The Same ~ Jessica Mauboy
Better Than Me ~ Hinder
Tonight I Wanna Cry ~ Keith Urban
Stupid Boy ~ Keith Urban
One Last Breath ~ Creed
My Sacrifice ~ Creed

Maps ˜ Maroon 5
Say Something ˜ A Great Big World
Dayum, Baby ˜ Florida Georgia Line
Love's Poster Child ˜ Keith Urban
Who I Am With You ˜ Chris Young
Can't Stand The Rain ˜ Lady Antebellum
Get To Me ˜ Lady Antebellum
Unstoppable ˜ Rascal Flatts
Hands On You ˜ Florida Georgia Line
Boom Clap ˜ Charli XCX
Thunder ˜ Jessie J
Broken - Featuring Amy Lee ˜ Seether
Brave ˜ Sara Bareilles
Ready To Love Again ˜ Lady Antebellum
This Means War ˜ Nickelback
I'd Come For You ˜ Nickelback

ROXIE

I'm excited to share a couple of chapters from a new story I am writing, Roxie. Some of you are already following this story through my newsletter or blog. If you sign up for my newsletter you automatically receive the chapters that way. The other way you can read this story is by visiting my blog. All the links for these are at the end of this book.

So, just to clarify, this is currently a story that I'm releasing for FREE in chapters. Once it is complete, I will publish it.

Enjoy Roxie!

Nina xx

CHAPTER 1

ROXIE

"You're not listening to me, J." Seriously, how the hell Madison managed to be married to this man eluded me at the moment. He was overbearing mixed with a side of asshole.

He breathed out a long, frustrated breath. "Trust me babe, I'm listening; I'm just not fucking liking what I'm hearing."

Was this guy for real? "Yeah well it's my life, my decision, and I say no." I dug my heels in.

He shook his head, pulled out his phone and made a call. I waited, resolute that I wouldn't budge on this. Not taking his eyes off me, he spoke into the phone, "Madison, your girl here doesn't want our help. I've got better shit to do than to stand here arguing with her so I'll give you five minutes with her and then I'm outta here." Without waiting for Madison to reply, he handed the phone to me.

I raised my eyebrows at him and then said to Madison, "How the hell do you live with him?" He didn't even flinch at that; I bet he knew what an asshole he could be, but just didn't care.

"Roxie, I'll share that secret with you another day but for now just listen to me. Your hairdressing salon has been broken into three times in the last three weeks, you and the cops have no clue who's doing it and you could really do with the help that J's offering you. I know you prefer to do things your way and I know you can be a stubborn bitch, but don't do that this time. Accept help for once in your life."

"I'm fine on my own, really I am," I promised her. The last thing I wanted was for a bossy man like J telling me what to do in my own business. No, I'd sort this shit out on my own.

She sighed. "I do love you, but you're hard work. You know that, right?"

"You wouldn't be the first person to tell me that," I muttered, and handed the phone back to J. He wasn't the only one who had better things to do than to keep going over this.

He was silent while Madison said something to him. A pained look crossed his face and then he said, "Fine, I'll see you at home tonight and we'll talk about this then." He ended the call and shoved his phone back in his pocket.

"Good, that's sorted," I said, my hands on my hips, waiting for him to leave.

His angry glare didn't leave my face and he replied, "If you think that's Madison done, you don't know her very well. As far as I'm concerned we're done, but when my wife gets an idea in her head she doesn't let it go till she has her way. And unfortunately for me, and you too, if she doesn't end up getting what she wants, she has ways of making me come to the party, so I doubt this is the fucking end of it, babe."

"Trust me when I say that I'm not a pushover either, J. I won't be pushed into something I don't want," I assured him.

"Well it looks like we're in for fun, fucking times then, doesn't it," he grumbled as he strode out the front door. He left without a backwards glance and I slammed the door behind him. Men!

★★★

Six hours later, I was elbow deep in hair colours, cuts and shitty customers. To say my day wasn't going that well was an understatement. As soon as five o'clock hit, I was locking the front door, heading down to the pub on the corner and drowning my sorrows.

"Roxie!"

I turned at the sound of my name. Bobby, one of my hairdressers, was motioning for me to come over to the front counter. I lifted a finger in the air to indicate I'd be with him in one minute. Shifting my attention back to my client, I decided not to rush. Bobby could be the biggest drama queen sometimes. I loved him to death but boy, he did my head in some days.

"Roxie, if you don't get that padded ass over here right this minute -"

I whipped my head around and glared at him. "Did you just say that my ass is padded?"

He fixed a smile on his face and nodded. "Yes doll, that's exactly what I said. Now get over here so I can show you something."

I stalked over to where he was, ready to punch him. He knew me well though, and raised his hands in a defensive gesture.

"I work this ass hard and you fucking know that -" I began to say before he cut me off.

"Settle petal, I didn't mean it. I just needed to get your bloody attention." He pointed outside. "Look at that beautiful specimen of man meat." He ended his statement on a sigh and I turned my gaze in the direction he'd pointed.

"Holy shit," I murmured; he was right. Walking towards us was a tall, well built guy who was covered in tats; he looked like sex on legs.

"Oh good Lord in man heaven, I think he's coming in here!" Bobby exclaimed. He narrowed his eyes on me. "He's mine sweet cheeks, and don't you fucking argue. You got to talk to that sinfully sexy biker dude this morning so it's only fair that this one is for me."

I rolled my eyes. "That biker dude from this morning might look hot, but he's an asshole. If he ever comes back in here, he's all yours."

"Thanks, but first I'm having this one." He shoved me out of the way as he fell over himself to get to the guy the moment he pushed through the door. "Why hello, gorgeous. To what do we owe the pleasure?" His voice practically purred the words and I stifled a laugh. I realised now that I'd actually met this man before; at Madison's wedding a few weeks ago. I couldn't remember his name though.

The guy flashed Bobby a huge smile and then blessed me with one as well. He reached out to shake Bobby's hand and said, "Hi, man."

Bobby just about melted on the spot. Goodness, this was too funny. The guy was obviously not gay but Bobby was so over the top confident that he always thought he had a shot with every man he met. "Lovely to meet you. I'm Bobby, and your name is?"

"Nash," he answered, and then looked at me, "And you must be Roxie."

That's right, Nash. "Yes, I'm Roxie. Let me guess, Madison sent you?"

His chuckle filtered through the room drawing my clients' attention, and they ogled him and all his gorgeous muscles. "Pretty obvious, huh?"

"Yeah, and the answer is still no."

"Sweet thing, it should be a no brainer for you. You've got a problem that we can help you with. You obviously need some help figuring out who keeps breaking in and that kind of work is my specialty."

I sighed. "You guys just don't get it. I don't want any help with this; I'm quite capable of handling my own shit."

He considered that for a moment. "Why are you resisting this? You and Madison have become good friends over the past few months; she just wants to help out a friend. There's no hidden agenda here, babe."

"I know. But let's just say that I have my reasons, and leave it at that."

Bobby decided to wade into the conversation at that point. "I vote we let Nash help you on this one, sweetie."

I scowled at him. "Shut it, Bobby. You just want an excuse to perv on Nash."

"You know me too well. Please tell him yes," he pleaded.

Nash chuckled and jerked his thumb at Bobby. "You should listen to your friend here."

"You're not hearing me. I've said no and that's the end of it. And please tell Madison not to send anymore men." I considered that for a moment. "No, scratch that, I'll tell her myself."

The smile that had touched Nash's lips a moment ago gave way to a perplexed look. "I swear to God, I will never figure women out. One minute you're screaming for our attention when you feel you're not getting it and then when we fuckin' offer it, you slam the door in our face."

I shrugged. "What can I say? We're a law unto ourselves. Plus we've gotta keep you men guessing; shit gets boring otherwise."

He shook his head. "Some days I'd just like shit to be boring, babe."

"Yeah well today's not your lucky day, hot stuff."

"You send me away, it might be your last chance at Storm helping you. You good with that?"

"I'm more than good with that."

He assessed me for a moment longer before saying, "Okay, we're done here." And with that, he turned and sauntered out, leaving Bobby open mouthed and stunned. He sent me a foul look. "Why the hell didn't you say yes?"

"Bobby, the last thing we need is those bossy bikers in our business. Like I said, I've got my reasons and for the moment it's best not to involve them."

"And what if you decide in the future that you do want them, what then? I don't think they'll be back; your chance is gone."

I had to smile at his naivety. I cocked my head to the side and asked, "Do you really think that if I begged Madison for help later on that she wouldn't be able to convince her husband to step in and help?"

Understanding dawned on his face. "I see your point."

"Right, so can we please get back to work now? I've got a date with a bar stool in about an hour and I don't want to be late."

★★★

Two days later, I was on my way to work when Madison called me. "How's my favourite hairdresser?" she asked.

"Tired and grumpy."

Her laugh tinkled softly through the phone. "You're always

tired and grumpy in the morning, Roxie."

"Yeah, well who the hell wants to be out of bed so bloody early? Not me, babe."

"Maybe you should have gone into a different line of work; something you could do at night."

"Perhaps I should ask your brother for a job at the strip club," I muttered. It was way too early to be engaging in conversation.

"Oh God no. You'd suck at that."

"Are you saying I couldn't shake my thing as well as the other chicks he's got working there?"

Laughing again, she said, "I've seen you shake your thing and you could definitely keep up with those girls. No, what I meant was that you wouldn't put up with the dirty men and the way they stare and try to touch. You'd be trying to punch them; you'd be bad for business, hon."

I yawned and scrubbed my hand over my face. She was right; there was no way I'd put up with men pulling that shit on me. Hell, I couldn't even understand how Harlow worked the bar in that joint. "You've got a point," I agreed before asking, "Why are you calling me so early?"

"I'm just checking in with you to see if you've changed your mind on Nash helping you work out who keeps breaking in and trashing your shop. Plus I need to reschedule my appointment."

"I haven't changed my mind and as for your appointment, I'm not at the shop yet so can you just text me what you want to change it to and I'll sort that out once I get there."

"Bloody hell, woman. Why do you have to be so damn stubborn?"

I was just about to answer her when I rounded the corner to my shop and discovered to my extreme anger that someone had smashed my window yet again.

"Motherfucker," I snapped. "Sorry Madison, I've gotta go," I said and ended the call. I took in the mess before me. Broken glass every-fucking- where and graffiti on the one window they hadn't smashed.

Whore.

Shit. That didn't quite fit with the message he'd left me the other day and now I was left wondering if my theory was right.

"Mean something to you?" a deep voice rumbled from behind me and I jumped in shock. I'd thought I was alone.

I spun to face whoever was there and sucked in a breath at the sight in front of me. He was tall. He had muscles trying to shove their way out of the fitted black tee he'd covered them with. His hair was black, thick and slightly wavy so that it fell across his eyes. And good, fucking gracious, the scruff on his face just about made my legs collapse under me.

"Who are you?" I breathed out.

He whipped his sunglasses off to reveal an intense set of green eyes. Without answering me, he pulled his phone out of his jeans and strode over to the window with the graffiti, and took a photo. He then returned to where I was and began taking photos of the rest of the mess.

I grabbed for his arm and hit rock hard muscle on his bicep. "I asked you a question," I said, annoyed at being ignored.

He stopped taking photos and focused those gorgeous eyes on me. There was a flicker of something there; I wasn't sure what though. It was like an untamed energy; something definitely swirled beneath the surface of this man and it unsettled me while at the same time unleashed butterflies in the pit of my stomach. And damn, for the first time in a very long time, I was unsure of myself.

"I'm Liam," he stated as if that answered any and all questions I might have.

I raised my eyebrows. "Care to elaborate?"

His eyes shifted between mine, and it appeared that he was

carefully scrutinising everything in front of him; the shop, the mess and me. Most definitely me. And it unnerved me even more than he already had. Eventually, he spoke, "Zane sent me to help you with your security issues."

I threw my hands up in the air. "And who the hell is Zane?"

His phone rang at that moment. "Yeah," he answered it. He listened to whatever the person on the other end said and then he replied, "I've got Roxie in front of me and they've smashed her windows again. I'm just about to take a look inside." He listened some more and then said, "Later, man." His phone was shoved back in his jeans and then he stepped around me and entered my shop through the broken window.

I swivelled around to see what he was doing. My patience was wearing thin; who the hell did he think he was just waltzing in like this without giving me any answers as to who he was? Stepping through the window, I followed him and repeated my question, "Who is Zane?"

He didn't answer; instead he turned his head to look at me, gestured at the inside of the shop and instructed, "Don't touch anything before I take some more photos of the inside." He then turned back around and kept walking.

"For the love of God, tell me who the hell Zane is!" I yelled, having reached the end of my tether.

He came to a halt and laid his gaze on me again. His energy rippled through the air and filled the room. It hit me hard and caused that fluttery sensation in my stomach again. *Damn.* That was the last thing I wanted to feel for this exasperating man.

"Zane is my boss. He runs Stone Security and we were called in on this job by Scott Cole. Any other questions you have while we're at it?"

"Those bloody bikers," I muttered under my breath.

He stood still, assessing me and waiting to see if I had anything else to say. When I didn't say anything else, he continued, "We're good to go?"

Oh hell no, we were so far from good to go it wasn't funny. "No, we're not. I never asked for you to be given this job so you can just leave now before we go any further." I crossed my arms in front of me and waited for him to go.

He quirked a brow at me. "So you're going to just keep letting this shit happen then? This is what, your fourth break in this month? Seems to me that you could do with the help, sweetheart."

There was that damn energy of his again, radiating out from him. It was confusing my senses and I couldn't think straight.

Before I could say anything he spoke again, "I hate to break it to you but this doesn't look like a random break in to me. Given that it keeps happening and that they aren't stealing anything. And that graffiti? That's the first time they've done that, isn't it?"

I hesitated for a moment. I really didn't want to admit my suspicions to him. "Yes, that's the first time they've graffitied the building."

He nodded. "Right, so this is escalating and I'm taking over the investigation. No ifs or buts because this shit can quickly turn nasty from here on out."

He resumed poking around while I stood like a stunned idiot and just let him take over. I decided I needed coffee to deal with this; he could go jump if he thought I wasn't touching the kettle. It was way too early for this shit and I needed sustenance.

CHAPTER 2

ROXIE

"HOLY SHIT ON A STICK, YOUR GIRL MADISON IS WELL connected," Bobby said as he gazed lustfully at Liam. He'd arrived at work ten minutes ago and had hardly taken his eyes off the man ever since.

I thrust the broom at him. "Stop eye fucking him and go and make yourself useful. We've got glass that needs to be swept up."

A devious grin spread across his face as he took the broom from me. "Yes ma'am."

I watched him go, wondering what the hell he was up to. Bobby operated from one angle only; do anything and everything to get the guy in bed. The look he'd just given me told me he was up to no good. Oh well, it was Liam's problem now, not mine. And maybe, if Bobby annoyed the shit out of him, he would pack up and leave.

My other hairdresser, Tahlia, breezed in just as Bobby began his little performance for Liam. She gawked at him as she walked through the shop and managed to hold in her laughter until she reached the back room where I was.

"Oh my God, Bobby has no shame," she said, as she shook her head in disbelief.

I eyed him, and she was right. He'd turned his task of sweeping up glass into a kind of dance and was sashaying his way around the shop, bending and shaking his ass in front of Liam as he went. Liam seemed oblivious to it though which I needed to rectify if my plan of Bobby scaring him off was going to have any chance at success.

"I think you've got an admirer," I pointed out as I made my way to where he was.

He'd been engrossed with something on his phone but looked up at me as soon as I spoke. "Sorry?"

I nodded my head in Bobby's direction. "You've inspired him."

Liam's gaze followed mine and he spent a moment watching Bobby as he gyrated his hips and puckered his lips in a kissing motion. Not an ounce of surprise registered on Liam's face before he turned back to me and murmured, "Perhaps some of his enthusiasm for me could rub off on you."

Well, holy fuck, now I was the one who was surprised. And not only at what he'd said but also at the shot of desire that coursed through me. But I stood my ground; this man would not get to me. "The only enthusiasm I'm feeling is for you to go back to your boss and tell him that I've got this situation under control."

"It looks like we've got some work to do on your enthusiasm levels then, sweetheart, because this situation is not under control and I'm not leaving."

His tone was commanding; the kind you didn't dare mess with, but I wasn't one to be messed with either. I was just about to tell him exactly where to go when Bobby interrupted.

"Oh my, I do love a bossy man," he sighed, while taking a break from sweeping. He ogled Liam instead. "I, for one, am glad you're not leaving, Mr. Bend-Me-Over-And-F -"

"Bobby!" I hissed, "For once in your life, zip that mouth." Bobby and I commenced non-verbal communication; the type where we said what had to be said with our eyes and flicks of our head. After two years of working together, we had this down pat and knew exactly what the other was saying.

After our quick dialogue, Bobby turned in a huff and stomped out to the back room. I gave my attention back to Liam who was now casually leaning against the front counter, feet crossed at the ankles and chin in hand. His amused eyes were focused solely on me.

"What?" I snapped. I didn't like the fact that he found this funny because I sure as hell didn't.

He lifted his chin in Bobby's direction. "You should go easy on him; he's just looking out for your best interests."

"Some part of that statement might be true but mostly, Bobby just wants you to stick around because you're hot." My mouth opened before my mind had a chance to even think about what I was saying. Story of my life. I mentally berated myself for my honesty.

Liam chuckled. "So you do have some enthusiasm for me?" His eyes twinkled with mischief and it had to be said, when Liam stopped being so serious, his hotness rating went through the roof.

His new playful mood flustered me and I dealt with it the only way I knew how; cranky Roxie took over. "Just because I think you're hot doesn't mean I'm enthusiastic about you sticking around. Tell me what you need from me and then we can all get on with our work."

He assessed me for another moment or so and then pushed off from the counter where he was resting. His serious face was back on. "I need to know if you're aware of anyone who may have been following you or if you've been harassed by anyone lately."

"Why?"

"Because if you have been followed or harassed, they might be the ones doing this."

"No."

His forehead creased. "What do you mean, no?"

"No, I haven't been followed or harassed."

He thought about that for another moment before asking, "Are you seeing anyone?"

"What does that have to do with this?" He was really starting to irritate me with all these personal questions.

"I'm just trying to get the background here, Roxie. I believe these break-ins have to do with either you or one of your staff so I need to know who is in your lives who might be responsible for them."

As much as it irked me to admit it, he did have a point. I had my own suspicions but after this last break-in, I was beginning to doubt myself. "When you say, am I seeing anyone, what exactly does that mean?"

He looked puzzled. "Last I knew, it meant are you dating anyone."

"No."

He opened his mouth but quickly shut it again and paused before continuing, "Okay, you're not dating anyone but are you involved with anyone in another capacity?"

"Do you mean, am I fucking anyone?"

His eyebrows arched. "Yes, are you fucking anyone or are you spending time in any way with anyone," he said with a slight shake of his head. I was pretty sure from the look on his face that I'd managed to frustrate him. Score one to me.

"Why yes, Liam, I am. I fucked a guy three nights ago and I also fucked him early last week," I informed him in my sugar sweet voice I reserved for when people really pissed me off.

The fucker didn't even blink. "I'm going to need a name."

"Well, I don't have a name. I never stopped to ask him."

He blinked.

Score two to me.

I smiled sweetly at him and waited for his response.

Finally, he muttered, "Fuck."

Score three to me.

We stared at each other for a minute or so and then he said, "Well, you're going to have to find him because I need to know who he is."

My eyes widened. "You're kidding, right? I have no idea who he is or where he is."

He smirked at me. "Yeah you do; we just have to go back to wherever you found him before you screwed him."

The bastard. He knew what I was doing and now he was playing with me.

"Ah, no. There's no we in this, Liam. I'll go back by myself and find him."

He shook his head. "No, sweetheart, we'll both go. If you think I'm letting you out of my sight during this investigation, you can think again."

My mouth dropped open.

Score one, two and three to Liam.

★★★

LIAM

JESUS CHRIST, SHE was something else. The little minx was fucking me around and doing a damn good job at it.

My instructions for this job had been clear: get in and get out fast. Zane was sure he knew who was behind the break-ins at Roxie's hair salon so when Scott had called in a favour he hadn't hesitated to agree to it. However, I'd just spent the last hour going over this particular break-in with a fine tooth comb and I was convinced this was the work of someone else, not the crew that

Zane thought. I was also sure that Roxie had an idea of who was committing these break-ins. Why she was keeping that to herself, I was yet to figure out.

She was currently glaring at me after I'd just informed her I'd be going with her to find this guy she'd slept with. *Fuck.* I had no idea why I'd said I would go with her and I also had no clue why she hadn't challenged me on it because she sure as fuck had challenged me on everything else this morning.

Bobby broke the tension between us. "Sweet cakes, your first client will be here in about ten minutes. You right to do it or do you want me to take over?" He winked at me and then suggested, "I could always take over here with Liam while you look after the clients."

I had to hand it to him; he was persistent. A good quality to have, but it wouldn't get him far with me on this; I was one hundred percent a pussy man.

"I think that Liam and I are finished here." She looked back at me. "Is that right?"

"For now. I've gotta take off to get to another job but I'll be back when you close so that you and I can take care of the matter we just discussed."

"You want to do that tonight?"

I nodded. "We need to find him as soon as possible."

Bobby was confused. "Who do you need to find?"

I didn't answer him but rather waited for Roxie to tell him; it wasn't my business to share her personal information.

She glared at me again; what for, I wasn't sure. "Apparently we need to find that guy I slept with the other night. Liam's convinced he might be the one breaking in."

Women and their exaggerations never failed to shit me. "I never said that, but I would like to clear him from the investigation," I said calmly; much more calmly than I was feeling it on the inside.

My phone rang which made my fucking moment; I needed a break from Roxie and her attitude.

It was Zane. "Liam, you nearly finished with the hairdresser?"

"Yeah, but it's not Red's crew doing these break-ins so I'm going to have to spend some more time on this one."

"Fuck," he muttered, "Was hoping you wouldn't say that."

"I'm just about to leave and head over to the other job you emailed."

"Good, I told them you'd be there in about twenty."

"I'll call you once I'm finished that one and let you know how it goes," I promised and we ended the call. I'd been working for Zane for about three years now and we had an easy work relationship; our thinking patterns were fairly similar which meant we didn't have to explain ourselves too much and there were pretty much no miscommunications. Just the way I liked it.

I turned back to Roxie but she'd left me and it looked like she was getting ready for her client. This gave me a reprieve from her smart mouth; it also gave me a moment to rake my gaze over her. She was unlike any woman I'd ever met; in looks and attitude. She was so far from my type it wasn't funny, and yet, the bulge in my jeans disagreed. Roxie had long hair that was a mix of pink and purple, and a face full of makeup; far more makeup than I usually liked on a woman. Her arms were covered in colour tattoos, as was the part of her chest exposed above her tank top. And Christ, there were even more fucking tattoos on her neck. I wasn't a fan of tattoos on a woman; didn't find them attractive at all. She had on the tightest black jeans known to mankind and a loose, black tank top that flashed more of her breasts than I'd ever want a woman of mine to flash. And those heels she was wearing? How the hell a hairdresser stood for eight or more hours a day in heels that high was beyond me.

Zane had told me that Scott and his boys weren't keen to work with her on this but that his sister had bugged them to help her. After spending as little as ten minutes with her, I could see why they felt that way. She was difficult, and full of attitude, but there was something else there; something I hadn't put my finger on yet but I'd work it out. Not to fucking mention the fact that her challenging nature turned me the fuck on. God knew why, because it also frustrated the hell out of me. Tonight would be interesting to say the least.

REMEMBER

Sign up for my newsletter to receive each chapter of Roxie as it is released.

OR, check my blog regularly for the new chapters.

ABOUT THE AUTHOR

Nina Levine is an Aussie writer who writes stories about hot, alpha men and the strong, independent women they love.

When she's not creating with words, she loves to create with paint and paper. Often though, she can be found curled up with a good book and some chocolate.

Signup for her newsletter: http://eepurl.com/OvJzX

She loves to chat with the readers of her book so please visit her or contact her here:

Website: http://ninalevinebooks.blogspot.com.au
Facebook: https://www.facebook.com/AuthorNinaLevine
Twitter: https://twitter.com/NinaLWriter
Pinterest: http://www.pinterest.com/ninalevine92/
(check out my boards full of the pictures that inspired me while writing Storm)

I would also love it if you would consider leaving a review for Revive on the site you bought it.

Reviews mean so very much to me xx

THE BEGINNING

A DUET BY JANI KAY

If you love biker books, you will LOVE this series by USA Today Bestselling author Jani Kay!

THE BEGINNING: A Duet is the story of The Princess & The Biker.

A modern day Romeo & Juliet story.

Ryder Knox wants freedom from the hatred churning in his gut. Saved by the Scorpio Stingers MC boys, he owes his life and allegiance to them—they are his family. He doesn't need a smart mouthed woman who pushes every one of his buttons. But he can't get Jade out of his head.

Jade Summers is a good girl. She wants a man just like her lawyer daddy. Not the alpha male biker who storms into her life, who looks like a sex god with tattoos and piercings. He's demanding, controlling and won't take no for an answer.

Their chemistry is off the charts and they are drawn to one another like magnets. Neither can resist the other.

Two worlds collide. Their families are determined to tear them apart. With everything stacked against them, is what they have strong enough to overcome the odds? They must choose: family or one another. The ultimate price may be too high.

Will their polar opposite worlds destroy and rip them apart forever?

This book is intended for mature audiences (18+) due to language and adult sexual situations.

THE BEGINNING: A Duet contains:

Book #0.5 RYDER (Prequel)
PLUS Book #1 TWO WORLDS COLLIDING
PLUS 5 BONUS Chapters

BOOK #2: UNCHAIN MY HEART IS OUT NOW
The story of the Beauty and the Beast: Can Eva unchain Harrison's
cold and unyielding heart?

Add to your TBR on Goodreads.

The Beginning: A Duet
https://www.goodreads.com/book/show/22500535-the-beginning----
a-duet

Unchain My Heart
https://www.goodreads.com/book/show/20985987-unchain-my-
heart

·